MURDER HAS NO CALORIES

◉

Corinne Holt Sawyer

DONALD I. FINE, INC.
New York

This book is dedicated to the two people in my life who work
the hardest
to make me into their idea of a perfect human being,
two people to whom — in consequence — I am a constant
disappointment:

Madeline Holt Campillo
and
Wayne Stroup

1

◉

It got so that Dorothy McGraw hated the word "plucky."

When her husband, Harvey, died of pneumonia and Dorothy was left to raise their son alone, her friends and relatives had said, "Oh, Dorothy will make it. You'll see. She's plucky." When her son was killed by sniper fire in Vietnam, the friends and relatives had tried to comfort her by saying, "Dorothy, it may not seem like it now, but the sorrow will ease in time. You're a survivor . . . you're plucky." And when, ten years later, her financial manager absconded with the funds of several of his clients—including Dorothy's—and when, after a comfortable adult life on the modest income from her late husband's investments, she had to find a business to support herself, they had all said again, "Don't you worry about Dorothy. She's a survivor. Strong as an ox, that woman. Plucky, that's the word for her . . . plucky."

The problem, as even Dorothy conceded, was that she *was* plucky. She was strong. She was a survivor . . . just as they had said. But she had spent so many years yearning to be seen as soft and feminine, the kind of woman to whom a man automatically extends a hand as she steps out of a car, the kind of woman who wears linen suits and pearls (and doesn't wrinkle the linen), the kind of woman who joins the Junior League and pours tea at the receptions following charity auctions organized by someone else, that she didn't like the notion that underneath that genteel exterior, she was constructed like a steel spring: resilient and nearly unbreakable—and not likely to rust early.

But as always, her survivor's instinct took over, and Dorothy gritted her teeth and pluckily turned her lovely old farmhouse in

1

the hills near San Diego into The Time-Out Inn, a spa where harried housewives could come for a week or two of pampering and weight loss, and stressed-out businesswomen could escape from telephones and secretaries and let the muscles and the mind unknot.

Dorothy's spa was small and luxurious, though she charged well below what many other such enterprises charge their clients. She brought in and trained a fine staff to give total service. She redecorated the old place from top to bottom in delicately flowered chintz and summer whites and installed central heat and air conditioning. Comfort was to be the watchword for her guests. She served highly flavored gourmet food, though it was cooked without salt and without fats so that even if clients refused the exercise regimen the spa offered, they would probably lose at least a little weight. And she advertised cleverly in several national publications.

Within a year The Time-Out Inn was supporting Dorothy adequately and showing a small profit, which she prudently plowed back into the business, buying a whirlpool for every guest bath, down pillows for the guest beds, extra thick Turkish towels and matching bathrobes, towel warmers, and triple makeup mirrors. Dorothy also gave her staff a raise.

At the end of her second year in business, Dorothy formed a corporation and made her chef/dietitian a vice-president. She offered staff raises again and upgraded the decor of the seminar rooms and lounges (the old parlors and the sewing room of the farmhouse) to match the elegance of the bedrooms and the dining room. She ordered lavender leotards in a variety of sizes with Time-Out Inn logos on them and loaned one to each guest on arrival. (Dorothy also developed a profitable sideline selling duplicates of the Turkish-toweling robes and the leotards so the guests could take them home as souvenirs or to continue their exercise programs—nobody was indiscreet enough to ask which.) Dorothy's pluck was beginning to pay off. But she still hated to hear the word.

The hated word notwithstanding, not once during the darkest sorrows of her life—not once during the most frightened and panicky times she'd ever dealt with—did Dorothy ever really doubt her ability to survive. She had from time to time wondered if she would ever feel happy again . . . but she had known she would continue. Until the murder. And then, somehow, Dorothy began to doubt her own strength and even the likelihood that she would be able to spring back, to carry on. It all began to seem just too much to cope with. The thought even crossed her mind that what she would really like to do would be just to quit. And then she had an inspiration. She came to call on Angela Benbow at Camden-sur-Mer.

Angela Benbow was just under five feet tall and nearing eighty. White-haired, with piercing blue eyes, she was not used—despite her age and lack of height—to being ignored. In fact, as an admiral's wife, she had been used to people jumping when someone (preferably, in her view, herself) commanded. When she was widowed and moved into the one-time luxury hotel, Camden-sur-Mer (which had been turned into retirement apartments), it had been difficult to adjust to the demands of communal living: trying not to complain too loudly and too often, even about one's gradually fading strength and health; trying to adjust to the schedules and preferences of others, rather than setting one's own and asking all else to conform; trying to tolerate the shortcomings of others, especially when—as is true with many who are aging—those shortcomings become exaggerated.

In age, the firm of resolve can become mulish; the careless, slovenly; the meticulous, picky; and those who habitually stand up for their rights can become downright curmudgeonly. To live among others—all of them with strong personalities set over a lifetime—was difficult, but Angela had managed, after years of carefully stifling her tendency toward abrupt truth-telling and her bent to sarcasm, to be accepted, even to make a few friends. In short she had, though she would never admit it, mellowed with age.

One of the friends she had made was Dorothy McGraw. Since Dorothy had opened her little spa some miles inland from Camden, it was unlikely that the two would ever meet. Dorothy seldom came to Camden; when she had shopping to do, she drove to the nearest mall or down to San Diego, while Angela seldom left the retirement home. As a hotel, Camden-sur-Mer had entertained the royalty of stage and screen in its day, but the hotel had pined and faded nearly to the point of death with the coming of the freeway system, which rerouted traffic away from the Coast Highway. Foresighted investors, however, had reopened the hotel, turning it into one- and two-room apartments for the elderly and staffing it with caring and dedicated people, including the best chef on the West Coast.

From time to time, as an advertisement for potential residents, the old hotel held an open house and invited the town's residents to look the place over. Visitors were served lunch (at a modest fee) and there was a pianist in the lobby—usually Frenchie Webster, a resident who, though nearly blind, could still bang out a tune. That nobody much listened during affairs like the open house didn't bother Frenchie, for nobody much had really listened when she used to play for the silent movies, as she explained to anyone who commiserated. During these open houses, the resident ladies also set up a booth where they sold the handmade products of their expert sewing and knitting, crocheting and embroidery.

All in all, the open house was usually a very satisfying affair, though not to Angela, who claimed to despise the interruption of her private life by what she likened to the crowds at a public hanging. "They only come to gawk at all of us senile old fools and wonder how we lived so long," she once grumbled. "And they nod their heads and say they'll age better than we have, or they say how can we stand living cooped up together like this . . ."

Nevertheless she had somehow been talked into agreeing to help out at the crafts booth as a cashier one year. "I don't know how I got into that," she had mourned to Caledonia Wingate, also the widow of an admiral and as huge as Angela was tiny. This unlikely pair were the best of friends, so Angela was not at all surprised when Caledonia was totally unsympathetic and made fun of her complaint; only the best of friends could afford to do that. A stranger or a mere acquaintance would have made sympathetic noises while thinking how annoying Angela's whine was. Caledonia was a close enough friend that she simply snorted and told Angela to "quit your grousing . . . you got yourself into this! Now go to that sale and do your duty!" And Angela meekly took the rebuke, and even smiled an apology.

Thus it was that Angela was at the tin box that served as a cash register when Dorothy McGraw came through the open house and stopped at the craft booth to buy four frilly white aprons for her dining room waitresses. "Such beautiful work on these," she said. "The girls ordinarily hate wearing aprons, though I insist. But they'll like these. I don't really understand their vehemence about aprons. When I was young, you always wore an apron in the kitchen, and often when you were doing the housework, just dusting and vacuuming."

"In our day," Angela agreed, deftly tucking the twenty into the box and counting out four singles in change, "in our day we wore dresses, though. In case someone came to the house, you know. Nowadays women wear old blue jeans and outsized men's shirts when they work around the house. They'd feel like fools protecting outfits like that with aprons. Especially frilly aprons."

"Not at my place," Dorothy said firmly. "Aprons on all the dining room staff. Spots of food look so bad on a uniform—even if it's a shirt and trousers! And when they try to pick up something hot—a casserole, say—why, they never have a hot pad anymore, either. I wish you could have seen what happened the other day." Purchase forgotten, Dorothy launched into the story of a waitress who dropped a heated plate, and Angela responded with flattering attention and amusement.

The two women liked each other from that very first meeting—they were similarly educated; each had a good sense of humor; and though Dorothy was about fifteen years Angela's junior, they shared many common memories—more than they might with a younger person. About three weeks after the open house, Dorothy phoned Angela and they went to lunch together in town. From then on the two had seen each other every few weeks, sometimes a lunch in town, sometimes tea at Angela's and at least twice at Caledonia's, for Angela had happily introduced her two friends to each other.

Angela was not really surprised, therefore, when Dorothy came to call. But the object of Dorothy's visit on this particular day did take her aback.

"Dorothy, I can't do that! I'm not a detective, private or otherwise. I mean, I've had a bit of luck . . ."

"But the police are not going to be helpful in this at all, Angela. They came out and peeked around in the shrubbery, upset everyone by asking a lot of personal questions, tracked mud onto the living room rug, upset the staff's routine, told the guests to stay put—to finish out their four weeks and not to leave—which was probably a good thing, incidentally, or the spa would have been absolutely empty the morning after they found the body!

"Anyway, they seem to be getting nowhere. They don't tell us anything at all. And we're left trying to keep things jolly for our guests . . . As more and more time passes, they're going to scare all my business away! I mean, who wants to come for a relaxing week or two to a place where the police tramp the halls night and day, and people get roasted to death in the steam room?"

"Dorothy! Really!"

"I'm sorry, Angela. Did that sound too frivolous? I hardly know what I'm saying anymore, I'm so worried. Not only are my current guests stuck at the Inn, but they're the last group of guests I'm likely to have. Ever. Do you understand what I'm saying? The business simply can't survive if the police don't find out who did this. I just want them to pack up their notebooks and their fingerprint dust and go!"

"There, there, Dorothy. I'm sure they'll find out who's responsible, and—"

"But they're not doing it! They're just asking more stupid questions. They're trampling the flower beds, rooting through supply closets, blundering into the beauty parlor while my masseuse is working—you can imagine the embarrassment—and letting the cold air out of the freezer . . . What on earth were they doing in the freezer anyhow? Did they think the killer was hiding between the slabs of bacon? Honestly! The fellow in charge is nice enough, but the others . . . Angela, you've *got* to help me. I'm at the end of my rope."

Angela shook her head. "Why me? That's really what I'm asking, I guess. You could hire a professional detective, couldn't you?"

Dorothy made a face. "Oh, I looked in the Yellow Pages. 'Ace McClaren,' 'John Trumpet'—colorful names, but not the sort to inspire confidence. Not in me. And all *men*! This is a 'Women Only' spa and the men—our handymen, the police—they stand out like sore thumbs. Nobody can forget they're around, even when they're being unobtrusive. I need a woman who can sign in as a guest and pretend to be legitimate—undercover she'd find out a lot of things from her fellow guests and the staff.''

''Aren't there any female private detectives? I should think in this day of equal opportunity . . .''

''There's one. Just one. And I did go to see her. 'Kitsey Summers'—there's another colorful name. Angela, she wouldn't do at all, for what I had in mind. She looked like a dance hall hostess, all bleached hair and short leather skirt. Not the look of a spa client. Not my spa, anyway. My clientele tends to be well-to-do, middle-aged, and a bit pudgy. Why, she was younger and leaner than some of my exercise instructors. Nobody would ever believe she was there to lose weight and get in shape. Now you, on the other hand . . .'' She held a hand up to stop Angela from speaking, for Angela was twisting in her seat and obviously about to add something to the conversation.

''You'd blend right in! You're—well, you're more the class of my clients. And you've had a lot of success working with the police. You've solved several murders, haven't you?''

''Well, not exactly. We—Caledonia and I—have had some incredible luck. And the police will be glad to tell you that's all it is: luck. We know the people here, you see, and we can figure things out that outsiders—even people who come to know us well—can't figure out. At the spa, I'd be an outsider just like the police, and—''

To Angela's dismay, Dorothy began to weep, her face turning beet red as she tried to hide her tears behind a tiny hanky. ''Oh, Angela, *please*. I understand what you're saying, but I don't know what else to do, where to turn.''

Angela felt absolutely helpless. But instead of the sense of frustrated anger that usually possessed her when she was swept along by events, unable to chart her own course, she was experiencing an odd thrill of pleasure. Nobody could really accuse her of trying to interfere where she didn't belong this time, not when Dorothy had begged her to help. Nobody could say Angela was just an aging busybody, not when she'd been approached as though she were a serious professional in the business of detecting. The future seemed to beckon to her, bright and entertaining, and Angela could hardly disguise her fascination and delight.

"I'll want to talk it over with Caledonia . . . you remember having tea a couple of times with Caledonia Wingate, don't you? My special friend here? I'd want her to come with me, of course. She's as much responsible for what we've been able to do in the past as I am," Angela said generously.

And so it was arranged. It only remained for Angela to talk Caledonia into the trip.

2

⊙

"**Y**ou must have taken leave of your senses! Me? Me go to a fat farm?'' Caledonia's entire bulk was quivering, and the thunderous roll of her voice was likely to register at least a 5.5 on a Richter scale.

"But I promised her,'' Angela said tremulously. She made a woebegone face and held one hand before her eyes, as though to hide tears, a gesture that had never failed to melt the late Admiral Douglas Benbow. It did nothing at all to Caledonia Wingate, who stood up, towering over Angela and glowering mightily.

"Absolutely not. Forget it, no way, in a pig's eye, when hell freezes over, you should be so lucky . . .'' Caledonia seemed able to go on indefinitely expressing the idea that she was not going to Dorothy's Time-Out Inn—as a detective or as anything else—so long as she was conscious.

"Cal, please. She's desperate. Her chief assistant was boiled to death in the steam bath. Or maybe it was 'broiled.' Which one do you do with water? I haven't cooked for myself in so long I—''

"Angela!''

"Oh. I'm sorry. I'm rambling, aren't I? Well, anyhow, the police aren't making any headway, and Dorothy may end up losing her business. I mean, she'll lose it as soon as her guests are allowed to leave. She says that right now they're in the midst of a four-week program, and the police told them to stay right at the spa. So all we have to do to join them is move in pretending to be guests there for a two-week short course and try to find out what's going on. It'll be fun. And a new experience. You've never been to a spa, have you?''

"Me? Hah! You're kidding!" Caledonia's retort was explosive.

"Well, neither have I! I always thought it might be kind of an adventure. And we can help Dorothy. You know we can."

Caledonia sat down heavily on the love seat, her orange and fuchsia sateen caftan swirling out to cover most of the little couch on either side of her. Caledonia's bulk demanded large clothing, and she liked everything to be generously sized on her, so that in the huge caftans she always wore, she often seemed to be sitting on absolutely nothing, the garment covering every bit of whatever chair was sagging beneath her at the moment. It was sometimes an amazing sight—not that anyone would have dared to comment. Caledonia was big enough to enforce respect, even though she was hardly likely to have to use such force, since she was the most popular of Camden-sur-Mer's residents and as such was likely to get affectionate good manners from all she contacted.

"Suppose it's true? I mean, suppose we *can* help her? Does that mean we ought to? We've been effective with our playing detective here, but that's mainly because we knew the people involved—or most of them. And we've been lucky, too. But in a strange place among strange people, how would we be any more efficient than a professional detective? Why doesn't she look in the Yellow Pages, for Pete's sake?"

"I told her all that, Cal. Honestly. But she needs somebody who looks like they belong at her spa. Goodness knows it would be logical that I'd be a client. And you . . ." Angela didn't finish her sentence, but the wave of her hand toward Caledonia's immense expanse of sateen was eloquent.

Caledonia groaned. "I can't think of anything I'd less rather do than exercise. All that jumping around and waving your arms. And as for eating diet meals . . ."

"Oh, the meals are superb, Cal. She makes a point of it. The only thing is, they don't cook with fats. You see? You won't find a reason to complain about the food."

"Well, maybe not the food, then, but it's the whole idea. Besides, in this heat I don't really feel like going up to our main building here, let alone moving out entirely, even if only temporarily. And

I certainly don't feel like going inland where it's even hotter than here.''

There was a Santa Ana wind blowing out of the desert, one of those rare times during each year that Camden was not cooled by an ocean breeze. When inland towns like Escondido and Poway were roasting in the summer heat, Camden—like the rest of that golden crescent of ocean shore just north of San Diego—ordinarily enjoyed a mean temperature of 70, with the mercury varying not four degrees in either direction between the 2:00 A.M. low and the 2:00 P.M. high. It was one of the few stretches of coastline in the world and the only one in North America to boast a true Mediterranean climate.

But during a Santa Ana wind the temperature soared, the vegetation burned brown, shirts stuck to backs, glasses slid off noses, and tempers grew short. A Santa Ana doesn't last more than three or four days at most, but when it comes, one isn't wise to pick a quarrel, plant a garden, enter a marathon, or throw a party that would demand one's staying in the kitchen to prepare a fancy meal that nobody would want to eat. Business mergers have fallen through and marriages have foundered on less.

"Oh, she's got air conditioning," Angela said. "You couldn't have a place inland without it, even if there wasn't a Santa Ana."

"I forget about air conditioning; haven't had it in years," Caledonia muttered, wiping sweat from her brow. "We could use it today, though. I wonder if my old electric fan is still in the basement storage. I could dig it out and . . ."

"You're avoiding the issue. You're coming with me, aren't you, Cal? You wouldn't want me to go alone, would you? And I'm certainly going, whatever you decide. I mean, it could be kind of interesting, you know? Please, Cal! I'll find a way to pay you back. And I promise you won't have to do any of the exercise things . . . all you have to do is pretend to be a guest."

"Air conditioning, you say?" said Caledonia, and mopped her expansive brow.

And so it was that Caledonia Wingate, swearing and sweating in the late morning sunshine, found herself the next day laboring up the front steps of The Time-Out Inn, toting two of her several suitcases and followed by an excited Angela, jabbering and chattering with anticipation.

The old house would have looked more at home in New England or the Midwest than it did in Southern California, but then that is true of most California houses built away from the coast before World War II. The two-story structure and most of the outbuildings were of board siding, now painted stark, shiny white, and the house—originally a square block of a building—rambled erratically with additions on the right front (an enlarged parlor) and on the left rear (private apartments for Dorothy McGraw) and a huge, double-level porch across the back and wrapping halfway around the side.

The rutted old cart track that wound past the main house, skirted the outbuildings, and led eventually to a wooded lake off to the east had been paved for a short distance and widened to provide parking places near the house to the left and to make a semicircular driveway that could bring guests and their luggage directly to the front door.

The inn had been redecorated inside so that it was no longer a farmhouse in any sense. At least, no son of the soil would have felt comfortable past the front porch, where an old-fashioned swinging bench hung from chains and springs hooked to the ceiling. Even then, a real farmer would have felt ill at ease with all the pots of crimson artificial geraniums lining the railing and the spotlessly neat blue-and-white braided rugs covering the porch floor. He would have snorted with dismay at the old dinner bell hanging in a frame by the entry: the clapper was missing, and the several coats of glossy black paint on its surface would have deadened the sound in any case. The whimsical plywood cow holding a WELCOME— WALK RIGHT IN sign by the door would have turned that farmer bilious. It was all too obviously a city decorator's idea of American "country style."

As Caledonia achieved the front porch and stared in distaste at the welcoming cow, two women in lavender pantsuits with "Time-Out Inn" embroidered on the left breast pocket came rushing out and wrestled her luggage from her.

"Welcome to The Time-Out Inn," the younger woman said, smiling widely. "Mrs. McGraw told us you'd be coming in for a short course. I'm Betsy, the daytime maid. And that . . ." she pointed to the other woman, silently carrying Angela's bags ahead and up the hallway stairs, "that's Helena. The other maid. She doesn't say much, but she's a good worker and anything you want, one of us will get for you. Phone's in there—the little booth at the back—"

She gestured to her left as they walked along the hall. At the back of a small lounge was a closet with an open door, and Angela glimpsed a phone table and phone just inside. But she didn't have time to gaze. Betsy was moving quickly and turned left at a staircase. "Your room is here at the head of the stairs . . ." and she led the way up.

Puffing slightly and fighting the folds of her floor-length caftan, Caledonia followed. Angela had skipped ahead on the heels of her luggage. The artificially chilled air flowed over and around them, and Caledonia began to feel a little more kindly disposed toward the project they'd undertaken.

"Oh, look, Cal," Angela said happily, just as Caledonia finally made it through the door. "We have our own bathroom with a shower and a *huge* tub, one of those big, old-fashioned ones with claw feet. It's plenty big enough for you to soak in . . . Oh, and two wardrobes, so we have plenty of space for our clothes. Two double beds, as well . . ."

"We're sharing one room?" Caledonia said incredulously. "Nobody told me that. I thought . . . surely there's room enough for us each to have a room . . ."

"I'm sorry," Betsy said, as she opened Caledonia's bigger suitcase on the luggage rack at the foot of one of the beds. "The other rooms were all assigned earlier. Mrs. McGraw thought since you two came together it would be all right . . ."

"Of course it is," Angela said firmly, glaring Caledonia to silence. "Here." She touched the arm of the silent Helena, who was unfolding Angela's case on the other luggage stand. "I'll take care of unpacking. No need for you two to interrupt your duties. Here," and she held out two folded dollar bills. Helena backed away toward the door, shaking her head.

"Oh, no, didn't they tell you? Nobody tips here," Betsy volunteered. "It'd be worth our jobs if Mrs. McGraw knew we'd taken a tip. Thank you for the kind thought. We both appreciate it, don't we, Helena?"

Helena nodded vigorously, still retreating out the room and into the hallway. "But we're happy if you're satisfied, aren't we, Helena? That's our job. Now, I'll be glad to help you unpack if you change your minds."

Angela and Caledonia shook their heads. "Well, suit yourselves," Betsy went on. "It's nearly time for lunch. You shouldn't be late. We'll see that two places are set for you. Look for your place cards. After lunch you can tour the place before you get started with any of the activities, if you like. Or you can join right in. There's an exercise class at one. You'll see it on the schedules we've left you."

Betsy gestured toward two large envelopes lying one on each bedside table. "There's a schedule sheet in there, with times you could have a manicure or a facial or a massage. Mrs. McGraw explained that those services cost extra, didn't she? The masseuse and the fellow who does the facials and hairdos and manicures and all, they come out from town whenever anybody's made an appointment. They're not regular staff like Helena and me."

She checked her watch. "Hope it won't crowd you too much, but lunch is served right on time at twelve, and you have only fifty minutes till noon, as of now."

"Oh, that'll be fine," Angela said, and saw Betsy out the door, closing it after her. She listened a moment as the maids' footsteps sounded on the stairs, growing fainter and disappearing as they neared the bottom. "I thought she'd never stop talking! I won't remember half of that," she said, turning her attention to her unpacking.

"I'm not sure I'm going to like this," Caledonia said, as she mopped the last drops of perspiration from her brow. "I'm feeling a little more human, with the air conditioning, but I'm not used to sharing a room."

"It's perfect, Cal. We can get together in the evening, if we don't have a chance before, and compare notes about everything we've found out. You'll see. It's the best way . . .''

Caledonia looked skeptical and turned to her own unpacking.

By eleven-thirty, Angela had emptied her cases and changed into slacks and a loose-fitting cotton camp shirt. In the heat of the Santa Ana wind she was tempted to leave the shirt hanging out the way the young girls always did around Camden's beaches. But even when it included slacks (which wasn't very often), Angela's clothing was meticulously neat, and flapping shirttails went against the grain with her.

"Even though," she muttered skeptically, looking at her image in the full-length mirror on the door of their wardrobe, "it would help disguise my waistline. Goodness but I've gained weight. And it really shows when I wear slacks. I'd prefer to wear a skirt, but I want to fit in here." She turned sideways to survey her profile, tweaking the shirt out a bit to blouse over the slacks' belt line and provide at least a little camouflage.

"Go ahead and put on a skirt if you like. Why bother to wear the slacks?" Caledonia asked lazily. She had finished her unpacking and now sat in a wicker armchair reading through the packet of materials the maids had left on each bedside table. She herself wore her habitual caftan, though in deference to the informal setting she had left off the rope of pearls she usually wore as well. "I know it says here we've got an exercise class right after lunch, but if we're going exploring . . ."

"Well," Angela said, "I think perhaps, you know, I just might do at least some of the exercises. I mean, why not take advantage of our time here? We want to look like we are legitimate guests, of course. And I was thinking . . ." She patted her rounded tummy and frowned at the mirror. "I was thinking that it wouldn't hurt to play the part convincingly. I could stand to lose a pound or two."

Caledonia wisely did not comment. There are times, she knew, when even the best of friendships cannot survive total candor, especially about such topics as weight and age. Sometimes, as Caledonia had learned over the years, the kindest course was not to tell a lie, which might be horribly transparent and therefore patronizing, but to say nothing at all. The two often teased each other, but Caledonia thought she caught a wistful note in Angela's voice this time. Thus, "I think I'll roam around and get the lay of the land, myself," was all she said.

Even if Caledonia had wanted to say more, she was forestalled. The sound of a brass Chinese gong, stroked just once, sounded from the foot of the stairs. It was lunchtime.

Caledonia grinned and heaved herself up from her chair and rolled out the bedroom door, meeting almost head-on with a plump, graying woman of about fifty who was also heading toward the top of the stairs, but from the other side of the hall. "Oh, you must be the new ones!" The woman's gray hair was overcurled, so that though she had held it back away from her face with a bandanna folded over and tied around her head like a hair ribbon, the hair still struggled loose in wisps and frizzled around her face in untidy ringlets at which the woman poked and pushed almost constantly as she talked.

"I'm Belinda Terry," she said, beaming at them while she struggled with the wayward coiffure. "Just call me Belinda. We all go by first names around here. I'm a lawyer's wife from Escondido . . . grown children . . . and my husband is away for a convention. It seemed the perfect time to do something for myself." She made a little face and poked at her hair again. "Considering what's happened, I wonder if I made a good decision. You're Angela and Caledonia, aren't you? Dorothy told us you were coming. But she didn't say which was which."

"That's Angela," Caledonia rumbled cheerfully, "and I'm the other one. I'm not awfully good on names, but I'll try to remember Belinda."

"Oh, you'll learn us all, by and by. Don't let it worry you," Belinda said happily, heading down the stairs at a good pace. "You'll meet us a few at a time and the names will come. Believe me, we're a distinctive group. This way." She gestured to the left, down the corridor. "Dining room's here. Knowing where the food's served is much more important to learn than people's names."

As they came into the room, they realized that although they had responded to the gong immediately, they were the last three to arrive for the meal. Three tables for four were set up; one had only one vacant place, the others each had two. The women who were already seated glared at the new arrivals.

"You're late!" one barked out. "It's three minutes past twelve. Lunch is at twelve!"

"That's Marceline Richardson," Belinda said, not in the least upset by the hostility in the other woman's tone. "I see I'm at her table today. She's just annoyed because she has to wait. The rule here is that everybody has to be seated before anybody can start on the food."

"Right! And I'm hungry!" Marceline snapped. "Do the introductions later and come sit down, for heaven's sake, before I eat my napkin!"

Belinda seated herself and Angela and Caledonia took the two vacant places at the next table. They had scarcely reached to pick up their napkins when the other women in the room had spoons in bowls and were greedily ladling in a clear, rosy soup with tiny carrot strips floating in it.

"I'm Angela Benbow," Angela said firmly, "and this is Caledonia Wingate. And you are . . ." There was no mistaking the question in her voice, or the tone of command.

One of their table companions, a fortyish, round-faced redhead with bright blue eyes, paused in her assault on the soup. "Francesca. Francesca Cziok." She pronounced it "Chuck" but kindly spelled it out for them. She had a thick accent, slightly reminiscent of the Gabor sisters'. "Call me 'Frankie.' And before you ask it, I am from Czechoslovakia. But many years ago. And she . . ." She pointed at her table companion with her spoon. "She is Margaret Randall. Maggie. You simply must forgive us for starting in the immediate, but we have been at the exercise all morning and we are *very* hungry. You will find out how is it. Do please excuse me . . ." And she bent her head and plied her spoon again.

"Women after my own heart," Caledonia said with a grin, and began to work on her own soup. "I have a hearty appetite and I sympathize . . . Oh, gosh! This is marvelous!"

"It is!" Angela said, trying her own. "Goodness, I think we may even have a better chef here than Mrs. Schmitt. She's the chef at our place," she explained, "and a genuine genius in the kitchen. I never thought I'd find anyone who could rival . . . well, but this is exceptional."

She said the same thing over their salads, which were served with a delicately flavored sweet-sour dressing redolent of dill. And she repeated herself over the main dish, a chicken Stroganoff accompanied by broccoli done in lemon. And she said it all over again when dessert was served: a deep parfait glass filled with some kind of cranberry-colored fluff.

"Fresh fruit," she said, "but what on earth have they done with it? Isn't it marvelous, Cal?"

Caledonia was content to nod as she scraped the last bit of dessert from her dish.

Margaret Randall was the first to finish her meal. If Francesca sounded as if she was kin to the Gabors, Maggie looked the part, though her silky hair, waving down to frame her softly pretty face, was inky black. Most of the women in the room wore untidy sweat suits and no makeup, but Maggie wore a color-coordinated designer "active wear" suit of French terry, and her face was carefully made up. But if her face and hair were soft, her voice was not. She spoke with a slightly nasal tone in the accents of the American city dweller, an accent almost identical on the streets of Detroit and the streets of Los Angeles—as though the children all learn to talk from teachers trained in New York.

"You'll have to look the other way if you don't like our table manners," she said cheerfully. "We get so hungry we could lick our plates. We're all here to lose weight . . ." She pinched her own soft jowl line and shook her head until the loose flesh vibrated. "See? But wanting to lose weight doesn't mean we want to deprive ourselves. Personally, I can't do without my creature comforts. Especially after I've been bending and stretching all morning . . . Well, you'll see."

Francesca looked up from her dessert, the last bit of color scraped out of the glass. "You," she said accusingly to Caledonia. "You are not dressed for exercise! What do you think you are going?"

"I beg your pardon?" Caledonia blinked.

"You'll have to forgive Frankie," Maggie said. "She's trying to improve her English, but over the years, all she's learned is more words to mispronounce and more old sayings to mangle. You'll learn to interpret, after a while."

Francesca ignored her. "What I have tried to say is, if you intend to kick the legs into the air, you must change to something more properly. Not a skirt. Or," she said, looking Caledonia over more carefully, "or a tent, neither. Even one so pretty that it has every color under the rainbow."

Caledonia shook her head slightly. "Pardon?" she said. "I didn't quite catch . . ."

Francesca was nonchalant. "If I have the English incorrected, please say so. Maggie has right. This is a difficult language and I am slow to learn. I fractuate the grammar and my sayings are sometimes not in the right. Well, what I say is, if you understand where I am getting at, it doesn't matter about the exact, does it?"

"Of course it doesn't matter," Angela said soothingly, and touched her toe warningly against Caledonia's ankle, under the table. "Cal didn't mean to sound critical, my dear. You say you're from Czechoslovakia?"

"Yes, my family got out just before the Iron Curtain was louvred." She hesitated, thought a moment, then corrected herself. "*Lowered*, I mean. Here in America—in San Diego—we have open a pharmaceutical company. I got *that* word right, didn't I?" She grinned and Angela nodded.

"I have not learn English so well, perhaps, but I do not make mistakes with things where money concerns. None of my family do that. After my father died, my husband—also a Czech, you see—became the headsman with the company, and we have been very successful. The orders have come rolling in like hotcakes! We have made money hand over feet. So I can afford to come to this place, where I spend some of the money to lose the weight I put on eating the good food I can finally afford to buy. Isn't it ironing?"

"Ironic!" Angela said, without thinking. "Oh . . . I didn't mean to correct you."

"Ironic. Very good," Francesca said, absolutely undismayed. "I must remember that." She pulled a little spiral-bound notebook and a pencil from the pocket of her sweat suit and wrote busily. "It's no used asking that one . . ." She pointed her pencil at Maggie. "Absolutely no used asking *her* how to used words. She only learned a couple of years ago herself to talk like the upper deck."

Maggie nodded, undismayed. "She's right. We're another family that struck it rich, but in dirt, not in drugs."

"Dirt?" Caledonia was skeptical.

Maggie smiled. "Dirt. We don't put it into your house, we take it out! Teams of maids and cleaners, mostly for working wives who got no time to do their own cleaning up, see? We started doing all the cleaning ourselves. Here . . . look." She held up hands that were roughened and calloused, though now they were carefully manicured and no longer reddened. "Real housemaid's hands, right? Because I *was* a housemaid. But finally we got to hiring teams we put together from people like us, right out of our old neighborhood. So my husband and I stopped doing the cleaning ourselves and just ran the office. Then after a couple of years we could even afford to hire people to run the office! Now we got more money than we know what to do with. Ain't it a kick in the head?"

"Oh," Francesca said, delighted, and pulled out her notebook again. " 'Kick in the head' . . . I heard that last week and didn't write it down and I had forgotten it. You know, I thought it was 'kick in the heel.' "

"That doesn't make sense," Maggie said, with a touch of annoyance.

"Well, but it does, sort of," Angela said. "You can figure out the idea of what she wants to say—"

"What about the murder?" Caledonia had enough of socializing and wanted to get to the point of her visit.

The other two women looked at each other, and Francesca shrugged. "We thought perhaps you had not hear all that. Because if you had hear, you would not come here. I for sure would not myself—but the police said we cannot leave, so we are make as best we can of it by the pretend that it all never happen. And we go on the body system."

"The . . . the body system?" Angela was puzzled.

"We do walk everywhere in pairs, at least at night. And as often as we can manage in daylight, too. And we stick around in groups, too," Maggie explained.

"But the 'body system'?"

"She meant the 'buddy system.' "

"Body—buddy . . ." Francesca shrugged. "We have agree not to walk alone."

"But she . . . Belinda . . . she was upstairs alo—" This time it was Angela who felt the touch of a warning toe against her ankle. Caledonia was frowning mightily, and Angela realized that it might be unwise to start by criticizing a fellow guest. She covered her gaffe with a fit of coughing. "Sorry," she whispered in a strangled voice. "I must have swallowed the wrong way . . ."

"Do you wish a bat on the pack?" Francesca asked kindly, poising a hand above Angela's hunched shoulders.

"No-no-no," Angela wheezed, waving off the threatening hand. "Just give me a minute . . ."

"About the murder," Caledonia intervened. "We heard about it, of course, but I thought the police were here dealing with all that."

"And you weren't afraid to come here?" Maggie asked.

"Well, it really had nothing to do with us, did it? I mean, we're just two aging widows from over in Camden . . ." If Caledonia hoped to sound small and innocent, she scarcely succeeded. Even her voice was big, and it boomed out across the dining room. "We weren't here when that woman died, and obviously we have nothing whatsoever to do with her. So I think we're probably as safe as anyone could be, here."

"Makes sense," Maggie said, nodding. She pushed her chair back. "Frankie," she said, "you gonna convoy me to the second floor and the little girls' room before we go to exercise?"

"Of course," Francesca said, pushing her own chair away from the table. "The body system, you see?" she explained to Angela and Caledonia. "Well, I am pleased to meet your acquittance. We shall see you at exercise class." And she left with Maggie, as most of the other women were leaving.

"Whee-ooow!" Angela said, freed of her pretense of coughing

and taking a deep breath. "Well, Cal, are you coming to exercise class? You could sit and watch."

Caledonia groaned. "Not me! No way! It's almost worse to sit and watch people leaping about than to have to do it myself!"

She dropped her voice to an undertone, a low rumble that could not be overheard from the remaining tables. "No, I'm going to nose around here in the house and out at the steam room—look over the scene of the crime, as it were, and find out what I can from the staff. You go play at being a real guest, and you get to know people. Then this evening we'll compare notes. Up in the room after dinner. And incidentally, you were right about these meals being top of the line. I'm looking forward to the next one already!"

"But the buddy system . . ." Angela began.

"Angela, forget the 'body system.' I told the truth when I said you and I were in almost no danger at all. The dead woman was killed for a reason that not only has nothing to do with us, it isn't even something we could guess at yet. Furthermore, whoever killed her must know that, and we represent no threat at all to him."

"Her, I should think. The odds favor its being a woman, don't they?"

"That's right . . . I haven't even seen a man since we arrived, though I understand they're around here somewhere. At least the handymen Dorothy mentioned. In the meantime, I'll try to keep an open mind, but I suspect you're right—the law of averages says the killer is a woman. So, Angela, while you're out there jumping around with the others, watch your step. I guess what I'm really saying is, watch your *tongue*! You know what I mean?"

And the two friends pushed away from the table and went their separate ways.

3

◉

Caledonia headed first toward the back of the house by way of the kitchen, and Angela, surveying her friend trudging in the opposite direction, felt a slight qualm at being left alone. But she bravely headed in the opposite direction: out the front door and toward a small, rectangular, cement block building that looked from the outside like the headquarters of a one-man auto repair shop. This, according to the map that had been in each packet they found in their room, was the "Health and Fitness House," and if Angela had been in any doubt, she would have been reassured by the fact that most of the other women who'd been at lunch with her were heading in that direction as well, most of them wearing their sweats, and several carrying small towels slung carelessly around their necks.

"That alone should have given me a clue what the class was going to be like," she said sourly to Caledonia that evening when the two were comparing notes. "I should have known that, air conditioning or no, we were going to be mopping sweat!"

The air conditioning was indeed going full blast inside the little building, and the cold air hit Angela like a shower of ice water as she entered. Angela looked around her with interest and with some apprehension. Mirrors from floor to ceiling lined one end and one side of the one-room building, and stout wooden bars were fixed in front of the glass. The floor was thickly carpeted and a line of chairs stretched the length of the room opposite the mirrors. In the entrance end of the room was a forest of exercise equipment: cycles and rowing machines and miniature trampolines and two stair climber machines. Angela's apprehension grew.

"We usually start on those in the mornings after breakfast. Easy does it till the food gets digested, first thing in the day." Angela looked around and found the speaker, the hard-faced woman with the black-rimmed glasses who had been so cross at lunch. Marceline Richardson, she remembered, just as the woman, apparently unaware that Angela had been told her name, quickly thrust out her hand, shook Angela's, and introduced herself.

"Richardson. Marceline. And don't worry," the woman went on, talking as she pulled off her sweats and revealed herself to be heavy but firm, her lavender leotard straining over the imposing hips and granite bosom, "we start afternoon exercise slow, too. You won't get an upset stomach or anything. We'll stretch and bend first. Hard on the muscles if you're not used to it, but nothing that'll jar you too bad. That comes later."

"Oh? It does?" Angela tried not to sound too anxious.

"Here . . . meet a couple of the others." Marceline took hold of Angela's elbow and propelled her down the line of chairs to two more women, apparently twins, when one saw them from the rear: chubby, jiggly figures in gray sweats, and with their gray hair cut in short, no-nonsense styles. When they turned at Marceline's command, however, Angela was surprised how different they looked. One had pale blue eyes, startling in a heavily tanned and deeply creased face, while the other had an unusually young-looking, unlined face of such a startling shade of pink that Angela suspected a recent face-lift and chemical peel.

"You're from Camden, aren't you?" the pink-faced one said. "I used to live in Camden, too. When my husband was working in San Diego. Didn't I hear you say at lunch you were from that retirement center, Camden-sur-Mer?"

"She and the big one both," said the blue-eyed woman. "Where is your large friend, by the way? Isn't she going to exercise with us? She can't pretend she couldn't use it."

"Oh, she's going to ease into the program. Maybe tomorrow," Angela said, feeling, to her own surprise, a little apologetic and defensive. "Her name is Caledonia Wingate, by the way."

"That's Tilly Warfield—from Sacramento," Marceline said, waving at the blue-eyed woman and taking over the introductions with an air of sharp command. Marceline adjusted her slanting spectacles as she spoke, and the light reflecting from their lenses made her eyes seem to slant rather wickedly as well, looking knowing and aware. "I'm from San Diego, by the way."

Tilly Warfield bent to remove her outer clothing, and as she balanced precariously on one foot and stripped off the voluminous sweatpants, Angela saw that Tilly's ample curves and soft bulges were squeezed into one of the spa's lavender leotards, one apparently several sizes too small. The spandex rolled and quivered as though, Angela thought, Tilly were wearing a layer of lavender Jell-O!

"She's a state senator's wife," Marceline whispered. "And I can tell you he's not a bit happy about the police making her stay here." Tilly Warfield was tugging hopefully at her leotard bottoms, as though a rearrangement of the spandex might also result in some miraculous rearrangement of her accumulated fat cells. "He calls the police about every day to see when she can get out," Marceline went on. "Of course, he never bothers to call *her*. I suppose that's why she's here . . . to get her figure back, so he will pay attention. Maybe he sent her here!"

"Did your husband send you?" Angela asked.

"Maybe he would have—if I had one," Marceline said sharply. "I've been a widow since 1975. I find living alone suits me fine. And I don't need a husband to send me here. That's one of the few joys of being a widow: being able to make your own decisions without having to consult someone else. Not having somebody try to order you around."

"My husband doesn't really order me around," the face-lifted lady volunteered. "But he did suggest I come here. I really need it, of course. And he's worried about me, too, by the way. He wants me out of here. He's called the police. But he just owns a chain of movie houses in Phoenix, and if a state senator can't get his wife out of here, *he* certainly can't!" She began to peel off her own sweat suit, revealing that her hills and valleys were also being pinched and reshaped by lavender spandex. "Oh, my name is Cmmn Strkmmf," she said, into the folds of the sweatshirt.

"Pardon?" Angela was startled. "Commons Turkey?"

"No-no-no . . ." The pink face emerged from the swaths of gray sweatshirt. "Carmen Sturkie. I had a bit of cloth in my mouth, somehow. I'm really pleased to meet you . . . oh darn! Look at that." She was pointing to a bulletin board hanging just above the chairs. The board bristled with newspaper cuttings about diets, ads for walking shoes, letters from grateful clients, and a forest of schedules and lists, most heavily annotated in red pencil and flow-pen markings.

Angela was startled again. "What's the matter with her?"

"Carmen's annoyed," Marceline explained, "because she's just seen that we're getting Trudi as our exercise instructor this after-noon." She pointed to a typed schedule with "Trudi Locher's Tone Up Time" scribbled into the 1:00 P.M. slot.

Marceline continued, "We have a hard time with this one. Too energetic. Ginger—she's the other one here—she at least under-stands how it is with us at our age, doesn't push us so hard. She's good."

"So is Trudi," Tilly Warfield said. She had joined them after removing her sweats and folding them carefully on a chair. When Marceline glared at her, Tilly's voice became apologetic. "Well, I mean, she's probably good. But of course I agree with you that she's far too hard on us."

Marceline seemed satisfied by the explanation and started across the room toward another pair of women, also getting ready for the exercises to come. "You need to meet these girls, too," she said, beckoning Angela to follow her. "Girls, this is Angela Benbow from the retirement center over in Camden. Angela, first meet Be-linda Terry from Escondido . . ."

"We met back at the main house," Belinda beamed, tucking a strand of frizzled hair under her bandanna. "Before lunch. Where's your friend?"

"Oh, she's going to skip exercises the first day," Angela said quickly.

"Shouldn't do that," a faded woman of about forty said, moving out from behind Belinda. She was tugging on a pair of knitted leg warmers, and Angela was of the opinion that her legs were the only part of the woman that was decently covered. She wasn't fat, but she was soft, her figure drooping here and there in a dispirited way. Nevertheless, she had defied the dictates of good taste to wear a tiny bodysuit with French-cut legs. Angela thought she looked positively appalling—far worse than the heavier women with the tight leotards. This one had a tired face that sagged like her figure did, and her hair was mouse brown and stringy. "Judy Daggett," the saggy woman said. "From Austin, Texas."

"Goodness, you're a long way from home," Angela said with polite curiosity. (Privately she was thinking that those memory experts would have a field day with this combination: saggy Daggey, or saggett Daggett.)

"I read about this li'l ol' place in a magazine," Judy said with a sigh. "It wasn't as expensive as the grand one Neiman-Marcus runs. I'd have loved to go to that one, sure 'nuff, but the money—"

"Well," Marceline interrupted, "I bet they don't have murders at Neiman-Marcus's spa! And they're not charging a bit extra for the entertainment here!" Nobody laughed at her little joke, and she shrugged and turned to the next woman, a butterball who had not even attempted to ease herself into a leotard: she was still garbed in gray sweats and looked as though she meant them to stay. "This is Clara Graham . . . we call her Cracker."

"Pleased to meet you," the Graham woman said, and Angela was amused to see that her face dimpled in a number of places at once—cheeks, chin, and just at the outside corner of the eyes where they sank into the well-padded temples. There seemed to be no bone structure of any kind under that translucent skin, but the complexion was a wonder, as is the complexion of so many heavy women. "Do call me 'Cracker' like the others do . . . Cracker Graham, you see?"

"Oh, yes. Of course," Angela said, uncertain how to proceed, since she hated nicknames and really would have preferred to use "Clara," if she addressed the woman at all. "Very cute," she added.

She was saved from further comment by the Cracker's gasp of dismay. "Oh, lordy, here she comes," Cracker whispered.

A tiny girl with long, glossy brown hair bounced into the room

through a door in the far end and clapped her hands. "Ladies, ladies . . . are we all ready now? Let's move forward into position
and each take an exercise band, shall we? Where is Frankie?
Where is Maggie? Come along, come along—you're wasting
time."

The women inched reluctantly forward along the matted floor,
moving with depressed expressions toward the front of the room
where they would be closer to the floor-to-ceiling mirrors and
where their exercise instructor stood waiting. Angela felt enor-
mously uncomfortable gazing at her own image in the mirrors and
wondered if the others were as self-conscious as she. They certainly
didn't seem so. At that moment the back door opened again and
Frankie and Maggie, Angela's luncheon companions, came hurriedly in, stripping off sweatshirts as they came.

"I'm sorry we're late," Frankie panted. "We had to make a
pitch stop."

"A pit stop," Maggie corrected her, grabbing one of the large
rubber bands that lay off to one side. Each of the other women
already had one in her hands, so Angela, modestly positioned toward one edge and the back of the group, took hold of one as well.

"And then the torture started," she complained to Caledonia that
night. "The music was too loud, of course. I knew it would be as
soon as I saw the age of that instructor. She is of the newly deaf
generation that plays music full blast straight into their eardrums.
About twenty, I'd say. Trudi something-or-other. Not an ounce of
fat anywhere on that child, and her muscles were incredible. She
could bounce and kick and pull, all at the same time and without
stopping for breath, and never seem tired."

"Sounds exhausting," Caledonia said, and yawned inadver-
tently. "But I did suggest you skip the exercise, didn't I?" She
yawned again.

"You know, I think I know what the motive would be for mur-
dering an exercise instructor! The woman's a sadist! Ooooo . . . my
thigh muscles haven't been this sore since I bicycled twenty miles
with the other kids in my Girl Scout troup sixty-something years
ago! Hand me that liniment stuff again, will you? And while I
suffer, tell me about your day."

While Angela had been bending and leaning and turning and pulling and twitching and kicking in time to a thunderous disco beat, with the voice of Trudi shouting over the music, "Now reach it left . . . left . . . left . . . Now to the right . . . right . . . right . . . Now left again . . . left . . . left . . . and now to the right . . ." Caledonia had been viewing the scene of the murder.

She had intended to poke around the kitchen as she went through on her way to the pool, where her sketchy map of the grounds had told her the steam room was located. "I thought it was my big chance to get acquainted with the working areas of the house," she told Angela.

"But I hadn't realized the kitchen would be full of people. I guess they were cleaning up the mess from lunch and getting things ready for supper. Anyhow, it's really an anthill out there—the two maids scurrying around, the chef and her assistant at a dead run— I don't know who all, coming and going. Somehow I thought that all went on while we ate, or something, and the kitchen would be empty when I wanted to look around."

"Oh, Cal," Angela reproved. "You haven't done your own housework in years! You've forgotten that normal people clean the kitchen right after meals! Here, can you rub that stuff into my back and shoulders, please? I don't know how I got through dinner feeling this sore. Concentrate on my left shoulder, will you? I think I pulled those rubber bands harder on that side for some reason." She rolled over onto her stomach and Caledonia talked on while she applied Ben Gay to her friend's aching muscles.

"Well, anyhow, one of the cooks asked me what I wanted. Polite enough, but you could tell she thought I wasn't supposed to be there at all. I was trying to think of a reason to be nosing around, and then I got lucky. Our hostess came in . . ."

"Dorothy?"

"Dorothy. She came over and said, 'I suppose you wanted to see me, Mrs. Wingate?' And all I had to do was say yes. So I said it. And she walked me out the back door."

"You'll have to forgive my being so formal, Caledonia. They don't know why you're here, of course," Dorothy had explained, when they were on the porch, well away from the listening ears in the kitchen. "I don't want them to realize that I know you from outside the spa."

"You suspect your staff, then?"

"Not really. Some of them have been with me more than three years, ever since I opened. I just want to be a little cautious. After all, I *thought* I knew the girl who was killed. But I'd have said she was just a very lovely, completely harmless young woman, quite ordinary in many ways."

Caledonia nodded. "And obviously she wasn't merely lovely and harmless, was she? Or at least somebody didn't think so. Very wise of you to be cautious. Actually, I was on my way to see the scene of the crime. You said it was in the steam room, and that little map of the house and grounds you gave us said that would be out back here somewhere."

"I'll lead you. Follow me." Dorothy moved down the steps of the porch and started across the back lawn, ducking through a hedge that circled and hid the swimming pool. "It's for modesty," Dorothy explained, pointing to the hedge. "The pool could be seen from the house and from the road, before, and you'd be surprised how shy most of my guests are about their size. That is . . . I beg your pardon . . ."

Caledonia was amused. "I'm not embarrassed about my own size, so don't pussyfoot around and we'll get along just fine."

Dorothy nodded and managed a tiny smile. "Well, anyhow, we bought a lot of mature red-tips and dug them in close together and it makes an attractive hedge. It hides the ladies from people driving past. Unfortunately, it also hides the door to the steam room, so nobody can see who comes and goes from that place. Well, of course somebody in the pool could see. But the murder certainly didn't take place when there was a witness having a swim."

They were picking their way around the edge of the pool, walking cautiously on the wet concrete surround. "Somebody's been in having a swim already," Caledonia said.

"Oh, I don't think so." Dorothy shook her head with regret. "One of the workmen has been here, I think, raking leaves and small trash out of the water. Though why the guests seem to think a leaf from the hedge makes the water too dirty to swim in . . ." Then she laughed ruefully. "There speaks the miserly business-woman in me. I can't look at the pool and that spill without think-ing of money. I worry about the hourly wages required to keep the water free of leaves, I worry about the cost of the chlorine mix I'll have to add when more water goes into the pool, I worry about someone's slipping on the wet walkway here and suing me. I used to be so normal. In the old days, a spill was just a spill—just something to be mopped up."

She sighed and pulled a ring of keys from her pocket, selecting one as they stopped directly in front of three small frame buildings.

"The cabanas to the left and right are just dressing rooms," she said. "I suppose we could tell guests to change in their rooms, but it seemed more elegant somehow to have changing rooms down here. We put in bathing suit dryers and lockers where the ladies can leave their things and a dressing table in each . . . you know . . ."

Caledonia opened the door to the one at her right and peered inside. "Oh. I see. Pretty bare, except for the dressing table and the lockers. Not likely to be the hiding place for a murderer. Uh— you don't lock them?"

Dorothy wrestled with the key, unlocking the door to the center cabana. "Just this middle one, now. None of them, before, and now we still leave the two dressing rooms open so people can use them when they use the pool."

"They don't stay away?"

"Oh, certainly. From the steam room. Nobody will even go in there anymore. But nothing bad happened in the other two cabanas or in the pool, did it? I keep hoping somebody will feel like going swimming again. So far they haven't," Dorothy said sadly and turned on the light so Caledonia could see.

The central building was small, but larger than the other two, with an anteroom outfitted as a changing room—lockers, mirrors, a couple of dressing tables—and two doors in the back wall. Doro-thy stepped to the right-hand door and swung it wide. "This is where it happened. The idea, you see, was they would take a steam bath and then wash off with a swim. The pool water's heated, of course, but it would feel cool compared to the steam. The other cabinet looks exactly like this.''

Caledonia looked inside curiously. It was like a largish closet lined in redwood, and the floor was made of redwood slats. Metal gleamed up through the cracks in the slats—pipes of some sort. There were also two slat benches of redwood, one set high in the back wall, one set closer to the floor. Each was wide enough for five people abreast. "I'd get claustrophobia sitting in here with maybe eight or ten others," Caledonia declared. "It's too much like a—a broom closet!''

"Oh, we only expect maybe four women at the most at any given moment. We don't let them fill up both benches. You have to have room to move from the high bench to the low bench, when it gets too hot for you on the top level.''

Caledonia nodded. "There are two control panels here, I see— one outside and this one inside." She touched a dial and a couple of knobs set in a stainless-steel plate on the inner wall. "But if the person inside can control the heat, how could anyone be steamed to death in here?''

"That's how come we thought it was surely just an accident. A terrible accident. The inside control on this one doesn't work, you see. We found out the thermostat thing was broken a week or so ago, but we hadn't had time to get it repaired. It's something neither Bart nor Ernie can do . . . our own handymen. We should have brought someone in from outside. But we hadn't done it yet.''

"Good heavens!" Caledonia said, as she peered closely at the panel on the outside of the cabinet. "Somebody could turn this up to 'Deep Fat Fry' and set the timer for hours instead of minutes, and there's nothing the person inside could do about it?''

"Theoretically not," Dorothy said unhappily. "There's a panic bar. So the person inside can get out in a hurry. We do have the occasional guest who panics in small places, and sometimes they've used the panic bar.''

Caledonia saw that the wooden bar inside the door (a flat bar she had assumed was a large towel rack) was indeed designed to be pressed and to operate the heavy latch in the edge of the steel and redwood door. She gave the bar a push but it rattled loosely back and forth in its sockets, and the latch did not move. "It's broken. Detached or something. But that's dreadfully dangerous! I'm surprised somebody wasn't roasted in here long ago!"

"But it worked before. The police think someone must have undone it on purpose that night when Jenny was brought here. To be sure that if she woke up, she couldn't get out, you see. When the police found the loose panic bar, that's when they decided her death wasn't just an accident. Somebody brought my little assistant in here deliberately and used the heat and steam to kill her . . . Jenny. Jenny Adler was her name. I told you that, I think. Such a pretty girl." Dorothy bit her lip and Caledonia saw that she was fighting tears.

Caledonia turned and made a show of examining the controls and the door. "It only takes a screwdriver to loosen this bar thing, I see. Even I could do it, and I have trouble setting my digital clock for daylight savings, never mind fixing a door so it won't work right. You say the police thought it was an accident at first?"

"Of course. We had no idea it was anything but. Jenny was dressed for the steam room—or rather, undressed. She had only a towel on. And her hair was wrapped in another towel, wound around and knotted to make a turban, you know? But she was drugged, of course. They found out when they did the autopsy. Whoever killed her apparently brought her in here unconscious, set her down on the topmost bench, put the steam on full, turned the heat on as high as it would go, and set the timer to the maximum."

Dorothy hit the controls with the heel of her palm, as though to punish them. "I can't imagine why that stupid timer has a six-hour setting anyway! Who would want six hours in a steam room? But it will run that long . . . and after six hours at maximum heat, Jenny's heart couldn't take the strain, on top of all those drugs. Or something like that. Anyhow, she died. And I miss her. She wasn't just a nice person, she was a wonderful help. I never realized how much she did for me and for the business, till I had to do it all myself. Oh, Caledonia, I do so hope you can find out what happened . . ."

"So," Caledonia finished the story of her afternoon, "I reassured her all over again that we'd surely try. Though exactly what we should do next . . . One thing I'm glad we *didn't* do is go to that nutrition lecture in the lounge tonight. I meant to go—after all, I haven't taken part in any of the other group activities today. But the thought of having some food expert tell me to eat grated cabbage and bean sprouts and wheat germ pancakes would have done nothing at all for my disposition, and . . . Angela! Angela, are you listening to me?''

There was a snore from the recumbent figure on the bed. Under Caledonia's gently massaging hands, her friend's stiff muscles had apparently unknotted, and Angela was deeply asleep.

4

⊙

The next morning Angela's aching muscles were much improved. To her own surprise, she was able to move without much stiffness. "I'm in better shape than I thought I was," she remarked smugly to Caledonia as they came downstairs to the dining room. "The only problem is, all that exercise and this deliciously cool, air-conditioned air has given me the most ferocious appetite! I can't imagine why they say you'll lose weight on two weeks of . . . Oh, for goodness sake, where is everybody?"

The dining room was empty. The three tables were laid for breakfast, but nobody else was in the room. Caledonia, who had been yawning her way along behind Angela, looked incredulously around her. "I can't believe nobody's here! They did say breakfast was at seven-thirty, didn't they? What time is it?"

She held her watch up close to her bleary eyes (she was not a morning person in any sense of the word). "It's almost seven-thirty now! Do you suppose something's wrong?"

Angela walked across the room toward the swinging door that led into the kitchen and called tentatively, "Yoo-hoo . . . anybody here?" There was no answer and nothing stirred.

"I never thought those women would be late for a meal, the way they were attacking their food yesterday, did you? Cal, you don't suppose something else dreadful happened and they've all got killed, do you?"

"Of course not," Caledonia said emphatically. "That doesn't make sense. Well, maybe *one* person got herself killed and everybody else is out looking over the scene of the crime. Or maybe somebody fell into a hole and needs rescuing and they're all out getting a rope. Or maybe today is a special breakfast schedule and they're all sleeping late.''

"Or maybe," a voice came from the kitchen door, to which both Angela and Caledonia turned quickly, "or maybe they're just out for their morning walk down by the lake. Why aren't you ladies with them?''

It was Helena, the usually silent maid. She had entered the dining room with a tray of fruit juice glasses, which she brought to the tables and set at the places as she talked. ''You ladies didn't read your schedules fully, I think. There's a three-mile walk before breakfast every day.''

"Three miles!" Caledonia was appalled. "Before breakfast? Great aardvark on a tricycle! What time do they get up, anyway? I barely made it myself for a seven-thirty meal!''

Helena allowed herself a tiny smile. "You'll change that pattern around here, if you plan to join in with things. They get out in the parking lot beside the house at six-fifteen to do warm-up exercises with Ginger, our trail leader. She gets them nicely stretched out and they're on their way by six-thirty.''

Caledonia closed her eyes and groaned. "That's inhuman!" Angela just stared.

Helena relented slightly at the horrified expressions of her two listeners. "I may have exaggerated just a little. Three miles would be very brisk walking. Maybe it's closer to two and a half miles.''

"Oh, that helps a lot!" Caledonia's voice dripped with acid.

"Coffee's ready, ladies," Helena said, ignoring the sarcasm completely and pointing to several large thermos servers on the sideboard. "There's NutraSweet in the sugar bowl and reconstituted powdered milk in the creamer, in case you take them.'' Caledonia made a strangled noise deep in her throat.

"The newspapers are over there." Helena pointed to a small table beside the door to the hall. "But there'll be no food till everyone is here. It's the rules. So find your place cards at the tables and have your juice, have your coffee, and read a paper, ladies. I expect you'll go for the walk tomorrow morning," she added firmly as she left through the swinging door.

"Hah!" Caledonia was snorting with indignation. "I'm starving and she's talking exercise. I'm sound asleep, and she's recommending a little walk through the woodland wild! Pour me a cup of that coffee while you're at it, Angela, and don't forget the cream and sugar. Or whatever inedible ersatz concoction they're foisting on us.''

Angela, who had been silently working at the sideboard, came across the room and delivered the two cups of coffee to the table where Caledonia had seated herself. It was a tribute to Angela's habitual early rising that she was awake enough to traverse the room without spilling a drop, her hands steady. But her face was not nearly as serene as her gait. "Oh, Cal, I never counted on that walk. I always have breakfast before I go for a stroll. I'm not sure I can manage on an empty stomach."

"Well then, don't do it. I can assure you I'm not even going to try! And, Angela, two and a half miles is no stroll. You've got hold of the wrong term, there. I think maybe . . . Say, this stuff isn't half bad, in spite of all the artificial this-and-that," Caledonia said, sampling her coffee. "Surprises never cease!"

"I mean," Angela mourned as though Caledonia hadn't even spoken, "if we're going to look like legitimate guests, we have to participate in at least some of the activities. After dinner last night, we both just went off to bed."

"Well, you were aching in every joint and I was tired from all my sleuthing during the day. Not to mention being relaxed by having cool air to breathe, for a change. The only program we missed was that nutritionist talking about problem eating, and I didn't need that. I have no problem eating . . . none at all."

"They don't mean it that way, Cal!" Angela reproved, but absentmindedly. "You know, something else is bothering me. We've found out where the other guests are for the moment. And I'm sure they'll be back just any time now. But in case you haven't noticed, somebody else is missing."

"Oh?" Caledonia heaved herself upward and lumbered toward the thermos once more. "Time for a second cup. You ready yet?"

"No . . . not yet."

"Well, go on. Who do you think is missing?"

"The police. Didn't Dorothy say the police were here?"

"So you reported," Caledonia agreed as she stirred additives into the coffee until it turned the correct shade of caramel. "Oh, I see your point. If they're really here, where are they?"

"Closer than you think, Mrs. Wingate," came a voice from the door to the hall, and the ladies looked in that direction to see an old friend: Lieutenant Martinez of the San Diego County Police.

"Lieutenant!" Angela trilled, her voice light and girlish with her pleasure. "How wonderful! We had no idea you would be here."

"And I certainly had no idea the two of you would be here! What in the name of all the saints are you doing at the Inn?" Martinez eased his way across the room with that graceful stride the ladies admired so much and seated himself at the table where Caledonia had returned to join Angela.

Caledonia was beaming at him as warmly as Angela was. "I must say this is a pleasant surprise!"

"I wish I could return the compliment. Not that I'm not glad to see you. I am always glad to see you. But at the scene of a vicious murder? Ladies, I repeat, what are you doing here?"

Angela seemed too rapt in the process of dimpling at him winningly to answer, so Caledonia told the story quickly. "Dorothy McGraw asked Angela and me to come and help her find out what's going on. They're friends, Angela and Dorothy. So we came."

Martinez's handsome face was solemn. "I'll say once more that I'm glad to see you, in order that you don't misunderstand what I'm going to say next. Ladies, this is not a welcome turn of events!"

"Why not, Lieutenant?" Angela roused herself from her worshipful gaze long enough to ask.

He took a deep breath. "This is an old song I sing. You've heard the verse and the chorus before. But murder is not a game, and you put yourselves into dreadful danger when you ask questions and act as though you are finding out truths. You put yourselves at a risk from which I may not be able to protect you, and you make my job harder, because in addition to finding out the answer to the puzzle, I have to protect my two friends."

"Nonsense, Lieutenant," Caledonia said. "You had me sympathizing with your position right up to that last 'and.' Then I knew you were just saying all this because you thought you should.''

"Oh? You don't believe I have to protect you?''

"Absolutely not,'' Caledonia said cheerfully. "Say, can we offer you a cup of coffee?''

"Oh, yes. That would be very nice. With cream and sugar,'' Martinez said.

"Angela, get the nice lieutenant his coffee,'' Caledonia ordered grandly, with a wave of her large hand. Angela rose meekly and without a word went to the sideboard to serve Martinez.

"Now, Mrs. Wingate, you were saying you don't believe I would be put to additional trouble protecting you?''

"That's about it. Because there are eight other guests here and a lot of staff—I've met two maids, I saw two cooks, and I understand there is an office clerk. There are at least two exercise instructors that I know about and goodness knows who else. And you've got to protect all of them, if you can. So what does it matter that we make two more to add to your burden?''

Martinez smiled fondly at her. "Ah, Mrs. Wingate, you reckon without my foolish emotions. I am devoted to you two ladies. I should be desolate if anything happened to either of you.''

"You mean we're special,'' Angela said coyly as she returned with his coffee.

"Indeed you are. But as well as being special friends, you are a special problem. For you two tend to . . .'' He thought a minute and searched for tactful words. "You tend to get involved. To ask questions, to look into places you should not go, to make dangerous guesses better left unspoken . . . you make people think you know a great deal long before you have the answers, and as a result, a nervous killer is bound to see you as a special problem to him—''

"*Her*, Lieutenant,'' Angela said.

"I beg your pardon?''

"Her, not him. We have decided that the law of averages dictates the killer will be a woman.''

"Now that's exactly the kind of thing I mean,'' Martinez said earnestly. "You mustn't say things like that where you can be overheard! Who knows what the guilty person would think you knew or had guessed, when in reality all you're doing is thinking aloud! Though, incidentally, I agree with you about looking for a woman."

"We haven't even *seen* the men on the staff, Lieutenant," Caledonia said, sipping her coffee, "let alone considered them as suspects yet. We're told there are a couple."

"Yes, Ernie and Barton, the handymen. Sometimes they drive the van and they take turns acting as night watchmen, as well. I think they're interchangeable, except they're totally different types."

He sipped his coffee a moment, apparently referring to some invisible mental catalog before he spoke. "Ernie Morrison's got a belly that speaks of hours spent in taverns with a mug of beer and a free lunch, and he's overindulged in both. He's fifty, has slightly graying hair, doesn't shave too close, has big jowls, and frowns a lot so he looks bad-tempered. I think he's probably just squinting because he's nearsighted. But he looks mean. Barton Travis, the other one, is every teenager's dream of a lifeguard. He's in his late twenties, and he's all white teeth, tanned skin, big muscles—the kind another man hates on sight. I was surprised at my own failure to be objective. I wanted to punch him directly on his big square chin!"

"Why, Lieutenant! I never knew you to let your personal likes and dislikes get in your way like that!" Caledonia said.

"Yes, you have," Martinez said ruefully. "My personal preferences get in my way every time I deal with you two. I don't suppose I can persuade you to pack up and go home and leave the investigating to me, can I?"

"Of course not, Lieutenant," Angela said, smiling up at him. "We promised Dorothy. But I am glad to see you here. It's a comfort to know we have a friend. Oh . . . you won't let on to the other women that you're acquainted with us, will you? Nobody but Dorothy knows we're anything but ordinary guests!"

"I won't give away your secrets," he said gently. "But I let you stay with regret and only because there's not a lot I can do about it. Just promise me that you'll be careful. And if you find anything, you'll let me know. You'll do that much, won't you?'' He stood and brought his emptied coffee cup back to a plastic tray on the sideboard. ''By the way, you haven't found out anything yet, have you?''

''Not a thing, Lieutenant,'' Angela said.

''Scout's honor,'' Caledonia said, giving a Scout pledge sign. ''I know you won't believe that, but after all, we've been here less than twenty-four hours.''

''So far, all we've really accomplished is to meet our fellow guests,'' Angela said. ''And by the way, Cal, I notice they separated us for breakfast, so I'm putting our place cards back at the same table.''

''What? What do you mean?''

''I mean they moved us to different tables. They move the ladies around at each day's meals, Lieutenant, so they get better acquainted with all the others. That's what it says in one of the brochures they gave us. We sat together for yesterday's meals, so today we've been shifted.''

Caledonia looked puzzled, so Angela stood up and began waving place cards around as she talked, moving them to where she wanted them put. ''I'm supposed to be at that far table, and you're here, Cal. Well, I'm taking my card—'' . . . she did so— ''and putting it on your table. And I'll take . . . Who's this? It says 'Cracker Graham.' Well, I'm taking Mrs. Graham's place card and moving it to the far table where I was. She won't know the difference and I'll be much happier.''

''That's all very fascinating, of course, but I have to find Mrs. McGraw, ladies,'' the lieutenant interrupted them. ''Where would she be at this hour, do you suppose?''

''Oh, in the office maybe,'' Caledonia said. ''We don't know our way around very well yet. You have news for her?''

''I do,'' Martinez said. ''We were doing some checking among the records back at the station house yesterday. It's where I was while you were moving in and having your first day here. And now I have something to tell her.''

''You won't tell us first?'' Angela said hopefully. ''Remember that we're here as her agents, really.''

He shrugged. "It's not going to be a secret for very long, I suppose. And it's a matter of public record. The woman who was killed, Jenny Adler, had a past. She was a prostitute in San Diego, or at least she was three-plus years ago. Not a streetwalker, mind you, but a high-class call girl. The city police went to investigate a shooting at a downtown hotel, and apparently they just sort of happened on her in the midst of one of her—uh—transactions. It was all fairly discreet, but there's no getting around the facts."

"Did she end up in jail?"

"No. The arresting officers had no real interest in her. She was run in almost incidentally. She paid a fine and was out in no time, and that was the last the police saw of her until she turned up here dead. At least, that's the last official record on her. And now I must find out if her past had anything at all to do with her present, if you see what I mean."

"Oh dear," Angela said. "Dorothy will be so distressed! She worked so hard to get a good staff here. A staff that would be, you know, professional!"

"Apparently they are," Martinez said with a smile, "but one of them was professional in a way other than the way Mrs. McGraw meant the word. Unless, of course, she knew about Jenny's past. That's an interesting idea, and another thing I'll want to discuss, if you'll excuse me. Besides, I think I hear your table mates beginning to arrive and I don't want to seem to know you well, do I? I'll be talking to you later."

Martinez eased out of the dining room just as the first group of five laughing, chattering women headed toward their breakfasts with the enthusiasm of schoolchildren heading for recess. He smiled and bowed to them as he passed, saying, "Ladies . . . good day, ladies . . ." They giggled and whispered as he eased around them.

"Isn't he just the most devastatingly good-looking man," Tilly Warfield sighed as she hunted up her place card and plunked herself down at the middle table.

"Ooooh, I declare, those big bedroom eyes!" Judy Daggett said as she joined Tilly, having determined that her place for the day was at Tilly's left.

Francesca Cziok was at the table with Angela and Caledonia

again, and she too sighed and looked after the lieutenant's square shoulders as he walked down the hall toward the front door, presumably headed for the little building next to the parking lot that bore the legend OFFICE over its door. "He is completely beautiful," she agreed. "So much like an actor. I keep thinking I have seen him before—"

"Gilbert Roland," Angela said. "He looks like Gilbert Roland used to look."

Frankie looked absolutely blank. "Who? I don't believe I know . . . But listen, do you suppose he used to walked a beep?"

"A beep?"

"Yes, you know, how the policeman in uniform does. Walks a beep." She sighed. "Would he not be lovely in a uniform?"

Their fourth chair was filled at that point by Carmen Sturkie. "The other girls used up all the towels in the downstairs lavatory," she said, her bright pink face puckered with apology. "I had to wait for the maid to bring me more. I couldn't come in without cleaning up after our walk. I . . ." She lowered her voice to a confidential murmur. "I sweat, you know."

Then, looking over her shoulder to see that they weren't overheard, she lowered her voice still further, and leaned forward. "What are the police doing here so early? No more trouble, I hope," she said, her whisper heavy with anticipation.

"Oh no," Angela began, but got a warning nudge under the table from Caledonia's huge knee. "That is, he—the lieutenant—was asking where Dorothy might be found. But he didn't seem to be in any hurry, so I'd say there wasn't much wrong. I mean, not today. Well, of course, murder's 'something wrong,' and he's here about the murder, isn't he? Or, at any rate, I think he is . . . He didn't say so. But he didn't say a lot, did he, Caledonia?" Floundering in her lie, Angela turned for help to her friend.

"He seemed relaxed while he was in here, and he even had a cup of coffee and passed the time of day before he went on, so there can't be much new that's gone wrong," Caledonia said smoothly. "What's for breakfast around here?"

Half an hour later the women were leaving the dining room, headed for the Health and Fitness House, and Caledonia was whispering to Angela, "Listen, I can put up with healthy food for lunch and supper, especially when it tastes as good as our meals here do. But damned if I'm going to eat oatmeal for breakfast! There's a limit! I can't believe that stuff is really good for you, all mushy and runny and lumpy like that."

"Well, we didn't specify a breakfast choice, Cal, and they just brought us something. From here on in we get to mark our menus for the day and you can tell them what you'd rather have each day and for the next breakfast. I saw the menus and order blanks on the sideboard. You can mark anything you want: Spanish omelette or hot applesauce or cheese toast. Not a lot of it, I suppose, but surely enough. Please don't fuss about food. We want to be inconspicuous."

"Oh, I'm not going to fuss even though I'm starving," Caledonia growled. "I wasn't able to gag down even two spoonfuls of that dreadful stuff! Why are we going to the Health House, by the way?"

But there was no time for Angela to respond. They were already entering the Health and Fitness House, and Caledonia's expression became even more dour as she realized that they stood in the midst of exercise equipment. Furthermore, most of the devices were already occupied and in use.

There was one trampoline left unused and an exercise bicycle that no one had taken. Angela started forward, then realized that Caledonia had turned on her heel and was headed back for the door to the outside. Angela grabbed her by the arm and held on with all her might. "Cal, don't go," she begged in an undertone. "You have to take part in *some*thing! You can't be a real, bona fide client here and do no exercise at all!"

At that point, a tiny, auburn-haired woman in a lavender jumpsuit—presumably Ginger, the trail leader from the six-thirty walk, now filling in as an exercise leader—turned on a tape player at the far end of the room, and sound poured forth, loud, brassy, and heavily rhythmic. "An hour of free exercise, ladies. Use whatever equipment you like. Then we'll have a structured session including aerobics. Move, ladies . . . move-move-move . . ." The other women were already rowing down an imaginary river or climbing to nowhere or cycling to infinity or leaping and jumping in place with that peculiar, slow-motion springiness that a trampoline imparts. Angela pulled harder on Caledonia's arm.

Caledonia hesitated and Angela pressed her advantage. "Please," she whispered, her voice barely audible above the music and surely masked from the others. "Please . . ." and she held Caledonia's hand tightly in hers. "Please keep up the pretense a little longer, Cal. Pretend . . ."

Reluctantly and slowly, Caledonia turned back. Her face was stormy with resentment, but she nodded sulkily, kicked off her sandals, and stepped gingerly onto the little trampoline, which squeaked and sagged under the unaccustomed tonnage.

Tentatively, Caledonia began to bounce, her caftan fluttering in her self-created wind. At every jounce, the trampoline's canvas sagged several inches, nearly to the floor, and its springs complained noisily; but it held bravely, and Caledonia began to jump to a steady beat, sailing gracefully up and down, up and down, with her garment belling out, making her look as though she were floating. Gradually a dreamy smile appeared on her face.

Angela, sweating unhappily on the stationary bicycle, was feeling the pull on her thigh muscles, and she was breathing deeply and painfully. Every time she looked over at Caledonia sailing up and down, up and down, and smiling a little, she gritted her teeth. "Next time," she muttered aloud, "next time *she* gets the cycle and *I* get the trampoline. Next time, I promise . . ." But the disco beat of the music was thunderous, and nobody could hear that promise.

5

⊙

"I really can't understand why you're so cross," Caledonia said, striding along the overgrown path that led through tamed woodlands toward the lake. Her caftan was flapping around her legs as she stumped stoutly along behind Angela, but even the multiple folds of silky material didn't impede her. Still, she found herself gasping and falling farther and farther behind.

"Angela, for Pete's sake, slow down, can't you? Even if you're mad, there's no need to run! I thought when we ducked out and left the others getting ready for aerobics, you were going on a little stroll. Kind of a cooldown, you know? I had no idea you were starting on a marathon race!"

Angela's mouth was set and her eyes narrowed with determination or rage—or both—and she looked as though she meant to go on forever. But her steps were not as firm or as rapid as they had been when she began, and her arms were starting to pump noticeably, as though to pull her forward with each step. Her breath had shortened considerably as well.

"Angela, I simply cannot help it that I enjoyed bouncing around on that trampoline thing, and that you had to work so hard on the cycle. I didn't ask you to go on the cycle, did I?"

Angela seized the chance to stop walking and catch her breath. "You didn't need (*GASP*) to grin like a Cheshire cat, Cal. You were so obviously having a good (*WHEEZE*) time . . . and I was so obviously suffering . . . Of course I assumed you were enjoying my . . . (*GASP*) my agony on that cycle."

"Oh, don't be silly." Caledonia's breath was heavy as well.

Walking was not her favorite pastime, and walking fast was something she reserved for emergencies. Well, in a manner of speaking, she told herself, this had been an emergency. If one's best friend is in a temper . . .

"And what you (*GASP*) said to me . . ." Angela went on.

"All I said was that I'm not going to ride the stupid cycle tomorrow morning and let you take the trampoline. I don't see how that's so bad. But I'll apologize, if it'll make you feel better."

"And you'll take the cycle next time?"

"Oh no! No you don't! Just for starters, there isn't going to be any next time. I will show up at the exercise building if I absolutely must, but only to keep up appearances. I'm through with the infernal machines. You can have my trampoline, if it makes you happy. In fact, if you get there early enough, you can have any trampoline you like. But there's simply no way on earth you'll get this giant rear end" (she held her caftan out to make herself look even larger) "onto that itty-bitty bicycle seat, or make these tired old legs rotate that flywheel. No way! It doesn't make any sense for me to suffer just because you suffered."

"Well," Angela said. She thought for a moment about continuing her pout a little longer, but decided against it. She moved over to a fallen tree that looked as though it would provide an adequate bench for both of them. "Well, I suppose that'll have to do. I just want to be sure you look authentic . . . like a genuine guest here." Her sulky mood was over. The walk had soothed her temper, and besides, she was tired of the pose that her annoyance had made her assume.

"Listen, I don't know about you, but I've got to rest a minute. Move over, will you?" Caledonia plopped beside Angela onto the log and sighed. "Pretty enough place. Nice quiet lake . . ." She gestured at the water that glimmered at them some twenty feet away, the sheen visible through the leaves of some aspen and a few pine. "This is where they walk every morning, isn't it?"

"So I'm told," Angela said. "How far do you suppose we've come? It feels—", she paused, rubbing her thigh muscles ruefully—"as though we've done the entire three miles."

"Only two and a half miles, I'll remind you. And I'm sure they just go half that distance, then turn around and go back to get in the full mileage. As for us, I'd say we've done barely half a mile."

"Oh, surely farther . . ." Angela stretched and yawned. "I suppose we ought to start back. We don't want to be late for lunch, do we?"

"Just another minute. I'm enjoying the quiet and the rest." Caledonia sighed again and stretched, looking around lazily. "The woods don't have too much undergrowth, so you can see the lake and the contour of the hill here, and there's no trash lying around. Most places you go these days have bits of Styrofoam and old Kleenex everywhere. Disgusting the way people just assume somebody else is going to clean up after them. Well, maybe I spoke too soon . . . there is a bit of trash over there . . ."

She pointed across the path where something dark and shapeless protruded from under a nondescript bush. "Looks like somebody dumped their jacket this morning."

"Oh, do you suppose so?" Angela got to her feet and wandered across to the area where Caledonia had pointed. "They'll want it back, then. If they . . . Oh, Cal! It isn't someone's jacket! It's some-*one*! I mean, there's a woman here . . ."

Aching legs forgotten, Caledonia was across the path in three steps, squatting down to lift aside the branches. A youngish woman lay crumpled there, face downward in the leaf mold. The twigs, small branches, bark, and torn leaves scattered over the body camouflaged it almost perfectly against the earth. Gently Caledonia touched the woman's neck.

"Oh, Cal, what are you doing?"

"I've seen them do this on TV," Caledonia said. "I'm trying to get a pulse. Maybe I'm not doing it right. I don't feel anything. Of course," she said, transferring her touch to the still cheek, "she's awfully cold. I guess she's dead, Angela. We'd better get somebody to come."

It took a while to decide how to sort things out. Finally, Angela took off in a half-trot for the Inn, leaving Caledonia on guard beside their find. "You're better at walking than I am," Caledonia had said. "You'd best go get the police and I'll stay."

Privately, Caledonia had decided that she was also better at defending herself than her friend would be, should the killer still be lurking around—though the cold feel of that dead woman's cheek told her that the killing had been done some time earlier, and there was probably little likelihood that someone was still hiding in the brush, waiting for another victim. She also thought she might find an important clue while she waited, some clue that would allow her to triumph over Angela, for she privately felt that Angela's past successes had gone in some degree to her sleek little white head.

"Serve her right," Caledonia said to herself, "if I broke this case myself. That's the term . . . broke the case." And she kicked at the sticks and rubble beside the path, turning over a few of the pebbles with her shoe and finding nothing, but not daring to do much for fear of disturbing things enough to show.

"Don't want to be bawled out by the good lieutenant," she muttered, peering under a few bushes without lifting their branches. She did not touch or go near the corpse again, feeling very self-righteous as she detoured several feet on either side of the crumpled body. Of course, if the truth were told, she was reluctant to go too near the body through a deep sense of dread, every bit as much as through any desire to preserve clues.

In fact, she had retreated completely from the woods into the path and was leaning perilously forward from that vantage point, trying to get a good sight of the body without getting too close, and looking as though she were about to dive headfirst into the turf, when Martinez arrived with Angela in a squad car. The car bumped along over the narrow, grassy track in an erratic pattern that rather suggested that its occupants were headed for a picnic and a day of fun, instead of serious business.

Charles "Shorty" Swanson, Martinez's gawky young assistant, was at the wheel. While Martinez got out of the car and went directly to where Caledonia was in the path, standing with her a moment to gaze sadly down at the dark heap of cloth under the shrubs, Shorty uncoiled his lanky six-foot-seven frame and gallantly handed Angela out of the backseat before he went over to join his superior.

"We'll need a crew, of course," Martinez said as he bent over

the still body on the ground, touching it gently as he felt for a
pulse. After a moment he shook his head, straightened, and walked
gingerly back to the path, taking care to disturb as little as possible
with his steps. Then he sighed. "What a waste an untimely death
is. Well, I'll get things started here. Swanson, take the ladies back
to the main house and do some phoning. Tell 'em to get a move
on with the crew. The faster we move, the better we'll do. I don't
wish to hurry you, ladies, but . . ."

"Wait, Lieutenant," Caledonia began. "We found the body, and
we hardly expect to be shut out of things at this stage."

"Mrs. Wingate, we're not shutting you out. Believe me. But we
have quite a lot of work to do. Just tell me how you found her."

They both did, Angela gladly putting in her version like a stage
whisper to Caledonia's monologue.

"And now, please," Martinez said, "go back and join the others.
Say nothing. Eat lunch, if you can, and forget about this. I'll talk
to you later, because I'll talk to all of the guests. But surely you
see that right now your continued presence here would just arouse
curiosity among the others."

"Of course. But, Lieutenant . . ." Angela seemed disposed to
argue, but Caledonia took her friend by the arm and exerted enough
pressure that Angela moved along with her to the squad car.

Swanson drove them back to the house even more quickly than
he had driven on the way out. The car bucked and swayed dan-
gerously over the rutted track, and conversation in the car was
limited, as though the occupants thought they could steady the rattle
and jounce by clenching their teeth tightly together.

"This road sure wasn't built for a car with soft springs. Nobody's
come down here in anything but a Jeep for years, I bet," Swanson
managed, as the springs groaned and Angela squeaked with alarm
at one particularly violent bump.

"I think," Caledonia gulped, taking a deep breath and grasping
at the back of the front seat to steady herself against the sway, "I
think the road is mainly used for walking. The guests do a three-
mile walk each morning."

"You do a three-mile walk? Ooooop, sorry . . ." Swanson swung
the car in a sharp arc to avoid another rut, and another small shriek

escaped Angela's tightly pressed lips, while Caledonia tightened her grip on the seat ahead of her.

"Not us. Some guests do. But it's really not a full three mi . . . Listen, aren't we almost there?" Angela's voice was very small indeed.

"Right here, ladies." The bouncing stopped, the sway settled down, and the car rolled easily the last few yards as it attained the paved section of road directly in front of the main building. Swanson opened the door and let his passengers out, then with a quick wave he sprinted for indoors and presumably the nearest phone.

"Let's catch our breath a minute," Angela begged, as they climbed the three steps to the front porch. "The others haven't come over from their aerobics yet. At least, I didn't see them when I came here and got the lieutenant. And I don't hear them now. We should have time . . ."

"Here on the swing, maybe . . ." Caledonia indicated the old-fashioned white-painted wooden swing, suspended by chains from the beams that held the porch roof.

The springs holding the chains sagged and squealed under Caledonia's weight, but they were stronger than they looked, and although the swing tilted heavily to the Wingate side, and Angela wondered for a moment if perhaps she shouldn't volunteer to sit on the railing, the women found themselves moving gently back and forth, stirring a breeze that felt comforting against their skin.

"I forgot how hot I was, what with everything going on," Caledonia said, grasping her caftan and pulling the material away from her body. "Whooo, that feels good."

"All right. It feels good. Now let's talk about that dead woman. Who was she?" Angela said.

"What do you mean 'who was she?' " Caledonia asked. "How should I know?"

"Well, did you recognize her? Was she someone from the Inn?" Angela asked.

"I don't think she was one of the guests, but I didn't get a look at her face."

"Well, how will we find out, do you think?"

"Wait for the police to do the finding, Angela. The lieutenant will tell us in good time. I certainly don't fancy asking questions directly and letting the others know we've discovered a dead body. Imagine the questions—what were we doing in the woods alone, how was she killed . . .''

"Well, how *was* she killed?"

"I haven't the faintest idea."

"You examined the body, Cal. Didn't you see *any*thing?"

"Listen, girl, you can handle dead bodies if you want to. Me, I just barely checked to see if she was alive or dead. I didn't waste time *examining* her. Be reasonable. You didn't even see as much as I did. You went nowhere near her!"

"I truly am a bit queasy about it," Angela confessed. "I couldn't look very close. In fact, I'm not even sure whether or not I can eat my lunch now."

Angela, of course, underestimated her own resilience. Refreshed by a quick wash and a rapid change of clothing, she confessed that her appetite seemed somewhat restored. Lunch started with a tiny cracker spread with caviar, the first salt she had tasted since she arrived at the Inn, and she nibbled it in tiny bites to make the salty taste last. There followed a meat loaf made with ground turkey instead of beef and delicately seasoned with Vidalia onions, fresh tomatoes, and dill.

"This dish is new to me," Frankie Cziok pronounced from the next table, "but the different it is, the more I like it!"

Cracker Graham, stationed this noon at Angela's table, chimed in. "I'm not sure what she said, exactly, but I think I agree. These unusual recipes . . ."

"What's this chef's name?" Caledonia rumbled. She was at Frankie's table, next to Angela's.

They hadn't arrived downstairs from their room a moment too early; the other women had returned from morning exercise, had apparently washed up quickly, and were all in the dining room at their places, waiting. Consequently, neither Angela nor Caledonia had been able to rearrange the place cards so they could sit next to each other. And perhaps, Angela told Caledonia later, it was just as well. "We need to get better acquainted with the guests, and not talk mainly to each other."

Angela found herself with Cracker and Carmen. She thought the two looked amazingly alike—both short, roly-poly, and graying—except that Cracker wasn't nearly as pink-faced as Carmen and Carmen didn't smile as often as the cheerful Cracker. "Didn't you say you used to live in Camden?" Angela asked Carmen, hoping to get the conversational ball rolling.

"Yes," was all Carmen said. She seemed mildly depressed today. Guilt? Angela wondered. Did that mean she knew something about the second murder?

"Don't you miss the climate, living there in Phoenix where it's so dreadfully hot?"

"Oh, yes." Carmen sighed and didn't talk anymore, her pink face solemn as she applied herself to her meat loaf.

"Personally, I love hot, dry weather," Cracker Graham said. "It's good for my sinuses. But when the level of dampness goes up, like near the ocean . . . well, you wouldn't know my voice, it gets so hoarse some mornings." She dimpled pudgily. "I say it's a whiskey tenor." She waited. "You hear that? A whiskey tenor . . ." Neither Angela nor Carmen responded. "That's a joke," Cracker said a bit petulantly. "Because I don't drink, you see?"

At her own table Caledonia was finding conversation equally balky.

"Why do you want to know the chef's name?" Marceline Richardson said sourly. "Her name doesn't make the food better."

"I only meant I'd like to thank her for all this great stuff we're getting. And it would be more gracious to call her by name."

"You haven't been to cooking class yet, have you?" Tilly Warfield asked. Tilly was the fourth at their table. Caledonia shook her head.

"Well," Tilly went on, "you'll meet the chef this afternoon about four, if you join us."

"I will?"

"Yes," Marceline said, reaching for a slice of lemon. As a salt substitute, the lemon found a lot of use, and there was a saucer full of fresh-cut lemon wedges at the tables for each meal. "She teaches us one new dish a day. Yesterday it was how to poach salmon. I noticed you weren't there . . ."

"Well, I don't often cook, so it never occurred to me I'd find the lectures interesting," Caledonia said apologetically.

"Interesting! They're fascinating!" Tilly's enthusiasm made her pale eyes sparkle. "I don't cook either, but I'm certainly going to bring these recipes back to give to our cook. And am I going to wow the guests at my husband's next reception with some of these goodies. I'll be the talk of Sacramento!"

"And low calories, too," Frankie said. "This food is better than no other I've tasted. Set assured, it's the best."

"Well," Caledonia said uncertainly. "I guess that means you like it."

"Like it? I'm simply infatuous with it," Frankie said enthusiastically. "But they'd have to serve good food at a place like this, wouldn't they? It just goes to follow."

"My glory, Frankie, you're absolutely babbling," Marceline said, putting down her fork. "I can't follow a word you say. Why don't you learn English? You've been in this country long enough, haven't you? I should think . . ."

"I try. I am really try. *Ing*! I mean, try*ing*! I mean, I correct myself when I find I have make a mistake, isn't it?"

"That's exactly what I was talking about. Frankie, I get so tired of trying to figure out . . ."

Marceline's tone was hostile, and Caledonia thought she was probably saved from breaking up an argument by the arrival at that moment of dessert, a kiwi fruit mousse that turned out to be both delicate and delicious. By the time dessert was finished, the potential argument was forgotten, and the ladies left the tables without much further conversation. But they didn't get far. In the hall waiting for them stood Lieutenant Martinez.

"Ladies . . . ladies . . ." He raised his voice slightly, and something in his tone caught their attention. "I'm going to need to talk to you again, one at a time."

"My pleasure, handsome," a woman's voice said from the back of the group.

Martinez bit his lip and went on smoothly. "I'm sorry to tell you there's been another . . . incident. The victim has been identified as the assistant chef."

"That kid Bunny? Bunny Rogers?" Angela couldn't see who spoke this time either, nor recognize the voice.

"Yes, I'm told that was her name. Benita—you called her Bunny—Rogers."

"Heavens above..." "How awful..." "My lord!..." "I can't believe..." The murmur of shock and concern rippled through the group.

"Ladies, I'll be obliged if you go about your normal afternoon activities. In that way I'll know where to find you when I want you for your turn at an interview. I'm going to be in the smaller parlor." Martinez gestured down the hall, away from the dining room door and opposite the main lounge. There, an oak door stood ajar leading into a room Angela and Caledonia had all but ignored in their coming and going about the Inn.

"I will be first," Frankie Cziok said cheerfully. "I have no mind!"

"I beg your pardon?" Martinez looked startled.

"I think she means 'doesn't,' Lieutenant," Angela interpreted. "Frankie, you should say 'I don't.' "

Frankie looked puzzled. "Oh. All right. I *don't* have no mind."

Martinez hurried on with his instructions, as though talking would help him control his face, which appeared to have developed a slight twitch just at the corners of his mouth. "In any event, I'll want you to come in about one-fifteen, Mrs. Cziok. I'm taking people in alphabetical order, for want of a better system. That means I begin—"

"With me!" Angela crowed delightedly. "With me!" And she scurried away from the group and into the little parlor. Martinez acknowledged her eagerness with a slight bow as she passed, and following quickly, closed the door behind them, which left the others milling about in the hall and buzzing with questions.

6

⊙

As Angela entered the parlor, she saw that Swanson was there as well, his gaunt length coiled into a straight chair, a notebook balanced on one of his skinny legs, ready for note-taking. "Officer Swanson," she greeted him with obvious delight. "I'm so glad you're here. I didn't get a chance to talk to you before, to ask how you are, how your romance is coming along . . ."

"Mrs. Benbow," Lieutenant Martinez interrupted. Or rather, he tried to interrupt.

"On the ride from the house to the woods, I was . . . you know. . . preoccupied. And I was far too rattled during the ride back. Literally and figuratively. What a dreadful road! It's a good thing I don't get carsick, isn't it?"

"Mrs. Benbow—"

"And, of course, finding a body is very upsetting. But that's really neither here nor there."

"At last!" Martinez sighed. But he sighed prematurely.

"Tell me how you and Chita Cassidy are getting on," Angela said cozily. "I always say I'm really responsible for your engagement. I knew Conchita before you did . . . I practically introduced you. Well, of course, I realize she works at our place, and you met her incidentally, while you were there investigating. But I was the one who always said what a good couple you'd make."

"I haven't had much chance to get over to Camden to see her lately," Swanson muttered, a distinct blush spreading over his neck. He ducked his head toward his notebook and raised his pencil, as though to remind Angela of the business at hand.

Martinez was less subtle. "Mrs. Benbow, please. The social

56

amenities can wait. Ask the lovely Miss Cassidy about the state of her romance when you return to Camden. Officer Swanson and I have a murder . . . no, now *two* murders . . . that need our attention.''

"Absolutely," Angela said. "I agree fully."

"You do?"

"Certainly. After all, I discovered this latest victim. At the very least, I want to know all about her. You said she was—"

Without asking his superior, Swanson flipped a couple of pages in his notebook and read aloud, "Benita Rogers, a.k.a. Bunny Rogers, a.k.a. Bunny DeVere, ran away from her home in Deming, New Mexico, to be a dancer in Hollywood. A couple of years later she shows up in the chorus line at a little club in San Diego."

"A chorus girl!" Angela was fascinated. "I don't believe I've ever had anything to do with a chorus girl before."

"She wasn't a very good one, apparently. She worked in a cheap club when she got to San Diego. We don't know what she did up in LA and in Hollywood. At least, not yet," Martinez said.

"Lieutenant, how is it you know even this much about her when we located the body just this morning? It took you several days to unearth Jenny Adler's lurid past."

"That," Martinez said, "was sloppy police work. And I take complete responsibility. You see, when we arrived here to look into Jenny's death, we naturally inquired about everyone's background, but the living first, since the dead could wait awhile. And Benita Rogers—this girl we found today—"

"I know, I know," Angela said a bit snappishly. "I'm not senile enough yet to forget that fast!"

Martinez had the grace to look embarrassed. "Well, this Rogers girl told us straight out about her past as a dancer. Maybe she figured it would look better to seem completely open—to seem as though she had nothing to hide. But I'm glad to say the pose didn't fool us. We found out about the rest of her record quite easily, especially since we had her alias to work with. And we came back here and faced her with it."

"Wait-wait-wait, Lieutenant, what record do you mean?"

Martinez opened his mouth to answer, but Angela blasted straight along. "And I don't really understand—if you could find out all that about Bunny, why didn't you find out about Jenny Adler right away, too?"

"Because it never occurred to my assistant here to search criminal records for Jenny's background. Of course, I should have done all that myself, or at least checked on Swanson. That's why I say the lapse is my responsibility. But then, Swanson used to be utterly reliable. I've never had to deal before with Swanson in love!"

Swanson glared ferociously at his notebook, and a red flush once more glowed beneath the short hair at the back of his neck. "I wasn't thinking of Chita. I told you, sir . . . it was just that everyone was telling me what a nice, quiet kid this Jenny was—what a lady—"

"Very possibly true. But you know better than to take that kind of thing for granted."

"Yeah," Swanson said. "I know. I really do know . . ."

"Whatever the cause, we eventually did find the record and traced Jenny back. But it took a while. And then when Benita was stabbed . . ."

"Stabbed?"

"Yes. The knife was there under her body where you found her. It was from a set in the kitchen here. And that raises the possibility that it was a weapon of convenience—that is, that the killing wasn't premeditated, but rather carried out on impulse with the nearest thing at hand."

"Lieutenant, you said a minute ago that this Bunny had a record?"

"Oh yes, Mrs. Benbow. Certainly. What she'd neglected to tell us in that first interview—maybe she thought we wouldn't find out—was that she had also worked, at least part time and while she lived in San Diego, as a prostitute."

"Oh, dear! Just like the first girl, Jenny!"

"Well, yes and no," Martinez said. "You probably don't know about this kind of thing, but there's a distinct difference. Jenny Adler was a call girl. That means, Mrs. Benbow, that she worked as a prostitute, but under vastly different conditions from the ordinary streetwalker. A call girl can be more like the Japanese geisha . . . hired to be a companion to a lonely man. Or she can be hired merely to act as his 'date.' ''

Angela seemed puzzled. ''But why would a man want to hire a date? Why not go to dinner alone if he doesn't have a friend to go with?''

''Some men measure their worth by the admiration others show. They spend too much on clothes, they spend too much on jewelry and cars, and they will even spend a lot to have a gorgeous woman with them at public functions, or in restaurants where they know they'll be seen by people who matter to them in business.''

''My word! Was Jenny Adler that pretty?''

''Apparently so. Hard to tell, when I saw her, of course.'' He hesitated and then thought better of enlarging on that subject.

''I said high-class call girl, and that's what I meant. None of this one-hundred-dollar-a-night 'escort service.' Jenny worked for people who charge five times that and more, and who guarantee beauty and brains in the women for whom they act as''— he hesitated and selected a word carefully— ''as agents. The night Jenny was booked by the police, she was with a powerful legislator.''

''How exciting. Who was it?''

''I won't tell you more than that. But he could afford to buy a companion who would make other men jealous of him. And he seems to have done just that. He had taken her to dinner at a good restaurant, and they had attracted plenty of attention. But then they went back to the hotel, and when the police found them, they were in . . . rather intimate circumstances.''

''What you're telling me,'' Angela said rather primly, ''is that as a call girl, Jenny made her favors available as well as her conversation.''

Martinez was amused. ''Yes, I suppose so. But frankly, I'm surprised that you know about that kind of thing.''

''I watch television quite a lot of the time,'' Angela said, still holding a rather prudish expression, her lips tightly pressed. ''I don't approve of these shows, but goodness I learn a lot about the real world!''

Martinez didn't show even a flicker of amusement. ''Well, anyway, both the women were active in the world's oldest profession, though apparently in a somewhat different class from each other. Not that Bunny was simply a streetwalker, either; apparently she sold 'her favors,' as you put it, to the occasional club patron who wanted company after the show, when the club closed.''

''She told you that?''

''Hardly. But that was certainly the case when she was arrested the last time. Bunny's 'client' that time was a college kid from upstate who ran into her at her club and thought he was pretty hot stuff when she agreed to go with him back to his hotel room. I don't think he realized he was just one of a series of cash customers. Not until the police started rounding up folks. It all came out then. She'd been arrested once before . . .''

''The most interesting thing about it,'' Swanson broke in eagerly, ''that last arrest of Bunny's was at the Kimbrough.''

''The Kimbrough?'' Angela was blank.

''The hotel where Jenny was arrested, and on the same night as well,'' Swanson said meaningfully. Obviously, he found the coincidence significant.

''My goodness! What does that mean?'' Angela said.

''We're working on it,'' Martinez assured her.

''Well, why did the police go to the hotel in the first place?'' Angela asked. ''Were they out rounding up prostitutes that night, or something?''

''No, it wasn't a vice squad thing. I thought I mentioned this to you before. There was a shooting in one of the rooms. Person or persons unknown disposed of a sometime resident there known as Peter Guns to his friends, Pedro Gonzalez to the police, although I suspect that was an alias as well. Certainly he used yet a third name to sign the hotel register: Gunnar Peterson, though with his black hair and dark skin, he looked about as Swedish as The Supremes did! He was a not-so-small-time drug dealer from Las Vegas, and he'd apparently taken a room at the Kimbrough to use as his headquarters when he was in town.''

''Drugs? He was selling drugs? Right there at the hotel?'' Angela was horrified. ''I think I stayed at the Kimbrough once some years ago when I first moved to San Diego . . . you know, before I went up to Camden to live. It was quite an elegant old place—a lot of potted palms in the lobby, brass railings, and dark oak—tremendously respectable.''

"The hotel is still old-fashioned, quiet and discreet. They wouldn't have tolerated any funny business—drugs, prostitution, any of that—if they'd known about it. And there really wasn't anything about Peter Guns, just to look at him, to suggest he was going to set up shop there. And maybe he wasn't.

"But he had neatly packaged drugs in his suitcase under the bed, and lying beside him on the bed there were more of the smaller packets, maybe ten-thousand dollars worth or so. Lying on the floor there was a one-hundred dollar bill, and we think that a deal was interrupted by a quarrel with a buyer, who ended up killing Guns. We think that after the shooting, the killer grabbed his money and maybe some of Guns's little packets of drugs and ran. We think he was in a panic to escape, and that's why he didn't search the room and find the rest of the supplies. The shot certainly roused everyone on the same floor—everybody milling around in the hall, the police arriving—whatever the case, we never found out any more. And now it's odd to think of it all starting up again, after three years.''

"You think the death of the two girls is somehow connected to the shooting at the hotel," Angela said wisely.

"Well, it seems an interesting coincidence, at the very least. We'll have to go back over the files on the Kimbrough murder now. But that's going to take us a while. There are pounds and pounds of papers to read," Martinez went on. "We spent a lot of man-hours trying to get to the bottom of that one."

"That does surprise me, Lieutenant. I'd have thought you wouldn't put out much effort when somebody does your work for you—getting rid of one of the 'bad guys.' I'd have thought you'd be delighted when one of *them* gets bumped off!"

"It's true I didn't exactly send a wreath to Guns' funeral," Martinez said, "but we don't encourage people taking the law into their own hands in our jurisdiction. Not even for a good cause. And if you wink at that kind of thing, the public thinks you're condoning it. Then where you had one before, you'll have a dozen tomorrow. One 'Subway Vigilante' can be either a hero or a menace, depending on your view. But a dozen like him, banging away with cheerful abandon at every imagined wrong, could decimate the population of our largest cities within months.

"Remember what happened when someone took a shot at another driver on the freeway out here a couple of years ago? Every member of our California lunatic fringe grabbed a gun and went out to avenge petty slights on the road. Accidentally cut a little close to another driver, and he was likely to level a .38 at you through his car window. Be slow putting on your turn signal, and a shotgun blast might take off your fender!"

"Lieutenant, all this still doesn't answer my question."

"Oh, I'm sorry, Mrs. Benbow. Did you ask a question?"

"Back about four topics ago," Angela said sweetly. "What was Bunny DeVere doing here? I mean, what were they both doing here? This is the kind of coincidence you say you distrust."

"I'm not sure about that," Swanson said. He seemed to have forgotten his earlier embarrassment. "Two hookers might get a notion to quit about the same time. Maybe their arrest after the Kimbrough shooting was just the last straw for both of them."

"Oh, I can believe that much," Angela said. "But can you believe they'd both end up here? On Dorothy's staff?"

"I don't know about Jenny Adler," Martinez said, "but I know what Benita told me a couple of days ago when I faced her with what I'd found out about her past. She said that just at the time she'd decided to leave San Diego and make a new start, this place was advertising in the paper asking for hired help. Two things appealed to her. First, the ad said 'No experience required—we will train you.' She liked that because she had no confidence in her own talents, and no special training."

"Her dancing?"

"She was barely hanging on in the chorus in some really second-string clubs, and that was enough to have given her doubts about her chances for success, all right. She thought she needed a job that would train her like this one would. And the other plus for her coming here—this being a spa for women only, she was unlikely to run into any of her old contacts here who might blow the whistle on her."

"Well," Angela said later to Caledonia and Dorothy, "that explains Benita—"

"Bunny," Dorothy corrected unhappily. "We all called her Bunny around here. Angela, I really didn't know any of this about her. She showed up and said she could cook, and she proved it to Paula's satisfaction."

"Paula's the chief cook," Caledonia explained to Angela. "I asked around for the name. The food here is so special I thought the cook had to be something special, too."

"Chef," Dorothy corrected.

"I thought 'chef' was a word you applied only to men," Caledonia said.

"Oh no," Dorothy said. " 'Chef' is just the French word for 'chief' . . . the chief cook is really what 'chef' means. So it could be a man or a woman . . ."

"Aren't you both a little off the track?" Angela's voice was tart. "You always accuse me of wandering from the subject, and listen to you!"

"Okay. I'm sorry. What were we talking about, anyhow?"

Angela had gone from her interview directly into the largest parlor of the old farmhouse, where the other women, including Caledonia, were all sitting, whispering and speculating, waiting to go one at a time to see Lieutenant Martinez. Shorty Swanson, consulting a list, had called Frankie Cziok, who hurtled along in his wake to face the lieutenant in private. "I am look forward to see the handsome lieutenant again," she chortled to Swanson's amusement. "He has me absolutely mesmatized!"

But Angela hadn't so much as found herself a seat when an energetic Trudi had come bouncing in to round them up for their postlunch session in the Health and Fitness House.

"Ladies, ladies, ladies . . . it's past time for afternoon exercise class. Your rubber bands are waiting for you. Come on, come on, come on . . ." Trudi clapped her hands in command. There was a modicum of grumbling, but one by one the women reluctantly hoisted their assorted tonnage to a standing position and began to straggle out toward their bends and stretches.

"We were just waitin' to see who would be called in for an interview next," Cracker Graham protested.

"I understand you're to be interviewed in alphabetical order, Mrs. Graham," Trudi countered. "You won't be needed for several minutes, and in that time you can burn enough calories to take care of your dessert from lunch. So let's go, let's go, let's go . . ."

And with reluctant steps the women had moved out. But just as Angela got to the hallway, Dorothy appeared quietly at her side and cocked her head in the direction of her own rooms. Angela raised her eyebrows in query and pointed silently to Caledonia, who was trailing along behind the group, heading out the door just behind them but with twice their reluctance in her dragging steps. Dorothy nodded, and Angela pattered quickly up to grasp Caledonia by a bit of her flowing caftan, just before she made it out the door.

"Psssst . . ." Angela gestured mysteriously with her head toward Dorothy, rolling her eyes at the rooms in the rear, jerked a thumb at the backs of their retreating fellows (now inching their way along the path toward the afternoon's festivities), and quickly did a "hush" gesture across her lips with her other hand.

Caledonia's chuckle rumbled through the hall, but she kept it a controlled mutter of sound until she was safely inside Dorothy's sitting room. Then she let go with a guffaw.

"I wish you could have seen yourself, Angela. You had so many messages to convey by expression and sign language, I'm surprised you didn't have to take off your shoes to do it! Do you realize you signaled 'Wait'—'She wants us'—'Go to Dorothy's room'—'Be quiet'—and 'Don't let the others know'—and all without saying a word? The kids at Gallaudet would be proud of you!"

Angela waved Caledonia to silence and started the meeting by delivering a complete report of everything she'd learned from Lieutenant Martinez. At last she reached the subject of her own immediate curiosity. "Dorothy—about Bunny DeVere—she really could cook?"

"Oh, absolutely. Of course, she had a number of shortcomings . . . she was a habitual absentee, for instance. Regular staff get only one day off a week, while one of our regular sessions is on. But she only managed to come to work an average of five days out of six. That's how come nobody went looking for her when she was missing from work this morning.''

"I'm fascinated that she was such a good cook, though," Angela said. "It somehow seems so unlikely!"

"Well, she wasn't very confident of her own abilities. When she came for an interview, she told us she had no skills. She suggested she'd be suited to cleaning duties. But then she said, sort of in passing, that she liked to cook. Paula put her through a test—had her make several fancy dishes—and the child really was a natural in the kitchen.''

"In the bedroom, too, probably," Caledonia muttered.

Dorothy ignored her. "She did a low-calorie béchamel sauce that would have fooled Escoffier into believing it had real cream in it. Her poached pears would make you weep. The girl was a talented chef.''

"Then why did she say she had no skills?" Angela wondered.

"I've seen it over and over. Women—maybe not the kids today, but the majority of women near thirty or more—tend to underrate the things they do every day around the house. Haven't you noticed? Skills they've built over a lifetime don't seem to them to be such rare gifts as they really are.''

"Sure," Caledonia agreed. "That's why women accept so little money to do invaluable jobs like being a nanny. Or a house-keeper.''

Dorothy nodded. "Some jobs—like being a practical nurse—just seem to come easier to women, whether it's by nature or, as the feminists would say, by conditioning. And so they sell themselves short, and they'll take less money than the job is worth because they believe they're just doing unskilled labor. Like poor Bunny . . .''

"Which reminds me," Caledonia said, "didn't you ever ask Bunny about her past?"

"Certainly. She told me she'd been a dancer. And that's all she said. It never occurred to me to ask if she'd been a . . .'' She hesitated.

"Well, I should think not, Dorothy," Angela said hastily. "Any more than you would have asked Jenny.''

"I didn't have to ask Jenny," Dorothy said. "She came to me three days before she was killed and told me she wanted to make a confession. She explained about her old life as a call girl and said she'd left all that behind her. She'd been thinking about breaking away—making a clean start in life—for some time, but my ad in the paper was what turned the trick for her . . ."

"An unfortunate choice of metaphor," Caledonia rumbled. "Perhaps you should just say 'made up her mind for her.'" Dorothy looked bewildered, so Caledonia just went on. "Listen, Dorothy, didn't you consider firing her after that confession?"

"Whatever for?" Dorothy was blank. "The past is past. And I already told you she was a really good assistant. In fact, I don't know how I'm going to manage without her."

"You didn't tell the police about Jenny's past, did you?" Angela accused. "Lieutenant Martinez said they had to find that out for themselves."

"No, I didn't. I didn't see how it could possibly be important. And I wanted—oh, I don't know—I just felt like she hadn't wanted people here to know, so I wanted to keep her secret, too. Do you see?"

"Do you think the girls knew about each other's past?" Angela said suddenly. "Jenny and Bunny, I mean."

Dorothy shrugged. "I don't think they were friends or anything. They didn't see much of each other here at work, anyway."

"They must have known each other before, though," Caledonia said. "It only makes sense. After all, they were both arrested at the Kimbrough the night that Thomas Magnum was shot to death."

"Peter Guns," Angela corrected her. "You have the wrong detective's name. I mean, the real one was called Gunn, not Guns. And, of course, it's only a joke, but—"

"Well, I knew the name was some kind of weapon." Caledonia dismissed the correction with a wave of her hand. "Anyhow, don't you both think they must at least have seen each other—in the paddy wagon or at the police station or somewhere like that? And when they got up here, each of them trying to outrun her past, I bet they met privately and agreed to keep that past quiet. Don't you think it's likely?"

"Certainly," Angela agreed. "It sounds just right, to me. But the dead girls are the only ones who could tell us if they were well acquainted, or just met casually as you say."

"I'm not sure there's any way to find out now, Angela," Dorothy said gloomily. "They certainly can't tell us."

"Maybe there *is* a way," Caledonia said. "Dorothy, you have records on your staff, don't you? Where are your people from? Are there any who have connections to San Diego, and therefore might have known the girls or might be involved in that Kimbrough Hotel business?"

"The police already checked on where everyone was from," Dorothy said. "My staff is from out-of-state."

"Isn't everybody?" Caledonia murmured. "That's the story of Southern California!"

"I mean," Dorothy said, "that at least as long ago as that hotel shooting most of my staff weren't anywhere near San Diego."

"Except," Caledonia corrected her, "for those two girls."

"True," Angela said. "So I suggest we concentrate on the guests. We don't know nearly enough about them to be helpful. Not yet. And we can't find out everything by just asking."

"We already know that Frankie Cziok lives in San Diego," Caledonia said. "She told us so."

"Mrs. Richardson is from San Diego, too," Dorothy said, entering into the spirit of the thing. "You remember which one she is—hard face, pointed glasses, cold voice . . ."

"And that Sturkie woman with the bright pink face, she used to live in San Diego. We need to find out how long she and her husband have been gone from there. They live in Phoenix now," Angela said. "Cal and I will have to find out more, of course. We'll have to look into the guests' rooms."

She jumped to her feet. "It's the perfect time, right now. The maids are having their lunch break and then they'll be setting up for dinner. They won't be upstairs. Our fellow guests have all gone to the afternoon exercise sessions. Or most of them have. They'll come back here one at a time to be interviewed by Martinez. And when they do, they have no reason to come upstairs."

"If one of them needs to stop in her room, though . . ." Dorothy said uncertainly.

Angela shrugged. "They probably won't. They'll be heading right back to the Health and Fitness House after their interviews. Martinez tells each of us to call in the next one, and each woman will have to go back across the lawn there to get the next interviewee. And once she gets there, she'll stay. Believe me, they're scared of Trudi. You really should tell her to tone down the drill instructor manners, Dorothy."

"One of them might need to use the powder room while she's here . . ."

"We usually use the one downstairs off the main parlor, between activities."

"But . . ."

"Dorothy, it will be all right. If one of them actually comes upstairs, Cal and I will get out into the hall and pretend we're knocking on a door, or something. It'll work out. I promise. We really need to see if there's anything—oh, you know—anything odd or incriminating or . . . Well, it just stands to reason we'd need to see their things."

"Oh, dear, I don't know. I feel funny about that. As though I were violating their confidence . . ."

"Why?" Angela said. "You're not doing anything. We are. Cal and I. And all the doors here are kept unlocked. That pamphlet you gave us when we came said we had to leave them that way."

Dorothy nodded. "Necessity. We bring in fresh linens and we do a check for illicit supplies every now and then."

"Illicit supplies?"

"Our clients are natural cheaters. That's why they come to us in the first place, of course—to get somebody else to take responsibility for their lives because they can't or won't do it themselves. Anyhow, when we started, with our very first group of clients, we found they had hidden food in their rooms: Hershey bars, Reese's Pieces. One woman walked down to the village every night and smuggled in a barrel of Colonel Sanders' best, right after she finished our dinner!" Dorothy's outrage was almost comic.

"Well, we took the locks off the bedroom doors and put bolts on the inside instead. For privacy's sake, you know." She seemed abstracted and unhappy.

"Look, Dorothy," Caledonia said. "Angela's right, this time. I admit she always snoops where she shouldn't, and I'm not really any fonder of our nosing through those rooms than you are, but Angela's telling you the truth . . . we really should check them out."

"That's something the police can't do, don't you see?" Angela said. "At least, not without a warrant. But we have an advantage: we don't need a warrant. Come along, Cal," and she spun out the door, eager to get started on her quest.

"I promise not to let her snoop through any more than we absolutely must, Dorothy. And I promise we won't tell anybody but you and the police what we find. Okay?"

Dorothy nodded reluctantly, and Caledonia headed out behind Angela, the good soldier following the leader into battle.

7

⊙

"First we make a list," Angela advised, when she and Caledonia reached their room and stopped off to make their plans, first closing their door against the accidental eavesdropper. Angela seized a pencil. "Let's decide which of our Inn mates we'll investigate. Well, for starters, not Frankie, of course. She couldn't have anything to do with a murder."

"Why? Because you like her?"

"Well, yes. Partly. But she's not the type, is she?"

"Angela, how many times will it take you to learn that there is no 'type.' Or rather, everybody seems to be the type, given the right provocation."

"But not" —Angela set her chin stubbornly— "Frankie."

Caledonia made a face of disapproval. "Put her on the list anyway."

"Oh, very well. And then let's see, we said Richardson. Marceline Richardson. She's from San Diego, right?"

"Right. And who else? Well, let's think about them . . . there's Judy Daggett . . ."

"She told me she was from Austin, Texas, and she certainly talks like a Texan. Southern idiom, slight twang . . . I don't think I'd put her on the list. Not yet."

"How about Maggie Randall? She's the fashion plate with the careful makeup, remember?"

"Of course I remember," Angela said in a huffy voice. "I've been listening. But is she from San Diego? Somehow I thought not. Anyhow, we're going to look into the pink lady, Carmen Sturkie,

70

too, because she used to live in San Diego. And Cracker Graham, because we don't have any idea where she's from.''

"Oh! Write down Belinda Terry. The first one we met . . . the one with the frizzy gray hair, remem—''

"Cal, I remember! But why her?''

"Well, she's from Escondido. And since Escondido is only twenty-five miles from San Diego and since this is the automotive age, I don't think you can say that's too far away to consider.''

"Well, then, I don't think we can rule out Saggy Daggett after all; an airplane would get her from Austin, Texas, to anywhere in the world in a few hours, let alone San Diego. And, of course, Tilly Warfield. And that's the whole bunch.''

"Tilly Warfield? Because Sacramento is so close to San Diego by car or plane?''

"Of course not, Cal. Because Tilly Warfield is a state senator's wife, and her husband might be the 'powerful legislator' who was found with Jenny when the police were investigating the Kimbrough shooting.''

"Good grief, Angela! What a jump in logic! And look . . . you've written down the entire guest list!''

"Well, then, we'd better get started, don't you think? We won't have a better time.''

Determining there was nobody listening in the hallway and nobody in the first room they chose—directly across the hall from theirs—was no problem. Finding anything significant, however, was a different matter. The room had been assigned to two women, as they discovered: Cracker Graham and Carmen Sturkie.

The occupants' purses were stored trustingly on the floor of two respective wardrobes that served this room, like several others, as closets. The first thing the searchers found was that Cracker was a resident of Oceanside. "Good address," Angela whispered. "She's got money.''

"We knew that," Caledonia answered, head down in Carmen Sturkie's things. "Or she couldn't afford four weeks here! Ah . . . letter from the husband . . . Better do your investigating now, Angela, and don't talk till later. There isn't time, and we don't know who might go past in the hall and hear,'' and she fell silent herself as she skimmed the letter, then rummaged along further through the purse.

Angela kept up her search of the Graham handbag, paying close attention to bills, letters, and a leather-covered pocket appointment book. Graham's purse proved that she bought her clothing at a very expensive shop in Costa Mesa devoting itself to disguising the figure problems of the hefty woman, that her recent physical had proved her to be in pretty good shape for an overweight woman of forty-five, and that her daughter, a student at Bryn Mawr, needed money for a spring vacation trip to the Bahamas with three people named Morgy, Mitzi, and Boopsy. Cracker's lipsticks were all worn down badly (*"Angela, you didn't take time to open all her lipsticks, for Pete's sake!"*—*"Well, of course, Cal. You never know where secret papers might be hidden."*—*"In a lipstick? Oh, grow up! We're not in a John le Carré novel!"*) and she was careless with her jewelry, for a strand of baroque pearls had been dumped casually into the bottom of the bag (*"Real pearls, Cal. Imagine mistreating them that way!"*), and in the pocket of a silk traveling suit Angela found a gold rope bracelet that must have exceeded sixty grams in weight.

The most interesting thing, however, was a half-finished letter still rolled into a small portable typewriter that Angela discovered in the back of the wardrobe. The letter began:

My darling Paul—
I miss you so much I can hardly bear to think it'll be another three or four weeks till I see you again. You mean everything to me, and—

There the letter stopped, interrupted no doubt, Angela said to herself, by one of those grim exercise sessions. The checks Angela found in Cracker's checkbook were inscribed "Gerald and Clara Graham." Obviously the letter to Paul was not intended for Cracker's husband; Angela made a mental note to find out by some judicious questioning who Paul was.

About ten minutes after they'd entered the room, they were ready to leave. Caledonia eased the hall door open a crack and peeked outside. "Nobody. Come on. Quick," she whispered, and they hurried out. "Still nobody around. Let's try the next one . . ."

The next proved to be assigned to one person: Belinda Terry, as Caledonia discovered. "I'll take this," Caledonia said, after she'd tapped lightly on the door, received no answer, and eased the door open silently. "You go down to the next one. And, Angela, don't take too long. Let's say nine minutes, and I'll meet you back here in the hall."

"Nine? Why nine? Why not ten? Or fifteen?"

"Because when you're late, you always pretend you forgot what I said. If I make it some odd number you'll have to admit you remember."

"Nine's an odd number, all right. But I remember even numbers just as well, honestly, and . . ."

Caledonia just glared. "Don't try to be cute! Check your watch now. Nine minutes . . ."

Angela scuttled to the third door in the row, tapped lightly on it, and hearing no response from within, entered a room that looked as though it had been hit by a strong wind. Silk and satin lay tumbled and twisted in the dresser drawers and spilled onto the foot of the bed. The occupant had apparently plowed hastily through the underwear drawer, making a selection, and had not replaced a thing. (*"Frivolous, fancy underthings, Cal, and really unsuitable to a spa vacation. Nothing guilty about that, of course, but it certainly shows a poor sense of . . . of fitness! Or possibly great vanity. Either way, sports bras and cotton panties would have been more appropriate."*)

The closet was likewise tightly packed with exotic colors, expensive fabrics, and an amazing number of items sporting beads and sequins. Angela clucked her disapproval of all the designer chic.

In the bottom dresser drawer Angela found an elegant leather handbag, and she wasn't really surprised—considering the clothing she'd just looked hastily through—that Maggie Randall's name was on the leather-sheathed checkbook in the bag. The checkbook showed a gigantic balance, and the engagement book with the matching binding showed a series of appointments with hair stylists, for tea, for dress fittings, with a broker—appointments that would have kept her busy every day. Her wardrobe and her jewel case showed excellent taste for cocktail party dressing, but perhaps some oddity if you considered that she claimed she'd come to the Inn to sweat herself thin. (*"Nouveau riche, you know, Cal. She'd definitely be the type to wear imported lace and real silks now that she's got it made."*) Maggie's makeup kit was crammed with moisturizers and beauty masks and bottles of seductive scents. (*"Cal, that woman is doing everything she can to preserve those spectacular looks of hers. She's not going to show her age without a fight!"*)

Finally, there was a pile of love letters in one corner of Maggie's leather suitcase, stored on top of the wardrobe. Angela had to stand on the vanity's bench to reach it and nearly fell getting the heavy case down, but she felt the effort had been worth it as she skimmed the letters.

"But no clue," she told Caledonia back in their room, "to who sent 'em. They were signed with X's and O's . . ."

Caledonia snorted. "I haven't done that since I was in high school! What did the envelopes say?"

"She'd thrown the envelopes away and just kept the letters. Notes, really. But, Cal, in my day, young men used to write about romantic things—the moon, the willows drooping over the water—they sounded a little soppy, like the lyrics of the songs back then. But they were lovely to read, like beautiful poetry. And years later you could go back and read them over and over again and sigh and remember . . ."

"So? How were these different?"

"Well, they were . . . Oh my. How can I say . . . They were . . . explicit."

"How do you mean?"

"He wrote about . . . you know . . . the physical things they did together. He described things in detail. Do you understand?"

"Oh, I understand, all right. But to me that would have been . . . well, offensive isn't too strong a word. And I certainly wouldn't have kept the letters to look at again and again."

"Oh, she's read them through more than once. The paper's all limp and crinkled. You know how cheap paper gets when you handle it and handle it . . ."

"Well, are these old letters from her husband, do you think?" Caledonia said doubtfully.

"It doesn't sound like letters from a husband to his wife, not to me. I think our beautiful Maggie's having an affair. In fact, I bet that's why she came here to lose weight, you know? To look younger and prettier for her boyfriend. Anyhow, she cares a lot about looks. You should see that makeup case!"

"Never mind the makeup. Those letters at least sound intriguing! My room was dullsville."

Caledonia was already in the hall waiting when Angela skittered out of Maggie's room and eased the door shut behind her. "Listen," Caledonia whispered. Below them the outside door was opening and female voices, chattering and giggling, sounded from the entryway. "Better get back to our own room."

As they cut across the head of the stairs, lunging toward their own room's door, they recognized Judy Daggett's tired drawl. The sound, which had been muffled to their ears as they crossed the hall, was perfectly clear when they reached the stairs, and though Caledonia went directly into their room, Angela paused by the stairs to listen.

"Cracker's in there with the police now, Carmen," Judy was saying. "She went in right after me. You'll have to wait awhile. You ever noticed there's a big jump in our alphabet? We go from B, C, D, and then G, right the way down to S, T, W . . ."

"Oh, I don't think so." Carmen Sturkie's voice, Angela thought, was as pink as her face. Sort of soft and puffy and feminine. "I think Marceline Richardson is next after Cracker . . . R, you see?" Carmen was saying.

"Oh. That's right. Well, then what're you doin' back here, if you're not next?"

"Cutting the exercise class, of course." And Carmen giggled. "Don't tell me you're going out to the Health House all eager to join the fun."

"Tell you the truth, I thought I'd just take myself a little ol' shower and a nice little nap. Besides, there's only about fifteen minutes of that jumpin' around left . . . be a shame to interrupt them by comin' in late.''

."Listen, Judy, since we're here anyhow with some time to kill . . . come in here and give me the lowdown. What did that policeman ask you in there, anyhow?'' and the voices trailed off. The women had obviously gone into the big parlor to have their chat. Caledonia, safe now with Angela inside their own room, eased the door shut.

Angela hardly waited to hear the latch click before she plunged into her report: what she'd found out about Cracker Graham, what she'd found out about Maggie. "Both women with lovers! Can you believe it?''

"Well, it's a remarkable coincidence, all right. But I don't see that it has a single thing to do with anything we're interested in.''

"We'll see about that.'' Angela was reluctant to dismiss her little discoveries as unimportant. "Well, what did you find out, then? Anything you think is significant?''

"Nope,'' Caledonia said. "The Sturkie woman has a lot of papers—bills, letters, stuff like that—all connected with Phoenix. Nothing that says a word about her years in San Diego. Her husband has a lot of money . . . you should see her bankbook! I didn't know people carried that much money just in their checking account!''

"Same for Maggie. But she had one of those accounts that gets interest. I know, because her bank and mine are branches of the same one, and I've almost decided to move my own account to one of those that bears interest. But I have to use up my old checks first, and . . .''

"Angela, you're rambling!''

"Oh dear. Again? Sorry. Go on with what you found, Cal.''

"Well, Belinda Terry's room was kind of disappointing, too. She had several pictures of her husband and her kids—three adult boys, apparently—but a bunch of pictures of one of them, both as a grown-up and as a little boy. Either he's her favorite of the lot or there's something a little different there. His name is Dennis. Dennis Terry. It was on the back of the snapshot. I'm only guessing, of course, but he may be dead.''

"What on earth makes you think that?''

"Belinda's a member of a support group for parents who've lost children. She had a schedule of club meetings in her appointment book. I forget the name of it, but I read about it last week in 'Dear Abby,' so I recognized it. And the boy may have been killed by a drunken driver or someone who was on drugs—she has a series of check stubs made out to various organizations that fight to get stiffer penalties for DWI, among other things.''

"How clever of you to look at old check stubs!''

"Well,'' Caledonia said modestly, "when nothing else is interesting—and nothing much was—you have time to see how a person's spending her money.''

"You know, I'm not sure I agree with your conclusions though, Cal. I don't think her donating to those organizations would necessarily be because of a personal tragedy. I mean, I support Mothers Against Drunk Driving every chance I get, and I haven't even been a mother, let alone having had someone killed by a driver with a nose full of cocaine or a stomach full of liquor. I just support them.''

"Sure you do. I do, too. But not a dozen of 'em . . . and for hundreds, rather than the occasional twenty or thirty bucks. Belinda's husband is a working lawyer, not Donald Trump, but she was sending several hundred to these outfits, and not just once but over and over.''

"All right, it may mean some personal involvement. But why assume it's the death of her son? You don't even know that the boy is dead.''

"Okay, then listen to this. She had a series of checks, right together—to Joe and to Melinda, to Harry and to Mary Ellen, and to Patsy—but that was it. She'd marked the stubs 'Gift' in each case. For some family occasion, I'd guess.''

"How did you know they were family?''

"Those family pictures, remember? She'd written their names on the backs. Those checks were to the sons and their wives. Anyhow, Patsy was Dennis's wife, and there was a gift check for her, but not a check to Dennis. You see? Something's wrong about Dennis.''

''Well, we can ask, of course. But I don't see what all this has to do with—''

''Drugs, don't you see? It's the only connection we've got so far. Something to do with drugs and with Dennis Terry. Well, maybe I'm just too fanciful, but it's worth asking about.''

Angela looked skeptical but decided against reminding Caledonia how tenuous a case she was making, and how often Cal had accused her of conclusion jumping. She would save that to defend herself, next time she felt she needed defending. For the present, she only said mildly, ''Well, when do we investigate the rest of our fellow guests?''

That chance came the same evening. There was a cosmetician visiting who had promised to do a couple of makeovers, hoping to sell some of her creams and lotions. The women were twittering with excitement through dinner, squabbling good-naturedly about who would act as the guinea pigs.

''You can't, Maggie. You don't need a makeover at all!'' Cracker Graham protested. ''Now me . . .''

''I think I qualify for the most needy,'' Judy Daggett said from the far table.

''No-no-no . . . look at my folds and fissures,'' Tilly Warfield argued. ''If she could disguise these, she could work miracles. I think I'm qualified to be a good model.''

''I adore cosmonetics,'' Frankie bubbled from the next table. ''They are so extensial. I buy them all. I simply cannot exist them!''

Angela and Caledonia, sitting at the far ends of the dining room from each other, managed to exchange meaningful glances, and after the meal they headed straight upstairs and waited breathlessly inside their door. No other footsteps followed on the stairs, however, and after a while they heard a burst of laughter from the direction of the main parlor and concluded that the demonstration had begun—probably with a few jokes to set a lighthearted tone.

''Time for us to move,'' Angela whispered, and they eased the door open and crept cautiously down the hall. "Let's start on this side of the hall first, okay?"

The first room next to theirs was a double, occupied—as they discovered when they set to work—by Judy Daggett and Marceline Richardson. "No wonder Richardson seems so cross all the time," Angela whispered. "Living with Saggy Daggett would wear me to a frazzle, and I'm sure my temper would get short."

"Hush up and get to work," Caledonia whispered from across the room, where she was going through a handbag.

Angela also found her subject's handbag in the bottom bureau drawer and set to work herself. It wasn't long before she felt frantic, hopelessly mired in trivia.

Judy Daggett was a pack rat. Angela pawed through torn ticket stubs, half sticks of gum, bobby pins, four or five sets of keys (some of which seemed to be identical to each other), three lipsticks and four small combs, two notepads, four pencils, three ballpoint pens, a pocket flashlight, an address book, at least a dozen crumpled shopping lists (*"Nothing interesting about 'bologna, bread, milk, wieners, catsup, Amer. cheese' repeated on every list, Cal. Except it shows a lack of imagination with her meal planning. And how she got so saggy in the first place!"*), four or five casual "how are you" letters from friends, an electric bill, a checkbook with a modest balance, a return airline ticket to Texas, a ball of twine, a crushed cardboard box of bandages, a tiny mending kit, a bottle of aspirin, two packets of allergy pills, a tape measure, six safety pins, a small pocketknife with a built-in nail file and screwdriver, a bottle of eyedrops, and three scuffed, tired-looking M&M's. (*"I swear, Cal, the woman never throws a single thing away!"*)

On her side of the room, Caledonia worked efficiently through the other handbag, paying special attention to the checkbook and a letter she'd found within. Then she examined the pockets of every garment in the wardrobe, the dresser, and the vanity in the bathroom. She was still ready to leave before Angela had even finished looking through Judy Daggett's purse.

"Keep going with what you're doing, Angela, but get a move on." Caledonia kept her voice low. "I'll do the room at the end here on this side. It's a single and it shouldn't take me long. But don't you dawdle with your work. Snap to it.''

Angela raised a flushed, annoyed face. "I can't hurry," she whispered. "Look at this stuff . . ." She flourished the bag, halfway open, to reveal the clutter inside.

"Don't worry about putting things back the way they were. Just dump 'em in as you finish looking them over. She'll never know the difference. Outside in the hall in four minutes, no more.''

"I'll try," Angela whispered, but Caledonia had already slipped out the door and eased it shut behind her.

Actually, it didn't take Angela that long to root through the rest of the purse. Its contents were a revelation of character and a good indicator of daily activities, but they failed to show a particularly guilty conscience, and Angela moved quickly on to the wardrobe on her side of the room.

The only thing she found in the pocket of one jacket that might be of some interest was a wedding band. Her eyes simply were not good enough to read the worn engraving on the inside, though she carried the ring over to the window to get more light. But she thought it said *"Something D to Something ((probably J) D,"* and the date was June something-or-other. The only clear part was the year, twenty years ago. "When Judy didn't sag so much," Angela thought to herself, unconsciously giving her girdled hip a little pat. Then she carefully replaced the ring in the jacket pocket and hurried into the hall.

She beat Caledonia back into the hall by nearly a full minute, and when her friend came through the door of the room she'd been examining, she was grinning. "Frankie's room. I'll tell you about it later. Let's do the last one on the far side now, the one we didn't get to this afternoon. Come on—while we have the chance.''

This was also a room occupied by one person, and that person had to be Tilly Warfield, or so Angela whispered as they entered. Caledonia found Tilly's purse on the bedside table and seized it eagerly, but its contents were as neat as Judy Daggett's had been messy. "I'll have to go slow with this to keep her from knowing I've been poking through her things," she muttered to Angela. "You go do the pockets and the luggage and stuff while I work.''

Neither woman noticed they had left the heavy room door standing ajar, until they heard footsteps and a soft, tuneless whistling. Angela froze. "There's somebody coming upstairs," she whispered. "And coming this way!"

"Oh glory—" Caledonia groaned and looked hopefully around the room, but the bed was set too close to the floor for her to squeeze underneath, and the wardrobe was too full to take her bulk as well as the clothing crammed into its narrow space. "Let's hope she doesn't want to go to the toilet," she muttered and bolted for the bathroom, easing the door shut behind her.

Angela had headed for the bed herself, hoping to duck behind it even if she couldn't roll underneath, when she heard a knock on the door of the next room. "Anybody in?" a man's voice called loudly. "Is this the room with the stopped up shower drain? Hello? Hello, anybody in?"

Angela paused with one foot half raised off the floor, ready to continue her flight to a hiding place, but in a moment she heard the door of the next room opening rather noisily, then shutting, and the sound of water running, a dull, rumbling, whooshing noise that was just audible through the wall.

"Come out, Cal," she whispered. "It's one of the handymen upstairs to fix the drain. But be quiet now so he won't hear you."

"He can't hear a thing, with that water running," Caledonia said. But she kept her voice down. "He wouldn't hear if we were banging on the furniture. We sure can't hear him doing whatever he does with his wrenches and things, can we?" She passed a hand over her brow.

"Good thing we left that door open so we heard him coming. My heart is simply pounding as it is. If that water had started running next door, just all of a sudden, without our having any warning, I swear I think my heart would have jumped right out of my chest! Come on . . . let's get to work and get out of here!" And she went head down into the handbag she'd abandoned in her flight.

Angela was keenly disappointed to find that the clothing in the wardrobe was as pristine of telltale odds and ends as the day it had been bought. (*"There wasn't even an inspector's tag left in one of the pockets. I always find 'em there weeks after I've started wearing*

the things, don't you? But she didn't even have lint!') The luggage
had been completely emptied, nothing forgotten in the taffeta pockets within, and the cosmetics and perfumes lined up on the vanity
table were so neatly sorted by size and content, Angela knew before
she looked that her search would yield nothing of importance.

"Why, Cal, she'd even wiped the snoots of the bottles."

"Snoots?"

"Yes. You know how bottles drip. I always put the cover right
back on. Then there's a rim of dried and crusted lotion—or whatever—around the edge of the bottle when I open it again. Really
yecky . . . but it's a habit I can't seem to break. This woman—this
Tilly—she wipes them clean before she puts the top back on. Can
you imagine? Now, that's what I call *neat!*"

"Never mind the bottles. Just come on." Caledonia listened a
moment at the door to be sure the water was still running in the
next room where the handyman was putting in his overtime, then
they slipped out, shut Tilly Warfield's door, and headed across the
hall. They'd just reached their own room and were opening the
door when the door behind them swung open and an unusually
handsome man peered out. "Oh, sorry," he said. "I heard someone, and I thought maybe it was Mrs. Randall. You know, the guest
here. I was going to warn her I was working in her bathroom so I
wouldn't scare her half to death." He grinned and flashed teeth so
even and white Angela's first impression was that they had to be
false.

"Well, you'd better find another way to warn her, young man,"
Caledonia said sternly. "Popping out like a jack-in-the-box that
way will give her a heart attack for sure. It nearly did me. Why
don't you leave the room door open?"

He grinned again and gave a mocking salute. "Sure thing. Good
idea. 'Night, ladies," he said and withdrew back into the room,
leaving the door ajar.

"My word," Angela said as they gained the safety of their own
quarters and closed the door behind them. "The lieutenant was
right: that is the most incredibly gorgeous young man! Goodness
but I'd be excited to find him here at an all-female spa . . . if I were
a little younger, I mean, or he were a little older. Now, to

business. Did you find anything suspicious in Tilly Warfield's things, Cal? I certainly didn't,'' and she launched into her explanation of the neatness of the cosmetics on Tilly's dressing table.

"That's one careful lady, all right," Caledonia said. "You found nothing misplaced, and there wasn't anything in the purse that was at all unusual—or of the slightest interest."

"But we still can't take her off the list. I mean, her husband is a legislator, and you'll remember that a legislator was involved with Jenny in the Kimbrough Hotel."

"There are hundreds of legislators, and maybe half of them are . . . " Caledonia hunted for a good word, " . . . concupiscent."

"What?"

"You know . . ." Caledonia hesitated again. "Sexy eager beavers. Like that."

Angela shivered delicately. "I wish you wouldn't say words like that, Cal!"

"Which word?"

"You know. That long one. It sounds so . . . so much like what it means! I don't even like you saying 'sexy.' What's wrong with a dignified word like 'lustful'?"

"I couldn't think of it! Besides, I don't believe 'lustful' is especially dignified. Anyhow, whatever word you use, the point is that there are a lot of illicit goings-on involving legislators. Or so *People* magazine would have us believe. Though I've never figured out whether it's the job or the locale—Washington, Sacramento, or whatever—that can turn so many men into unabashed satyrs."

"Satyrs, Cal?"

"Don't you start on my vocabulary again, Angela. Lechers, if you prefer. Wolves. Skirt-chasers."

"Actually, Cal, I think it's the position of power. A man who can pull strings and get to park anywhere without a ticket, or who can speed and not be stopped, I bet he gets to thinking he can get anything he wants, never mind the rules. Rules were made for other people. For the 'little people.' "

"Shades of Leona Helmsley, right?"

"Yes. Same thing. Anyhow, the point is . . . oops, what point was I making?"

"You weren't," Caledonia said. "I was. I was reminding you how many legislators there are, and that we have absolutely nothing to connect Senator Warfield with the Kimbrough Hotel mess."

"The coincidence—"

"There isn't any coincidence. I mean, there is just plain no connection. So unless we find out something else about her, I suggest we take Tilly Warfield off the suspect list for the time being."

Angela nodded a little sulkily. "It would have been a neat theory . . ."

"Neat, but not very sound. What else have you got?"

Angela reported on her safari through the wilds of Judy Daggett's purse with some distaste. "The problem is, it's all so innocent. The only things I found that might even be used in the murders were her flashlight and her pocketknife."

"Flashlight? Pocketknife? What's suspicious about those things?"

"The flashlight was a little pocket-size one. Somebody needed to have light to see when they fiddled with the latch thing in the steam room, didn't they? It was perfectly all right the day before the murder, you said."

"Dorothy said."

"Whichever. But it was certainly unworkable the next day. So somebody worked on it in the dark. And they needed a screwdriver, of course, and that pocketknife had a screwdriver for one of its blades."

"Daggett, huh? I don't know why that surprises me. Do you suppose Daggett's big enough to carry Jenny to the steam room?" Caledonia said doubtfully.

"Who said she was carried? If she was groggy but not fully asleep, anybody could walk her out . . . like, you know, if she'd been drugged or hit on the head or something."

"Sounds logical," Caledonia said. "Though I've been thinking in the back of my mind she was carried."

"You could have carried her, Caledonia. I couldn't. So I thought in terms of walking her along, half asleep. Anyhow" —she settled back into her chair— "what else did you find out?"

"Marceline Richardson is a blank, unless you count a huge deposit this month into her checking account,'' Caledonia said. ''I mean, she's been getting a monthly check that's the same every month—$6,000 even. I'd guess it was alimony.''

''She's a widow. She told me.''

''Okay, then it's from some sort of trust fund or something. Salaries and pensions seldom come out even like that. They're usually odd dollars and cents. Like $5,992.51 . . . not $6,000. Anyhow, the point is, that this last month all of a sudden she got a payment of nearly $200,000.''

''In her checking account?'' Angela said, and her voice squeaked slightly.

''Well, that's where she put it when it came in. Afterward, she wrote checks to a broker for something over $100,000 and to her own savings account for the rest. She didn't keep it in checking.''

''Was it the principal from the same trust fund that's been paying off every month or something?''

''Huh-uh. She got the usual $6,000 on schedule this month.''

''Well, that'll bear looking into. What else?''

''Frankie Cziok, your good buddy.'' Caledonia grinned. ''I didn't find anything suspicious, but the woman has a lot of money. You could sure tell by her luggage and her cosmetics and her checkbook balance. She's got a jewel case in that room, too.''

''Like Maggie. She brought jewelry, too.''

''I guess they found out after they got here that nobody was wearing their jewelry and they just left it in their rooms.''

''But that isn't funny, and you were grinning when you came out of Frankie's room. You're grinning again now, Cal. What is it you found out?''

''Nothing suspicious. But I read a letter from her husband. He'd written to encourage her during her stay here. And it's no wonder she can't speak any better English than she does—they do this to each other. He said he was 'exhubilant' she was going to be so 'skim' when she got out of here.''

''Skim?''

''He may have put 'skinny' and 'slim' into one word.''

''Maybe. Or maybe he got it off a milk carton. You know, nobody spells the word right any more. It's 'skimmed milk' but everybody just calls it 'skim milk.' Maybe he thought 'skim' was a word for being thinner than average—both milk and people.''

"Okay, I'll buy that. Anyhow, he finished by saying she'd be glad she came. It was a smart move . . . or,'' Caledonia went on, her smile growing even broader, "as he put it, 'You are crazy like an ox!' ''

8

◉

The next morning, while all the other guests at The Time-Out Inn were presumably out jogging, Angela (bright-eyed and perky) and Caledonia (yawning blearily) sat down and made out a list headed "Further Inquiries." Angela read it aloud when they'd finished.

"Okay now. Marceline Richardson—where does she get her money?"

"You mean, where did she get that $200,000—that big lump sum—don't you?"

"It would be helpful," Angela said primly, "to look into the regular monthly payments, too. She says she's a widow, and I suppose her husband left her money, so that—as you said earlier—they're just her regular payments from a trust fund or something. But knowing beats just supposing. So we ask. Next, Maggie Randall: love letters, question mark."

"Angela, are you sure that isn't just a matter of your idle curiosity?"

"I beg your pardon?"

"Oh, don't get huffy. I can't cope at this hour of the morning. I mean, I see no connection between Maggie Randall's having a lover, assuming for the moment that she does, and the shooting at the Kimbrough. Or, for that matter, any connection with the two deaths here. Do you see a possible connection?"

"Well, how can I say, until I know all the details of her affair?"

"Assuming there's an affair to know something about. Right?"

"Right. But we might as well ask about anything unusual, is the way I see it. Which brings me to Cracker Graham, Mrs. Gerald

Graham. I have another big question: who is the Paul she wrote a love letter to?''

''Yup, that's a biggie, all right.'' Caledonia didn't even bother to smother her huge yawn. ''If it matters one bit more than Maggie's affair.''

''Belinda Terry,'' Angela wrote down. ''What happened to her son Dennis, and is there any family connection with drunken driving or drugs or whatever . . . though I still think you jumped to conclusions there, Cal. I'm not blaming you—it's an intelligent guess. But it just goes to show that I'm not the only one who—''

''Gloating doesn't become you. Get on with the list.''

''And Tilly Warfield. We want to know if that was her husband the police found with Jenny during the raid on the Kimbrough, don't we? And that's about it.''

''Hey-hey-hey . . . hold it a minute. What about Carmen Sturkie who used to live in San Diego?''

''Well, we didn't find a thing.''

''Doesn't mean there isn't something to find, just because we didn't find it. Let's remember to keep our eyes on *all* these gals. And by-the-by, let's put these questions of ours to Lieutenant Martinez and ask him to investigate whatever we can't find out for ourselves.'' She grinned at her friend. ''Oh, get that pout off your face, Angela. We were always going to hand on our information to him and let him do the hard part of the digging.''

''But—''

''No 'but' at all. We'll give him our toughest questions and ask for his help. Like Richardson's income and her recent windfall of $200,000 . . .''

''It could have come from drugs, couldn't it?''

''I suppose so, but we have no logical way to find out by ourselves. You don't just walk up to some person and say, 'We peeked into your checkbook and saw a huge deposit recently. Would you mind telling us if you're involved somehow in drug dealing?' Not if we want to stay alive.''

''I know you're right, but—''

''I said it before, no 'but.' Oh, and there's no Judy Daggett on your list, either.''

"Well, being a sloppy housekeeper is no crime. And before you say it, I was referring to her purse and her closets and her dresser drawers and her makeup table. She left us hundreds of things to look at, but nothing of any significance—at least not so far as we could see."

"I'm not so sure of that," Caledonia said thoughtfully. "You said there were a flashlight and a screwdriver in her purse. And the murderer needed them to fiddle with that steam room door. We didn't find either a flashlight or a screwdriver in any of the other rooms, did we?"

"True. Of course, I'll remind you of what you said to me. Just because we didn't find them doesn't mean they aren't there. Or at least *weren't* there. They might have been disposed of."

"Anyhow"— Angela drew a firm line at the end of her list— "that's the whole lot."

"Not yet it isn't. Your friend and mine, Frankie Cziok . . ."

"We don't have any questions to ask about her!"

"Angela! Of course we do. We should ask Lieutenant Martinez to look into the connection between her family's pharmaceutical house and the drug trade. The illegal drug trade, I mean, of course. There couldn't be a better front for drug peddling than drug peddling, if you see what I mean."

"Oh, Cal!"

"Write it down," Caledonia said sternly, rising to her feet and standing over Angela in a position that, had they not been friends, would have spoken of infinite menace. "Write."

"Oh well . . ." Rather grumpily, Angela wrote. Then they heard the sound of the front door opening and the chatter of voices. The women were returning from their early walk, eager for breakfast. Angela tucked the note into the pocket of her slacks, and she and Caledonia hurried downstairs to the dining room.

Angela found herself positioned for her meal with Carmen Sturkie, she of the bright pink face, and Tilly Warfield. At the farthest table Caledonia sat with Judy Daggett and Cracker Graham.

"You girls have been skipping a lot of the activities," Tilly said in an accusing tone, after she'd polished off a bowl of hot applesauce and a slice of cheese toast (made with low-fat cheese). She added some of the reconstituted powdered milk to her coffee and stirred vigorously, disposing of an errant lump of dried milk that was bobbing about in the caramel-colored liquid.

"The kitchen's not being as careful as usual, are they?" Carmen remarked. "I suppose it's remarkable things are as organized as they are. The staff is all shook up over Bonnie's death. Of course, it's only natural. When they canceled yesterday's cooking lesson I should have guessed."

"Oh, dear! I meant to go to that and I forgot," Angela said.

"Tilly's right." Carmen reached for a half orange, one of the allowed breakfast supplements. "You and your friend don't take part in a lot of the things. You two didn't go to any of the exercise session yesterday afternoon."

"What did you come here for, anyhow?" Tilly snapped. "Just to gawk at the scene of a murder?"

"Don't mind her," Carmen said, her face glowing pinker than ever. "She's just annoyed because they caught her cheating on this morning's walk."

"That's not true!" Tilly's tone was vicious. "And I wasn't cheating. I was just . . ."

"She was taking a shortcut! We go along in a straight line beside the lake for about two-thirds of the way, then the path does a kind of do-si-do, a double hairpin curve around the outside edge of a little peninsula. We follow the path, of course. But there's a way to cut across through the woods. You'd shave off about a half mile. Well, Tilly was last in the line along that straight part of the path, and she just hung back and let us all go on ahead on the curved bit while she cut through the woods the short way, right across the neck of the little point."

Tilly turned her attention to her coffee, stirring again and refusing to look at Carmen.

"She meant to come out of the woods and join up at the end of the line," Carmen went on. "But she misjudged and came out of the woods ahead of us, just as we turned the corner. Last we saw she was behind us, and suddenly there she was ahead of us, almost at the end of the path."

"Well, I got tired," Tilly said defensively. "I loathe all the walking, but at least I do part of it. You and your buddy don't do *any* of it! And you never come to the self-help programs in the evening or the cooking classes . . ."

Angela could see the danger in this line of attack. She and Caledonia would simply have to try harder to look as though they belonged, and she said so, almost in those words. "We certainly haven't been involved in enough. You're quite right, and we must do better. Yesterday I meant to attend that cooking class, and I simply forgot, just as I said. We were . . ." She hesitated. "We were taking a nap in our room."

"How about last night when we were doing the makeovers?" Tilly pushed the point. "I really enjoyed that, much as I dislike the rest of the routine here. Even if they didn't choose me for the model."

"Who did they choose?" Angela's curiosity extended even to the demonstration she'd missed.

"Maggie Randall," Tilly said sourly. "As if she needed help! Well, we enjoyed the show anyhow . . . but you two didn't even come."

"Oh, gosh, I'd have come myself," Angela said, inventing rapidly, "but I had to stay upstairs. I mean, Caledonia fell asleep early, right after supper, and I knew she'd be so cross if I went and she didn't."

Angela explained the lie in full the moment she was alone with Caledonia after the others left the dining room, headed for the morning session on the exercise machines. "It was a pretty silly excuse, I admit," she said apologetically.

"Silly! It was ridiculous. You're the one who goes to bed right after supper and rises with the lark. I'm the night owl. At least you could have said *you* fell asleep."

"But it was all that came to me on the spur of the moment . . . and she seemed to accept it. Anyhow, we'd best get to the Health and Fitness House now. We don't want to arouse any more comment by skipping activities. We'll just have to fit our investigations in between the classes and seminars, that's all."

"Tell you what," Caledonia said. "One of us had better talk to Lieutenant Martinez as soon as possible about the list we made—

the things we found out and still need to find out—and I'll be the one to do that, since I have no intention of going back to exercise class. Not in this lifetime, at least. And not in any other life, either, if I have a say in the matter.''

''But, Cal . . .''

''It makes sense for me to go talk to the police, anyhow. They got through interviews with all the other women yesterday, but they never got around to calling me in, and if I'm supposed to look like I'm just another guest here, I have to at least pretend to go and be interviewed. In fact, you can make a point of telling the others I'm in getting my turn at the third degree, when you go over there to exercise.''

''But, Cal, I don't see why I should exercise, while you—''

''Angela, I deserve a break. You don't know it because you weren't at my table, but they served me oatmeal again! I'm *never* going to get an edible breakfast around here!''

''Oh dear, Cal, we forgot again to put in your breakfast request. We must do that today! Unless you want oatmeal for another brea—''

''I'd sooner go to exercise class. And you know I'll do that when the Devil's weather station puts out a frost and freeze warning! Here . . . give me that list to take with me to the lieutenant.''

Thus it was that Angela found herself reluctantly joining the other women at the Health and Fitness House. But she was able to claim one of the small trampolines this time, instead of an exercycle or a rowing machine, and before long she found herself smiling with enjoyment and floating up and down, up and down, bouncing in slow motion to the thunderous disco beat on the tape player Ginger had turned on at the far end of the room, adjusting its volume in the apparent hope of waking sleepers in the Hawaiian Islands.

Angela simply put her fingers in her ears and, finding she could still hear the music perfectly well (*''Wonderful thing, bone conduction, isn't it Cal?''*), kept time with her floating jumps until her breath became short and she had to quit. But when she glanced at her watch, she was amazed to see that she had been bouncing and jumping for about twenty minutes.

In the meantime, Caledonia waited in the lounge until she heard Shorty Swanson's voice in the hallway. "I'll take care of that, sir," he was saying out of the door. "See you later, then," and he went on to the small parlor across the hall, which the police had turned into their office.

"Oh, Officer Swanson, I'm ready for my interview now," Caledonia called out, hurrying to catch the tall young man before he closed the door behind him. "You didn't get to the end of the W's yesterday in the interviews. So let's get it over with now, shall we?" She kept her voice loud, in case anyone should be listening, and she closed the door to the little parlor firmly behind the two of them.

"Mrs. Wingate, we didn't need to talk to you. We got everything we needed from what Mrs. Benbow told us."

"Yes, but the others don't know that. Remember, I'm supposed to look like just one of the gang, right?"

"Oh. Oh, right. That makes sense. Okay. Listen, I was just going to have coffee and go over our notes on yesterday's interviews. You want some coffee while I work? Kill a little time so they'll think you're being asked questions, see?" His smile was conspiratorial.

"Well, I do have a couple of things I wanted to talk about . . ."

"Oh. If you want the lieutenant, he's on his way to interview the handymen. We talked to the whole staff except them yesterday."

"Ernie and Bart? They do keep out of the way, don't they? We've only managed to catch a glimpse of one of them. Of course, Dorothy keeps them busy. There are dozens of things to be done around an old place like this. And they're mostly here during the day. I expect they're home most nights."

"Oh no," Swanson said, handing over a cup of coffee. "Cream and sugar?"

"Don't I wish! You mean imitation sugar and dried milk!"

"No, real cream and sugar for us. We're not dieting." Swanson offered an overflowing sugar bowl and stifled a grin as Caledonia gratefully dipped her spoon in deeply, not once but twice. "Cream?"

"You bet. I must drop in to your place more often! Our lunches and suppers are great, but breakfast . . . I need real cream and sugar to enjoy my coffee. And these fiends keep serving me oatmeal for breakfast! Not once, mind you, but every day since I've been here!" She sipped and sighed. "Now, what did you mean when you said 'Oh no' a minute ago?"

"I just meant that you're wrong about Ernie and Bart being gone at night, Mrs. Wingate."

"Well, I know sometimes there's a special job. We saw the handsome one doing some plumbing last night. I just meant generally."

"I meant generally, too. One of them is always here. They need a night watchman, I guess, with all these women here alone. Whoever's watchman for that night sleeps in a room they have fixed up at the back of the Beauty Cottage. It's nice enough. They've got a microwave and refrigerator in one corner and a TV and chair in another. A decent bathroom, and, of course, two beds . . ."

"Two? I thought you said one or the other stays over."

"Yeah, but they take turns . . . alternate nights, you see? They don't want to make the bed up fresh every other night, do they? Ernie—he's the one who's a real slob—he might not mind sleeping in Bart's sheets, but I think Bart would object to Ernie's. Which one did you meet?"

"The beautiful one," Caledonia grinned. "Don't be shocked, young fellow, but seeing him, I'd have given my eyeteeth to be young and slim again. Not that I was ever really slim, mind you. But he's enough to start my imagination working!"

"Yeah, he is a beautiful object, isn't he?" Shorty said glumly. "I'm glad Chita can't see him. She loves me . . . I'm not sure why, but anyhow she says she does. But even another man can see that guy could tempt Chita."

"Don't undersell yourself, Officer Swanson," Caledonia said kindly. "On the other hand, don't volunteer to introduce the Beautiful Bart to your fiancée, either!" They smiled and sipped companionably for a moment.

Then Caledonia said, "I am really grateful for the coffee, Officer

Swanson. A wonderful lagniappe. But I came here with a purpose. You know Angela and I have been investigating, of course . . .''

"Yes, ma'am." Shorty Swanson had been learning tact from his lieutenant, and he kept a perfectly straight face and an expression of eager interest, though it was a real effort.

"Well, there are a few things we've discovered that we will be able to follow up on, and we'll share with you if they merit sharing. But there are a few items we can't really be expected to find out for ourselves. For instance . . ." She reached into the pocket inside her capacious sleeve and extracted a pair of glasses. She had long needed them for reading, and now could have used some help even in her distance vision, but she steadfastly refused to wear her spectacles permanently.

"It's not vanity," she explained ferociously when Angela teased her. "It's anger. I wouldn't really mind getting old if it weren't for all the inconvenience it foists on us! Like hearing aids and canes and glasses! Tiny aches and pains and things that don't quite work right. Aging brings us too many things that are just . . . just plain *annoying*!"

So she'd had an embroidered pocket sewn inside the sleeve of each of her many caftans and her glasses rested there, ready for use. Now she reluctantly perched them on her nose while she consulted her list. "Mrs. Richardson got a windfall recently of $200,000. We think that should be looked into. You might also check her source of regular income, while you're at it, just in case. We're grasping at straws, I realize, but if there's a chance that the money is related to drugs—"

"I see. Here, let me jot this down." Swanson put pencil to paper. "Is there anything else?"

"Yes. While you're looking for connections to drugs, check up on the company Frankie Cziok and her family own. It's a drug company, and we thought it might be a perfect cover." She didn't see Swanson's quick smile; his head was lowered over his notes and he just kept writing. "And we think you two should look into Senator Warfield, Tilly's husband, and see if possibly he was the 'legislator' the lieutenant said was found at the Kimbrough in Jenny's company."

Swanson wrote, but he said aloud, "Now, that I can tell you right away. He isn't the man, Mrs. Wingate."

"Oh. Oh, dear. Well, there's one good idea down the drain. Who *was* the man, if it wasn't Warfield?"

"That I can't tell you, Mrs. Wingate."

"Can't or won't?"

"Won't, ma'am," Swanson said and blushed. "The police have to know, but the lieutenant says there's no point in spreading around embarrassing facts, especially when they don't really have any bearing on these murders. I mean, not that we know of."

"Well, but . . ."

"No, ma'am. I'm sorry. That's confidential."

Caledonia shrugged. "Okay then, there's Carmen Sturkie. We haven't been able to find out a thing about her life in San Diego, before she and her husband moved to Phoenix. You and the lieutenant can find out about them, if you haven't already. We just want to know if there's any way to tie them into the mess at the Kimbrough Hotel . . . or anything else."

"Sure. That's natural, I guess. Is that all?"

"Nope. One more thing. We found out that Belinda Terry had a son, Dennis, and we suspect he may be dead now. No need to go into what makes us think so. But we wondered if you'd check that out. Belinda's from Escondido . . . husband's a lawyer."

"We know that," Swanson said. "Go on about the son."

"We wondered if there was anything about his death that had to do with alcohol or drugs . . . you know? Like, was he run down by a driver under the influence, or something? Would you look it up? We wouldn't know where to start to get the facts."

"Well, it should be easy enough for us to find out. I'll talk to the lieutenant and we should have some answers for you fairly soon, I'd guess. Anything else?"

"No, I think that's about it. I better wander over to the Health and Fitness House and see if the gang is still working out. If they're through, I might join them. If they're still exercising, I'll find something else to keep me busy for a while."

And with that promise she rolled herself upward to her feet and moved majestically out of the room, out the front door, and down the path Angela and the others had traveled earlier, her caftan flapping around her like a regal robe as she sailed serenely along toward the avoidance of exercise and physical exertion.

9

⊙

Caledonia actually had her hand on the doorknob, ready to enter the Health and Fitness House, when the door swung out toward her and a hurrying woman bustled straight into her, head down. They exchanged grunts of surprise, and as each recognized the other, exchanged a kind of greeting.

"Caledonia!"

"Maggie!"

Caledonia was the first to recover enough to say more. "Are you running away from Ginger and her cast-iron commands?"

"Yes and no. I have an appointment for a facial, and I don't want to be late."

"But you're cutting morning exercises."

"We're allowed to, when we have an appointment for any of the services—nails, hair, whatever. I've booked straight through for the rest of the day," Maggie said, and she sounded smug about it.

"You could book in the evenings and not miss any exercise classes," Caledonia said.

Maggie scowled. "Didn't you read that brochure they gave you? The masseuse and the beautician—they don't even come out from town unless there's an appointment set up. And then only during the day. As for missing the exercise activities," she added, confirming Caledonia's darker suspicions, "I'd rather miss the exercise class than the special lectures and things in the evening anyhow. So that suits me beautifully."

She checked her diamond watch. "I've got a facial this morning . . . right about now . . . manicure and pedicure after lunch, massage last thing in the afternoon. I won't stretch a single rubber band today, I'm afraid.''

She held up her wrist, as though she thought Caledonia could read the tiny watch face from four feet away. ''We'd both better hurry. My appointment is in two minutes, and you'll miss the rest of free exercise on the machines, if you don't hurry. There's about ten minutes left before they take a rest break. You'd only be in time for the floor exercises . . . you know . . . where they lie on the floor and do reaches and stretches.''

''Exercise lying down? I don't think I'd mind that quite so much,'' Caledonia said hopefully.

''Well, it doesn't last all that long,'' Maggie said smugly. ''Then we start the limber and tone-up exercises. That's what we usually do till lunch. You have to stand up for that. It's hard work. Of course,'' she said a bit sharply, ''you wouldn't know, would you? You've really managed to escape quite a lot of exercise yourself.''

''And I intend to keep right on escaping,'' Caledonia said cheerfully. ''I really wasn't condemning you when I suggested you were on the run from Ginger. In fact, I admired your good sense. And since they're still going on with the whatever-it-is in there, I'll just stroll along to the Beauty Cottage with you and see about an appointment for some of that good stuff myself.''

That wasn't strictly true, for until that exact moment, Caledonia had quite forgotten that The Time-Out Inn offered a variety of pampering services to complement the torture of diet and exercise. But it seemed as good an excuse as any to make better acquaintance with Maggie and perhaps to ask her a few questions.

''You have such smart outfits,'' Caledonia began, as they walked along the path, not exactly strolling but not rushing either. The Beauty Cottage wasn't fifty steps away, and Maggie didn't seem disposed to hurry for her appointment, despite her suggesting she might be late.

Maggie preened unconsciously. ''I'm glad you like them,'' she said. ''I bought all new clothes for my stay here. Of course, I didn't realize there was going to be . . . you know, trouble.''

''Oh, your clothes are perfectly okay. I don't think there is such a thing as an outfit designed especially for attending a murder.''

"I beg your pardon?"

"Just a joke, my dear. Not in very good taste, I suppose. I only meant . . . your clothes are marvelous. That embroidered velvet you wore to dinner last night . . . Magnificent!"

"Thank you." Maggie's smile was nothing short of smug.

"But what a nuisance to change every evening after exercise! The rest of the women all just wear their sweats. They wash up, but they don't change clothes, do they?"

"Well, I feel better if I get into something . . . different. Sometimes, of course, I don't change completely. I mean, I just add a bolero or a bright scarf or something . . ."

She seemed willing to go on indefinitely with her strategies for fashion, so Caledonia hastened to interrupt. "Well, they're gorgeous clothes, all right. Even if they make me feel a little frumpy. But then 'frumpy' is all most of us here can manage. Speaking of which, I don't really understand why you're here at all! You don't let go into slobbery, like the rest of us. You're certainly not fat . . ."

"Thanks again, but I'm about ten pounds overweight. And it's showing up in the strangest places. Right here . . ." Maggie put her hands against her lower abdomen, ". . . and here . . ." She slapped her hips on either side. "I had to buy a new belt for one of my Adolfo knits last month. The waistline of the dress was all right, but that snakeskin belt was in the last notch and straining. I never used to gain in the midsection this way."

"It's your age, my dear. That's tactless of me to say, I suppose, but when you get past forty . . ." Maggie stiffened and her mouth made a tight little line, but Caledonia went serenely on, ". . . you just do thicken up in the middle, that's all. Unless you're one of those born scarecrows, all bone and angles. Don't worry about it. You're still beautiful, and men prefer soft and round to hard and stringy."

Just at that moment they reached the door of the Beauty Cottage, and Caledonia cursed silently. She had just got around to the point where she could have turned the conversation to husbands and lovers. And with a little luck, perhaps she could have found out something useful. But Maggie had hurried in and sailed through the tiny anteroom into one of the inner cubicles, shielded from Caledonia's view by a curtain of white sheeting.

"Sorry I'm late," Maggie was saying. And a mellow tenor voice answered, "No problem at all, my dear Mrs. Randall. If you'll just lie down on the couch here and let me put this sheet over you and tie this turban over your hair, we'll begin. Upsy-daisy . . . tha-a-a-t's right . . ."

Caledonia looked around her. There were three easy chairs, two lamps, and on a small table, a stack of magazines: Elle, Vogue, Architectural Digest, House Beautiful ("*and one copy of* People *for plebeians like me, Angela,*" Caledonia reported later with amusement).

On a bulletin board hung five clipboards, each containing a chart with times written down the left side, days across the top, and women's names filled in. One board was headed "Facials," one "Manicures," one "Pedicures," one "Massages," and one "Hair Dressing"—and just as Maggie Randall had said, her name was down in several slots all through the day.

Caledonia shrugged. She wasn't all that keen on beauty parlors for herself, but maybe there'd be useful gossip. Or maybe one could overhear confidences being exchanged in the next booth. She grabbed the pencil and into one slot for each remaining time period through the afternoon and in two slots on the following day she firmly wrote: *Angela Benbow*. Her entries seemed to cover the full range of services, and a wide, self-righteous smile settled on her face. Now let Angela complain that she did all the hard work by going to the exercise classes! Caledonia, still grinning happily, let herself out of the Beauty Cottage and started back toward the main house.

She hadn't gone a dozen steps when she heard the sound of a mower starting up somewhere behind the Beauty Cottage. One of the handymen, she supposed. Then, curious to see one of these elusive creatures closer up, she left the path and walked around behind the building.

Her supposition had been right. A John Deere riding mower was cutting stripes across the lawn between the Beauty Cottage and the swimming pool's hedge, and on the John Deere was an untidy lump of gray cloth, an unshaven man in a sweat-stained work shirt and chinos who appeared to be breathing steam. As Caledonia got closer to him, she realized that he had the stump of a cigar clenched in his teeth, and she thought that if he didn't get rid of it at once he would blister his lips. In fact, as he focused his bloodshot, suspicious little eyes on her, he did get rid of the cigar butt, ejecting it with a puffing noise, then spitting heartily as a follow-up.

"Do something for you, lady?" he said, stopping the mower and pulling a handkerchief from his hip pocket, a rag stained as gray as his shirt and already dripping wet.

He honked mightily into the grimy cloth, then opened its folds to inspect the results. Apparently satisfied, he crumpled the handkerchief again and stuffed it back into his pocket. "Yes'm?" he prompted inquiringly.

"You have to be Ernie," Caledonia said.

"Don't have to be. But I am. So?"

"I . . . I'm one of the guests here, and . . ."

"No kiddin'! I thought you was one of them little exercise teachers," Ernie smirked.

Caledonia came close to grinning in spite of herself. "I was wondering about the nighttime arrangements. The security here, I mean."

"Yeah? How come?"

"Well, you have to admit there's been a lot of violence here, and it's all taken place at night. I wondered—"

"Listen, lady! You got plenty security here. If I ain't sleepin' over, Bart is, and we both got a gun. But we didn't hear nothin' the nights those girls was killed. Nothin'. Or they wouldn't of got killed. Somebody else might of . . . I'm a real good shot!" He spat energetically, aiming at a begonia in a nearby bed, as though to prove his deadly aim, which he certainly did as far as the begonia went.

"Well, who was on duty the night that girl from the kitchen died?"

"Me. I didn't hear nothin', I didn't see nothin'. Period."

"And when the first girl, Jenny, was killed?"

"Bart. Bart was on duty that night. Same thing. Ask him if you don't believe me."

"Where do you stay?"

"There. And if you'll let me get done with my mowin', I'm goin' back there to sit the rest of the afternoon in the shade. Too damn hot to work."

He waved at the back of the Beauty Cottage, and Caledonia saw that it had a door with an entry light and a small railed porch on which sat a tired-looking lawn chair and a small metal table with a radio and a can of beer, sweating as copiously as Ernie was. Caledonia smiled to herself; Ernie hadn't been out on his mower very long, or that beer can would have pretty well dried off. He probably ran out and jumped on the mower, she thought to herself, when he heard Maggie and me coming along the other path. Up to then, she imagined, Ernie had been resting himself on his little porch.

"Won't Mrs. McGraw object if you just take the afternoon off?" she asked blandly. Let him think she was deceived with his pose of hard work.

"Let her. I'd as soon get fired from this damn job as keep it. People gettin' killed, people yellin' at me to do this, do that all day and half the night . . . people askin' damn fool questions . . ." He glared at Caledonia. "Lady, you ain't the police and I'm damned if I need to talk to you one more minute than I already done."

And he punched the starter on the John Deere, then drove off on a path parallel to his last pass across the lawn but about two inches removed from exactly touching, so that once again he created a distinctly striped pattern.

Caledonia realized she was not going to learn more from him, so she cut across his stripes, walking an arc past the swimming pool and toward the main house. As she passed the opening in the hedge, she saw that the water in the pool was quiet and undisturbed, the concrete apron dry. No one had been swimming recently. Caledonia thought that despite Dorothy's brave attempt to keep the pool clean and heated and the dressing rooms open for the guests' use, swimming would not be a popular activity with this group. Too many unpleasant memories in the pool area.

She stumped past resolutely and climbed the three steps to the back door, then stood for a moment outside the kitchen trying to decide her next move. As she stood there, she glanced back the way she had come. To her surprise, Ernie had driven his mower to the corner of the hedge and sat there, staring intently at her. He was too far away for her to see his expression, but the direction of his gaze seemed unmistakable.

"I wonder what his problem is?" she muttered. Then she turned back to her own dilemma, albeit a minor one. She could cut through the kitchen again, but the sounds from inside warned her that the staff was moving rapidly forward in their preparations for lunch and would resent her intrusion. Or she could climb up the back stairs that led directly to the second floor from the far end of the porch. True, they were meant primarily for the staff's use or for emergencies and were listed on the map she'd been given as a fire escape, but they looked sturdy to her eye and wide enough to make climbing them no more difficult than were the main stairs.

As she hesitated, the back door opened and the maid Betsy came out. "Oh, hi, Mrs. Wingate," she called out over her shoulder, turning sharply and walking along the porch the opposite way from where the stairs were. At the far end of the porch she stopped and with great effort unlatched and swung open a huge, insulated door.

"Freezer," she called cheerily as she disappeared from Caledonia's view. "Oh, lordy, but it's cold!" Her voice sounded muffled and far away.

In a moment she came out again with a giant cardboard cylinder in her arms. She scuttled across the porch toward the kitchen door, which Caledonia opened quickly for her. "Mrs. Wingate, will you slam the freezer door after me, please? This tub of diet yogurt is giving my arms frostbite and I got to dump it . . . Here we are, girls . . . yogurt for the dessert!" And she hustled inside.

Caledonia walked quickly down the length of porch to the freezer. This would make two new places she'd investigated this morning, places she hadn't even seen before during her stay. Who'd have thought it, in a place so small! She peered interestedly inside.

Cold air was pouring out the door in almost visible waves. Inside there were shelves full of cartons, some of which she saw were marked "Eggs." There were cardboard tubs similar to the one Betsy had been lugging into the kitchen. There were chickens hanging from overhead hooks—presumably replacements for the ones that the police had allowed to spoil when they first examined the area. There were stacks of boxes Caledonia could not identify, and in one corner was an old-fashioned lunch box. Someone on the staff was making sure their sandwich mayonnaise didn't spoil, she supposed. Nothing that looked remotely suspicious.

Caledonia sighed. The chill air felt good against her hot, damp skin. But she dutifully slammed the door shut and swung over the locking lever, then turned back and slowly climbed the big wooden staircase to the second floor, puffing and huffing on the last few steps. At least the front steps had a landing where one could stop and catch a breath. The fire escape stairs led straight up to an upstairs porch like the one she had just left, and the door halfway down its length led into the upper hallway next to her own room.

Convenient, Caledonia said to herself, for any one of the guests to come and go in the night without going through the house itself. Dangerous, she said to herself, as she noticed that the bedrooms adjoining the porch had windows opening onto it.

"Anybody could slide those open and get in," she muttered. "Or get out," she added, after thinking about it. She opened the door. "But they wouldn't need to crawl out the window. This porch door's oiled so much it doesn't even squeak!" Convenient again, she thought.

But as she eased herself down on her bed, the thought "convenient" melted into "maybe there's time for a little nap," and within a few seconds, even that thought had melted and disappeared.

Angela arrived at the room about ten minutes before twelve, with only time enough to run a comb through her hair and change her shirt before lunch. She had been sweating, first through the machines, then after the all-too-brief respite of floor exercise, through a vigorously directed set of kicks and bends, pulls and stretches, and she was feeling breathless and completely hot and sticky, all of which did nothing for her temper. That Caledonia was resting comfortably, her mouth open and a tiny snore issuing through her nose, did not improve Angela's mood one iota either.

She slammed the bathroom door shut behind her, ran the water full force as she washed her face, threw the hairbrush onto the bathroom vanity so that it clattered, and kicked the metal wastebasket noisily as she passed. When she came out, a little cooler and less sticky, wearing her clean blouse, she felt somewhat better to see that Caledonia was sitting up, stretching and yawning.

"Sorry if I disturbed you," Angela said sweetly. "You looked so peaceful. Of course, it's nearly lunchtime anyway. It would have been a shame to miss your first decent meal of the day, since you say you didn't eat much of your breakfast."

"Right. That oatmeal . . ." Caledonia pulled herself upright and tidied her hair, straightened her caftan, and applied a bit of lipstick. "Listen," she said, consulting her watch, "there's just time for me to tell you about my morning's activities . . ." And she reported in full, finishing with the news that Angela had the afternoon off from exercise. "And tomorrow afternoon as well. You've got a massage at one-thirty and a manicure at three today. Then tomorrow you'll have a pedicure and a facial . . . You'll be a new woman from bottom to top, as it were."

Angela's smile became angelic, her spirits buoyant with the news that she did not need to look forward to more exercise that day to legitimize their stay. "I completely forgot about the beauty services. How clever of you!"

"Sure. Figured you'd be glad to sit and let someone knead and smooth and clean and paint you in various spots."

"And you'll go to the exercise classes this afternoon, then?"

"Oh no! Not me!"

"But, Cal, one of us has to show up. People were asking about you this morning as it was. I got grumpy working so hard and thinking of you *not* sweating, if you see what I mean. I admit it. But I wasn't the only one. I think Tilly Warfield is getting very suspicious, for one."

"Listen, I told you Maggie Randall had booked herself into beauty and out of exercise, and I bet most of them do the same, whenever they can. Nobody will think anything of it if I stay away. And if they do—well, I'll just have to live with that.''

''But, Cal, they mustn't suspect we're anything but regular guests like they are—''

Her argument was interrupted by the gong sounding softly in the lower hall, and Caledonia shrugged and headed toward the door. ''We'll talk about this later,'' she said.

At lunch Angela was at a table with Frankie Cziok and Cracker Graham, while Caledonia sat with Tilly Warfield and Belinda Terry. Tilly was silent, resentful of Caledonia's cavalier attitude toward the exercise classes. She said as much before she clamped her lips together and refused to make polite luncheon conversation. ''She's just jealous she hasn't the courage to cut out entirely herself,'' Belinda said kindly to Caledonia. ''But she manages to cheat a little, don't you, Tilly?'' Tilly glared and said nothing.

''Is fudging natural for a politician? Did she learn how from her husband, do you suppose?'' Belinda went on, all too obviously baiting Tilly, who kept her face turned toward her plate and continued eating in sullen silence. Caledonia felt that her own silence was the best course, and simply nodded vaguely. Soon Belinda, twisting an errant lock of hair back under her bandanna, resumed her own meal, and the table fell silent.

Two tables away, Angela was being treated to a long, involved story about a woman who, Frankie insisted, ''had to have her eucharist removed. So sad, not to be able to have more children! Children are such a blessing.''

''Oh, I don't know about that,'' Cracker said. ''Sometimes they're a sadness. I mean, you never know, do you, how a child will turn out? My own son is in a state hospital. They say the chances are he'll be there forever. Though they don't know about these things.''

''He has seekness?'' Frankie asked.

''Well, not exactly. It's . . . you know . . . mental,'' Cracker said. ''They don't have a specific name for it. It's like he's autistic, but it came on him when he was twenty-five. Autism is something children have, usually. So they aren't sure what it is with him. I can't even remember all the words they gave us . . . Paul hears, but he doesn't respond. He reads things, but we can't tell if they affect him or not.''

"You write to him?'' Angela asked gently. But she already knew the answer.

"At least every other day . . . sometimes every day. Like I say, Paul seems to read the letters, and maybe he likes hearing from me, maybe he understands I still love him . . . but we can't tell.''

Frankie managed to express her compassion without making it comic, for once, and Angela just shook her head sadly. Their lunch, a chicken Stroganoff that tasted rich with sour cream but was guaranteed to have no more than one-hundred fifty calories a serving, was finished in relative silence.

On the way out of the dining room, Angela signaled Caledonia, and they let the others go ahead of them.

"I can't stay, Cal. I'm due at the Beauty Cottage for that massage you booked for me. But I have some news.''

Caledonia listened with interest to the story of Cracker Graham's son. "So that's who Cracker's beloved Paul is. No love affair at all.''

Angela shook her head. "Really sad. Well, maybe some of our other clues will be as innocent. I hope so, anyway. I'm getting really fond of some of these women.''

And Angela whisked out on her way to the Beauty Cottage, while Caledonia started up the stairs. She wasn't quite certain what to do next, but she reasoned that something would present itself. Sure enough, as she came up into the hallway, she saw three women.

Helena, the silent maid, was just entering Tilly Warfield's room at the far end of the hall, her arms loaded with linens. Maggie Randall was coming out of her room, having hastily changed to yet another colorful, sophisticated costume, an ice-green satin overall affair that hugged her waist and shimmered like water as she walked. Nearly at the same moment, Judy Daggett came out of her room and sagged her way toward the stairs. She looked, Caledonia thought, more as though she were headed for execution than for exercise.

Suddenly Caledonia remembered her questions about the pocket-knife with its little screwdriver and the telltale flashlight. Quickly she dropped to her knees and made a show of searching the carpet near the corner by the door to her room.

"Hi," Judy said, slowing down her steps. "Something wrong? Lost something?"

"You need help?" Maggie asked.

"A contact lens," Caledonia lied. "Lost a contact lens. My eyes aren't good enough to see them in the half-light here, but I think it must have landed close by the corner."

Helena the maid turned away and went into Warfield's room, presumably to get on with her job, apparently deciding that the guests had the problem under control. But Maggie stopped beside Caledonia, bent over from the waist with a deep sigh, and began looking here and there without much enthusiasm. To Caledonia's delight, Judy knelt beside her and began to pat the carpet with both hands as Caledonia was doing. Her trap had worked for the right woman!

After a few moments, Maggie straightened her back. "Oooh, bending that way is hard . . . and I'm late for a pedicure, girls. You'll have to excuse me." And she moved languidly off down the stairs as though making her grand entrance to a ballroom.

"I can't find anything either," Judy said, straightening her back with a sigh. "I'm sorry."

"What we need is a light," Caledonia said slyly. "Do you by chance have a flashlight of some kind?"

"Gosh, no," Judy said, getting to her feet. "I meant to bring one, but time just got away from me when I was packin' to come. I tell you, somehow I just couldn't get myself organized."

"Well, then I suppose you can't loan me a screwdriver, either. The drawer pull in my room has got loose . . ."

"Would if I had one, but I didn't think to pack anything useful! Not that I'd bring a screwdriver with me, anyway. I'm not at all handy. All thumbs." Judy rubbed the small of her back and stretched a kink out. "Got to run now—exercise class. That li'l ol' instructor is so sarcastic if we're not on time. Sorry 'bout it . . ." And she was gone.

Slowly Caledonia got to her feet and went on into her room. She slipped her glasses out of the pocket in her sleeve and glanced closely at the notes she and Angela had made that morning before breakfast. There it was, big as life: "Daggett—screwdriver and flashlight—ASK!!!!"

Caledonia pulled out a pencil and put a big check mark beside both items. She hesitated and then scribbled a note as well: "She doesn't remember them. So how come they're in her purse?"

10

On second thought, Caledonia decided, it might be well to let Angela know right away about her clever investigating. She might, she told herself, be able to get a private word with Angela by simply going over to the Beauty Cottage and sending Angela's masseuse out of the room. "Crude, but if no better idea presents itself . . ." she muttered, as she stumped down the front stairs with the intention of heading straight out and across the lawn.

But she had no sooner reached the ground floor than the door to the smaller parlor opened and Lieutenant Martinez started out. "Oh, Mrs. Wingate. How fortunate. I was just on my way in the hope of finding you . . . perhaps at the building where they exercise."

"Lieutenant, surely you know me better than that. Exercise? Me?"

"But I thought you and Mrs. Benbow . . ." He lowered his voice, ". . . that you two were trying to seem to be ordinary guests. Surely . . ."

"You sound just like Angela! She can think of a dozen reasons why I ought to go out and jump up and down or stretch a rubber band. She's jealous because she does it and I don't, that's all. But this place is advertised as a haven for rest and relaxation, as well as for weight loss. Speaking strictly for myself, I'll make do with a little rest and a lot of relaxation, thank you. I gave up on the weight loss years ago. I have neither the strength of mind nor the strength of body to do what's necessary."

"Somehow, Mrs. Wingate, I doubt your assessment," the lieutenant said, stepping to one side and indicating the open parlor door. "Won't you join us for a moment? I have something to discuss." He glanced up the hall and across into the large parlor, but saw no one who might have overheard him so far. "Please?"

"Oh, Mrs. Wingate," Shorty Swanson called out, as Caledonia entered and seated herself in the largest (and most comfortable) of the parlor's chairs. "Can I tempt you with a bear claw? Fresh made in the kitchen here this morning, and about the best I ever tasted!"

"That really gets my goat!" Caledonia said. "Not you eating them, but me not getting them! Did I tell you that since I arrived they haven't given me anything for breakfast but oatmeal?"

"I think you said something about it," Shorty grinned, and he brought her one of the huge, sugar-encrusted sweet rolls. Then for a moment there was a pleasant silence in the room while she and young Swanson savored their sticky treasures.

Martinez watched with an indulgent smile until he judged that between them they had downed enough calories to furnish energy for a medium-sized power plant. Then he cleared his throat. "You asked Shorty to do a little research for you, Mrs. Wingate. Is that not true?"

"Absolutely. Except it was me and Angela. Angela and me. Angela and I. Both of us, anyhow. Though I did the asking while she put in an appearance at the morning exercise sessions. But that was just this morning! You don't mean you've done it already!"

Martinez smiled with just a touch of smugness. "You made your request early . . . we've had more than three hours to work on it. And some of the inquiries took only a single phone call. Of course, our knowing where to ask for the information made things faster."

"Well, I knew where to ask, too. I asked *you*! And look . . . as easy as pie—you should pardon the calorie-filled expression—here you are with the answers."

"Well, some of them, at any rate." He turned to Swanson. "Want to do the honors for us?"

Swanson pulled out his notepad and thumbed back a page or two, rather self-importantly. "You asked about the Cziok family business . . . All-American Pharmaceuticals."

"More like All Mittel-Europa Pharmaceuticals, if you ask me.

But I suppose immigrants would choose a name like that. They'd need to identify with the flag and the new country more than a native would," Caledonia said. "Well, what did you find out?"

"Nothing. That is, they seem to be perfectly legitimate."

"They've had a highly profitable business since the sixties, when the family arrived here," Martinez put in. "They made a reputation by startling honesty and fanatic reliability. If they say they'll deliver on or before a certain date, they do it or give full refunds. They make good on damaged orders and give quick service when there's a problem. And they are genuinely courteous . . ."

"Amazingly un-American, I'd say. Better investigate further," Caledonia said. "No, seriously, isn't it lovely that at least in their case, nice guys didn't finish last?"

"They've been so honest and upright, I'd rather accuse the Boy Scouts of dealing in illicit drugs! And the whole family has become moderately wealthy through the business. No Donald Trumps, no Sam Waltons, but wealthy by any normal person's measure. So what kind of fools would they have to be to jeopardize it all by turning to illegal sources for additional income? They're much too intelligent for that. Or so our sources of information tell us."

"The next question you asked," Swanson said, clearing his throat to serve as a warning before he began, and to be sure his superior had finished what he had to say, "was about the extra income Mrs. Richardson had. Now, that took some doing. Banks and other financial institutions, as you probably know, don't like sharing their records. But we have all kinds of inside sources. And the answer we got won't tell you anything. I mean, it's not a guilty secret or anything like that. If she's a suspect in this, if she has something to do with our murders, it's not because of her income. I'm sorry to disappoint you and Mrs. Benbow, but—"

"Oh, for heaven's sake, Swanson!" Martinez lost his patience. "Get to the point!"

"It's like you said it might be, Mrs. Wingate," Swanson said quickly, and his face went crimson. "Her regular income's from a trust fund left by her late husband. And the big payoff recently was from an annuity she had."

"A big one, even by today's standards," Caledonia said.

"Possibly," Martinez said. "But nevertheless, perfectly innocent."

"Well, there's two ideas down the drain," Caledonia said with a massive shrug she intended to be nonchalant, but which, because of her size, looked more ominous than casual. "Anything on my other two? Carmen Sturkie and Belinda Terry?"

"Nothing yet on this Sturkie woman," Swanson said. "Of course, we got people calling Phoenix, right now. But here near home? Nothing to speak of. We did find out what theater her husband owned—the old Downtown Palace. It's been torn down for several years now. One of those that started to go under when TV came in. He sold it to a development company who put in a shopping mall. And he bought himself another theater in Phoenix, and they've been there ever since. The only things we've found so far that aren't 100 per cent innocent are a couple of traffic tickets and a record that some patron brought suit after she choked on her popcorn while she was watching Tyrone Power and Basil Rathbone in *The Mark of Zorro*."

"Did she win the suit?" Caledonia asked curiously.

Swanson grinned. "Uh-uh. She carried on so much about the leading man, the jury figured she choked up over passion, not popcorn. They found for the defendant—Sturkie and his Downtown Palace. And that was that."

"Belinda Terry's son Dennis is the only thing you asked us about that might have a link to the business at the Kimbrough," Martinez said. "At least, there's an interesting coincidence there, if they're not actually connected. Dennis Terry died of an overdose of heroin . . . in a room at the Kimbrough."

"Good heavens! The same night that dealer was killed?"

"Oh no. Several months earlier. So, of course, there needn't be any connection at all between the two deaths, Dennis Terry's and Peter Guns's."

"Okay, okay. Maybe this will turn out to be just one of those strange coincidences where people end up saying, 'Small world, isn't it?' " Caledonia said. "Maybe. But maybe not, too. I think that this time I have hold of something worth investigating. Usually it's Angela who puts things together and comes up with the answers. I think this time *I* may have done it.''

''Well, at least it would pay us to look into the matter a bit more carefully, especially now that it's tied in with our present case. If it is.''

''What do you mean, 'If it is'? I thought that was the natural conclusion, Lieutenant.''

''Mrs. Wingate, we have no evidence at all that these girls' deaths are connected with that old case at the Kimbrough Hotel, even though both girls were tied in with the Kimbrough. All we can say is that we'll look into the death of the Terry boy again and see if we can find a connection to the drug dealer's death.''

''Lieutenant, that's enough for me. Angela doesn't think much of my idea . . . she never does unless it's a notion she gets herself. But I'm excited about this because I'm the one who made the discovery this time and the one who put two and two together afterwards.''

''You know, I'm curious. How did you find out about the Terry boy, anyway?''

''It's really just guesswork, of course,'' Caledonia said with suitable modesty. ''You see, Belinda has pictures of all her sons and their wives, but when she sent gift checks to them, she only sent checks to her other sons and their wives. And one to Dennis's wife. But not to Dennis. Do you see?''

''I see, all right. I see you've been doing more than just asking questions. You've actually had a look into her private things, haven't you?''

''I didn't say that!''

''You didn't have to. I'm a detective, remember? Let me spell out the deductive process here. Mrs. Terry might well have showed you her family pictures, so you'd know about the existence of her sons and their wives. But she didn't tell you about Dennis's death, and I know that because you had to ask us about it. That means you probably worked out your theory after finding out about those checks she'd written. But one thing she'd never discuss freely or show you voluntarily is her checkbook. So you had to look into that by yourself. And you did, didn't you?''

Caledonia nodded and said nothing.

"Mrs. Wingate, going through someone else's private papers is an invasion of privacy. Grateful as I am for information you may unearth, I don't want you taking such chances. If Mrs. Terry had found you rummaging among her things, she might well have suspected you of trying to rob her and she'd probably have called the police. Us. And if she'd registered a complaint, I might not have had any option but to arrest you on her complaint."

"But she didn't find us, did she?" Caledonia said smugly. "None of them did."

"None of them? I see. You looked through the possessions of the other guests as well, right?"

"Right. And a good thing we did, Lieutenant. We got all these marvelous ideas . . . all these questions for you to ask. But let me tell you, as far as the murders are concerned, my money now is on Belinda Terry, and I'll bet it has something to do with her son Dennis. Gentlemen, I wish you good day!"

And Caledonia swept grandly out of the room.

"Knows how to make a marvelous exit, doesn't she?" Martinez said. "Well, let's get back to work . . ."

Left by herself again, Caledonia thought of what she ought to do with her afternoon. "Nothing says I can't take a nap, I suppose," she said, and then looked guiltily around to be sure nobody had overheard her. Apparently she was still alone in the hall. So no one saw her as she toiled up the stairs to her room, to her bed, and to the Land of Nod, where she spent a happy three hours or so.

Angela, relaxed and expansive after her massage and pedicure and feeling virtuous after attending a cooking class that instructed the ladies on the tricks of producing a splendid veal piccata, found Caledonia still asleep and gently woke her in time for Caledonia to tidy up a bit—to throw a little water on her face and comb her hair—before supper. A newly wakened Caledonia had no inclination to talk about her day's activities and discoveries, however. But she did promise a full synopsis after supper, which she provided later as they readied themselves for bed.

They had dined well on the same veal piccata Angela had

watched the chef prepare in cooking class. They also ate wild rice, a pineapple and carrot salad, and a delicate pecan tart that the maids assured them used no sugar for sweetening. "Only concentrated apple juice," Betsy said brightly as she put one small tart before each woman's place.

After dinner, there was a film in the main lounge, an amusing little dramatized demonstration of how to order nonfattening items in a restaurant when one is a guest and doesn't want to make a fuss about dieting. Angela insisted that Caledonia accompany her to see the film. "We've skipped out on far too much," she urged. Reluctantly, Caledonia agreed and was pleasantly surprised to find herself entertained by the presentation. It was after the ladies bade each other good night and made their way to their rooms that Caledonia at last had the time and privacy to fill Angela in on all she had done, and all Lieutenant Martinez had said, and all she'd thought about it, and what she speculated about. Finally, she became aware that Angela was silent and yawning deeply. "Boring you?" Caledonia said with acid in her voice.

"Oh, no, Cal. Not really. It's just . . . the exercise this morning and the country air . . . and then relaxing with that massage this afternoon . . . I could sleep for a year, I think!" Angela yawned again. "Aren't you tired?"

Caledonia shook her head. "I had two naps today, girl. Two! That adds up to maybe four-plus hours extra of sleep. And I'm a night person anyway, as you'll remember. Our early-to-bed, early-to-rise routine around here hasn't gone too comfortably with me. Listen, I got a book from the shelves in the main lounge. Can you sleep if I leave the light on and read awhile before I try to close my eyes?"

"No problem," Angela said and yawned involuntarily. "Oh, dear. You see? Just turn the overhead light off and read by your bedside lamp. It won't keep me awake." She punched at her pillows and sank back into them with a happy sigh.

Caledonia opened the murder mystery she'd brought upstairs and, making her own pillows mound high behind her neck, leaned back for a read. The room was absolutely still until, in about five minutes, Angela's sleepy voice came softly from the other bed:

"Cal, did you by chance remember to tell them in the kitchen about your breakfast? That you wanted one of the other choices . . ."

"Oh, peanut butter!" Caledonia's favorite expletive hissed her annoyance. "I clean forgot. They'll try to make me eat oatmeal again, of course! I'll bet I have the healthiest colon in the state of California, with all the oats I'm packing away! Angela, why didn't you remind me?"

There was gentle, deep, regular breathing coming from the other bed. Caledonia glared over her book at her sleeping friend. "Well, at least she was generous—her last thought before she faded out for the night was of me and my breakfast. Blast their oatmeal. How am I ever going to remember to tell them about it?"

Grumpily she returned to her reading. But after a chapter, she realized that she hadn't remembered anything she read. Her mind was on her breakfast. "Or what passes for breakfast around here," she muttered, and went back to read the chapter again, but to no avail.

"Might as well get some sleep," she muttered, and put the book aside, flipped off the light, and rolled over. And over. And over. Nearly two hours of rearranging herself, her pillows, and the bed-clothes did absolutely no good. At last she threw the bedcover off, tiptoed into the bathroom, and holding a washcloth over the running water to muffle the sound, drew herself a warm bath.

A half hour's soak seemed to make her drowsy, and she returned to her bed, but with every bit as much futility as on her first attempt. She switched her reading lamp back on, grabbed the book again, and made another try, this time getting two chapters read before she finally gave up and reached for her robe.

"I think I'll go down to the kitchen and write out a note for the staff about my breakfast. I'll just leave it where they can find it. On the stove, maybe. Or in the toaster."

She slid her feet into soft, stretchy-cloth slippers and, trying hard not to let the bedsprings squeak under her weight, eased her way once more to an upright position. Even in her nightclothes, Caledonia made an imposing figure. Her gown was of a heavy cerise satin, and as large and flowing as any of her daytime caftans, except that it was sleeveless. Her robe—also of heavy cerise satin—made up for that, however, with full-length, bell-shaped sleeves. And the skirts of both gown and robe swept the floor. So Caledonia had to gather the folds of cloth into one hand to guard against tripping as she moved along.

"Might as well go down the back stairs and through the kitchen," she said to herself, and headed out the door at the end of the hall that led directly to the back porch and fire escape. There was a moment's rather noisy confusion as the swath of robe and gown in Caledonia's hand somehow got caught in the porch door, and Caledonia ended by slamming the door twice, once on a heavy fold of satin, again against its frame as the cloth was pulled free.

She hesitated a moment just outside and listened. Would the noise have wakened any of the other guests? Peering through the hall window, she could see a light in one of the rooms, spilling out of the crack under its heavy old door. She couldn't decide which room it was but it didn't seem to matter, since no bedroom doors opened and no other lights came on in the darkened rooms. So she assumed she hadn't made enough noise to be heard. Or if they had heard her, they had simply assumed it was the watchman *du jour* on his rounds.

Caledonia tiptoed forward and inched her way carefully down the stairs. She was glad to find there was sufficient moonlight coming from the pale night sky to make the steps visible without her turning on the porch lights. Lucky, so far, she thought.

Once safely down to the lower porch level, she gave a hearty pull to the kitchen door. There her luck ran out. The door stayed firmly shut. I should have known it would be locked, she thought. And who can blame them, what with a murderer running around? But how am I going to get that note to the staff?

Suddenly she grinned. Come to think of it, she hadn't even brought pencil and paper with her! She had simply assumed the kitchen would be open and she'd find writing materials once inside. Served her right! Well, perhaps the door to the kitchen inside the house—the door from the dining room—was the one she should have tried to begin with. She started along the porch, headed for the little steps that led into the backyard, thinking to make her way around the house to the front door, and suddenly another thought crossed her mind.

If I were home now, she was telling herself silently, I'd make a midnight snack. I wonder if there's something in that big freezer down there that would be good for a nibble. She remembered the lunch box she'd seen and her assumption that it held someone's sandwiches. A good enough midnight snack, if it was still there. She headed for the freezer door.

Opening the freezer was no problem. The big locking handle eased open, though it took a firm grip to move it, and the thick door swung out silently. She reached inside and found the light switch and sure enough, there at the far end of the room was that lunch box, still waiting for its owner to claim it.

The other guests may be dieting, Caledonia told herself, but I never said I would diet, too. Besides, that dreadful oatmeal at breakfast means I really only eat two full meals a day anyway. Not enough for me. I deserve that sandwich. And she walked into the freezer.

The lunch bucket proved to be a veritable cornucopia: a salami sandwich, a chicken sandwich, celery and carrot sticks, two deviled eggs, four chocolate chip cookies, a crisp Granny Smith apple, and a thermos of coffee. She spun open the cap of the thermos and tasted the coffee, then made a rueful face. The lunch box had been in the freezer too long. The coffee was cool to her tongue, and she closed the thermos with regret.

"Maybe," she said aloud, "there's something to drink around here that would be better than that coffee. Wonder if they keep anything . . ." She laughed aloud at herself. How often she'd mocked her fellow residents at Camden who walked about talking to themselves! How often she'd sworn she'd never do that. Oh no, not her!

Head down among cartons and tubs she searched. Yogurt, eggs, oranges—nothing to drink. She was all the way across the freezer in her search, and had just about decided she'd had enough of the cold and would go outside with her improvised picnic, even without anything fit to drink, when she felt rather than heard the door be-hind her swing shut.

Whirling about, she lunged toward the door, but it was already too late. The heavy panel had closed completely. And not by ac-cident, she realized with dismay, for when she reached toward where the handle should be and found only a flat metal plate held by bolts that had been countersunk out of reach, she could see the metal plate moving. The handle on the outside was being swung into the lock position. She pushed energetically against the door, but it was firmly closed and equally firmly locked.

"Hey," she shouted. "Hey . . . you've made a mistake. There's somebody in here. I'm in here! Listen, I'm sorry I left the door open and the cold air leaking away, but you better open up and let me out before I freeze to death!"

There was no answer.

"Hey! *Hey*!"

There was no sound at all from the outside.

And there wouldn't be, of course. She had really known all along that if the person who slammed the door had been innocent of malice, he (or she) would probably have reached in to turn off the light before he (or she) closed the freezer. This unknown person was not just trying to conserve electricity!

"But I wonder if they knew who they were locking in? No, surely not. This has to be a case of mistaken identity," she said aloud. (No point now in worrying about whether anyone would think her senile if they overheard her talking to herself.) Then she sighed. It couldn't be a mistake. There was nobody else on the premises who was of Caledonia's bulk and height. "Not even big Ernie the handyman, fat slob that he is," she muttered angrily. "No, one glimpse and they'd know it was me. And that means they were out to get me, and get me they did. Well, what can we do about it?"

What she did—or tried to do—was all the things she would have deplored as futile if someone had listed them as possible actions. First she pushed several more times against the door, including running at it and giving it a gigantic bump with her shoulder as she'd seen them do in movies. It didn't budge, of course, but her shoulder felt bruised before she gave up the effort.

Next she tried to summon help. She pounded on the door and shouted. She banged on the compartment's frost-lined walls. The sound of her own voice and the solid thunk of her fists against the walls told her they were thick enough to be virtually soundproof.

Then she scratched and clawed at those deep-sunk bolt heads in the metal plate that attached the handle outside and tried to work at them with makeshift tools—with metal staples that held produce boxes together, which she pulled out at the cost of several finger-nails, with hooks from the track that hung from the ceiling, even with the edge of the metal lunch box—none of those things did a bit of good.

At last, she went back and banged at the door again and shouted and shouted, over and over, her breath coming in great white clouds and her voice growing raw, even though she knew the sound wouldn't carry through the heavy insulation. And then she wept, rather embarrassed tears to be sure, for Caledonia was not was the kind of woman who cried when things got desperate.

But desperate they were. She was locked into a freezer in her nightgown. Strong as she was, she could not budge the door. Loud as her voice was, she could not make it penetrate the freezer's walls. And healthy as she was for her age, she was not proof against freezing cold.

"I doubt if I can last the night," she said aloud, resuming her monologue, more for the comfort of the sound than for any other reason.

"Silly old woman," she said disgustedly. "You know you hate those stories where the heroine hears a noise and goes down to investigate. But first chance you get, what do you do? You go walking around alone at night when there's a murderer loose, you don't tell anybody you're going, you don't even wear your shoes—" ... she peered at her own feet in the little cloth slip-pers— "and you walk into a ... a death trap!"

That was the bad side.

But there was, she decided at last, something of a good side, after all. There was apparently a sizable leak somewhere in the thick walls or around the door, for there seemed to be air to breathe. That meant she wasn't going to suffocate. There was the light, albeit a tiny bulb, which still shone bravely from the vicinity of the ceiling, casting heavy and ominous shadows over everything. "But even if it's ugly, it still beats total darkness by a country mile," she told the silent line of dead chickens that hung from the ceiling.

"Well, I always wondered how I'd meet my end," she said. "A frozen side of beef in a bright pink nightie—that never entered my head. Did you," she addressed the chickens again, "ever dream you'd end up looking like an airborne chorus line? I bet not. And I shouldn't complain about having on a nightie . . . you gals don't even have your feathers on! Poor little birds."

Caledonia sighed and turned her attention to fashioning a bench. "No need to die standing up," she said. She dragged together two wooden fruit crates packed with oranges, placing them in the middle of the room directly under the overhead lightbulb that swayed gently at the end of a cord, and tested her makeshift sofa rather gingerly. Somehow it bore her weight. She relaxed and reached over to get the lunch box she had earlier abandoned on a stack of egg crates.

"No need to die standing up. And no need to die with an empty stomach, either. That salami sandwich looked good, but I think I'll stay with the chicken for starters . . . Mmmmmm, chicken's pretty tasty. Sorry about that, ladies," she addressed the line of hanging poultry again. "Avert your eyes if it offends you," and she began on the second half of the sandwich with a gusto that, considering her situation, was nothing short of remarkable.

11

When Angela awoke to her alarm the next morning, she staggered into the bathroom to splash herself awake with cold water before she bathed and brushed her teeth. It wasn't until she returned to the bedroom that she noticed Caledonia was not in her bed. That wasn't like Cal, she thought to herself. "Where are you, room-mate?" she murmured.

At home Cal would much rather lie in bed until the last possible minute when she could still dress and make it to the dining room while breakfast was being served. Here Cal had to rise early, of course, since there was only one breakfast sitting. It had been one of the many things about the place that didn't suit Caledonia at all well.

I only hope, Angela told herself, as she pulled on clothes and gradually came more and more awake, I only hope she hasn't got so fed up with early rising, not enough food to please her, and me teasing her all the time about not exercising that she just up and left. Good heavens, maybe she's packed and waiting downstairs to go home right now!

Angela rushed to check Caledonia's wardrobe, but everything was still there, undisturbed, so far as Angela could see. Well, at any rate Caledonia hadn't gone home in a sulk. Perhaps, Angela thought, Cal was just out taking morning exercise after all. Perhaps, just for once, she had gone out to watch the dawn come up. She'd be back for breakfast, Angela was certain. And she headed for the dining room herself.

But Caledonia didn't show up for breakfast either. Betsy and Helena brought breakfast in to all the ladies and Betsy announced blithely, "You may begin, ladies," but there was still no Caledonia.

"Aren't we going to wait for Mrs. Wingate?" Tilly Warfield asked.

"Yes, please wait," Angela said. "Cal's bound to come for her meal."

"But there's no place set up for her," Carmen Sturkie said. "I don't see her name tag anywhere."

"It's still over there on the sideboard," Belinda Terry announced, craning her neck to be sure. "Yes, that's it over there."

"What's the big idea? Where is she?" Maggie Randall asked.

"Mrs. McGraw's orders. That's all I know," Betsy said, and whisked out.

"Well, orders are orders. I'm going to eat," Cracker Graham said, and piled into the small Spanish omelette that was her breakfast.

"I still think we should wait. She's not likely to miss a meal altogether unless something's very wrong," Angela said, but she tried not to sound too worried. She didn't want to admit that Caledonia might be out following up a hot clue. They were, after all, supposed to be ordinary guests. Skipping breakfast shouldn't have been a big deal, and there was probably nothing much amiss.

"I wondered why she wasn't at the table before us, as she usually is," Tilly Warfield said, spooning up the boiled eggs and grits that were her choice from the menu. "I'd say she didn't miss many meals, from the size of her. This must be something unusual to . . ."

"Could she just have gone for a walk on her own?" Belinda Terry ventured. "I did that one morning when I was worried about personal things and I just wanted time to think."

"I didn't think of that," Angela said. "I suppose she could have."

"She could use the exercise, okay. She is definitely obverse," Frankie Cziok put in.

"Pardon?"

"You know. Big."

"She means 'obese,' " Maggie said helpfully.

"That," Frankie said with dignity, "is exact the what I said!"

Maggie ignored her. "I don't know about a walk, though. There's really only the highway to town and that one good path, the one we take that goes down by the lake. But we didn't see her as we took our morning hike. Well, at least, I didn't see her."

"Me either," Cracker Graham said. Then she giggled. "And you couldn't help but see her!"

"Morning, ladies . . ." Dorothy McGraw's cheerful voice made them turn in their places, as she whisked through the room and disappeared through the swinging door to the kitchen. "Hope everyone's having a good breakfast." The door swung to and closed off any chance that someone might retort. And perhaps it was just as well. The women were unhappily polishing their plates and draining the last drops from their cups, as though to try to fill in with coffee the empty spaces left by inadequate amounts of food.

"Coming to exercise class?" Belinda asked, as she rose from her place and pushed her chair back under the table.

"No," Angela said. "I think I'll stay to talk to Dorothy. She must know where Cal is, if she gave the orders not to set a place for her."

"Oh, Angela," Judy Daggett said as she stopped beside Angela as the others filed out, "I notice you didn't eat but one slice of your toast this morning."

"I'm just too concerned to eat. Cal's being missing is a bit strange. I mean, I'm sure she's all right, but . . . well," Angela finished lamely, "you know how it is."

But Judy hardly noticed what Angela was saying. She stared at Angela's plate with a peculiarly fixed gaze. "Well, if you don't want it, can I have the other slice? These breakfasts leave me ravenous!" Angela waved her hand, and Judy Daggett pounced on the toast.

"I also am what she said: ravenses," Frankie put in. "I am so hungry I could eat a house!"

"Horse," Marceline Richardson corrected automatically. "Me, too. Smart work, Judy." But she sounded angry, and Angela reminded herself silently not to leave food on her plate again, lest the women actually come to blows over the leftovers.

The others filed out, and Angela was headed toward the kitchen door when it swung open and the two maids, Betsy and Helena, came out again, moving quickly, heading toward the tables to pile dishes onto trays.

"Betsy," Angela said. "Didn't you say earlier that Mrs. Mc-Graw had ordered that no place be set for my friend Caledonia?"

"That's right."

"Is Mrs. McGraw still in the kitchen? I'd like to ask her about that. I'm . . . I'm a bit concerned. It's just not like my friend to miss a meal."

Betsy grinned. "No'm. I'd guess not ever!" Then Betsy wiped the smile from her face. "But it's no use asking her, Mrs. Benbow. She told us to ask her no questions, and not to discuss it with any of the other guests, and I suppose that means you, too, or she'd have told me different."

"But surely . . ."

The maids had finished stacking trays and were headed for the kitchen again. Then Helena took pity on Angela, standing irresolute, undecided how next to proceed.

"Oh, Mrs. Benbow," she said as she passed. "You might ask Lieutenant Martinez. He might know. He's here early today. In the little parlor, or so Mrs. McGraw says. We weren't allowed to go in there."

"He's here already? But it isn't even . . ." Angela checked her watch. "It isn't even eight yet!"

"All the same . . ." Helena jerked her head in the general direction of the study, a pantomime that adequately finished the sentence. Then she was gone through the swinging door into the kitchen, leaving Angela to head for the parlor.

The parlor door was firmly closed, and she knocked lightly, almost timidly. On the one hand, she felt rather foolish to be so concerned. But on the other hand, she was puzzled, and Caledonia's place not being set had a certain ominous strangeness to it.

The door opened an inch or so and Shorty Swanson peered out. "It's Mrs. Benbow, sir," he said over his shoulder. "You want I should let her in?"

"Of course, of course. Come in quickly, Mrs. Benbow. And shut the door tight, Shorty."

To her surprise, Angela found herself literally pulled inside and moved hurriedly away from the door, which Swanson closed firmly behind her.

"Cal!" Angela's voice was a mere squeak. "Cal, what are you doing in here?"

On the couch lay Caledonia, covered in a bright quilt, which she clutched almost to her chin. Still, Angela could see the hint of cerise satin glowing from below a fold of quilting, and realized Caledonia was still in her nightclothes.

"Caledonia! You're not even dressed! How . . . how gauche!"

"Well, considering that I've been rescued from the cold hand of death—and I was trying to wait to go to our room till you were awake, just to be a thoughtful roommate, mind you—considering all I really wanted at the moment was to lie down somewhere and keep warm . . . all things considered, I think I can be forgiven for appearing before our friends in my nightgown!"

"Whatever are you talking about, Caledonia? You always accuse me of babbling, but you're making very little sense." Angela realized that the room was unusually warm, the air conditioning turned off completely. "It's stifling in here! Can't we get some cool air . . ."

"I think, Mrs. Benbow," Lieutenant Martinez said, "that you need to be filled in on Mrs. Wingate's adventures. Then perhaps you'll understand. Air conditioning is not a good idea right now. She really needs the warmth, I should imagine, though the doctor will be able to tell us better when he arrives."

"Told you not to bother with a doctor," Caledonia said gruffly. "I'm perfectly okay. Now. No thanks to my own stupidity, of course."

"Will someone please explain?" Angela said plaintively.

"Mrs. Wingate spent a good part of the night locked in the freezer," Martinez said. "It was by the grace of God she was found before she caught a severe chill, at the very least."

"In the freezer! Good heavens . . ."

"What saved me was three things," Caledonia trumpeted, taking over the story forcefully. She had no intention of being preempted, even by her favorite policeman. This was her tale, and she meant to tell it.

"First of all," she said, "that thing they call a freezer isn't."

"Isn't what?"

"Isn't a freezer! Oh, I have no doubt it would kill me just as thoroughly as a freezer would, given time. But maybe not as quickly. Maybe not at all. Though I didn't work that out for a little while."

Locked in, apparently for the long haul, Caledonia had finished the lunch in the metal box, then had tried to think her situation through more calmly. Panic, which she'd felt at the beginning, was certainly counterproductive. What was required was some reasonable planning—a strategy for survival, as she told herself. To begin with, she needed to calm her own fluttering heart, use her brains. She looked around her at the other occupants—the line of chickens hanging from the ceiling rack, the oranges and apples, the lettuce, the eggs. And then it hit her.

"If this is a freezer," she said aloud, "how come there's produce in here? Nobody keeps eggs and lettuce in the freezer! By golly, I think this thing isn't a freezer at all, even though everybody calls it one. It's just a big cooler . . . a walk-in refrigerator! I bet it doesn't get down to freezing at all!"

Considerably cheered up by that bit of reasoning, she got to her feet and began to pace. "Might as well move around a bit while I think. I probably think better on my feet anyhow," she said, grimacing ruefully, "much as I hate the notion. Now, the main question is, how long can I survive in a refrigerator, as opposed to a freezer? Well, maybe not for days, maybe not even a whole day. But maybe long enough . . ."

"Oh, Cal," Angela interrupted Caledonia's story. "Oh, Cal, little children suffocate in old refrigerators that get thrown into dumps! You read about one every few months or so! You were in terrible danger!"

"Well, the truth is . . ." and Caledonia sounded a bit sheepish, almost apologetic. "The truth is, that cooler isn't very airtight. In fact, it leaks like a sieve. That's the second thing that saved my life. That old cooler must cost Dorothy a fortune to run, it lets so much cold air out. And more important, brings fresh air in! I've told her she ought to do something about it, replace it or something. But I'm grateful that it does leak; otherwise, even though it's big, I might have suffocated.''

"Oh, Cal!"

"Anyhow, the third thing that saved me is that I finally figured out,'' Caledonia said, "that I'd be let out first thing in the morning. Really early in the morning, actually. Because the kitchen staff has to come in at least an hour ahead of breakfast to get everything ready. It may not take very long to make up the pitiful platefuls they serve us, but they have to feed the staff as well.''

"The staff begins to arrive,'' Swanson referred to his notebook, "between five and six, as a rule.''

"But even so,'' Angela said. "Even so . . . that's a long time in the cold!''

Caledonia nodded. "Absolutely. I agree. The trick, as I saw it, was to keep myself going till somebody came and opened that door. I figured it had to have been about one-fifty or so when I came downstairs, so maybe it was close to two when I was locked in there. All I had to do was survive maybe four hours at most, till somebody would come along and let me out.''

"But, Cal, what on earth could you do till then?''

"This is part of what saved me . . . and this part I'm very proud of. I survived,'' Caledonia said smugly, "the way animals do in the cold.''

"You don't mean to say someone had left a fur coat in there, or something?''

"No-no-no. It was—well, think about it. Sled dogs in Alaska stay warm by pulling sleds. Wolves stay warm by chasing moose. Moose stay warm by running away from wolves. Whales stay warm by the effort of swimming in the Arctic Ocean, icy cold as it is . . .''

"But they've got all that blubber . . .'' Behind Angela, Shorty Swanson made a strangled, snorting noise and Lieutenant Martinez cleared his throat sharply, then took out a silk handkerchief with which he touched the corners of his mouth, managing to hide any smile behind the fabric. Angela grinned widely in spite of herself and didn't manage to hide it at all.

"Oh, don't be so embarrassed, all of you," Caledonia said good-naturedly. "That's it, of course. That's exactly what I meant! I reasoned that I had plenty of fat to burn, to keep me from expiring of the cold. So—and here's the part I hate the most—so I did what the sled dogs and the wolves and all do . . . I burned it!"

"What?"

"I exercised."

"Cal!"

"It's true. I did jumping jacks and push-ups and I marched and ran and skipped around the room in a big circle. I had to stop for breath every few minutes, but I got so cold, I'd start pretty quick again jumping and clapping my hands—"

"Cal, you couldn't keep that up for four hours! You're so out of shape . . ."

Swanson snorted again, more softly. And Angela said rather defensively, "I meant, your muscles would ache! You wouldn't be able to keep going!"

"I suppose you're right. But I had powerful motivation, that's for sure. Anyhow, I didn't have to."

"The staff came in earlier than you thought?" Angela asked.

"No, ma'am," Martinez put in from his chair on the other side of the room. "She found a Lochinvar. A knight-errant on a John Deere."

"I don't understand . . ."

"She was rescued by the night watchman," Swanson said, as amused as his chief.

"By that handsome young man? How wonderful! Just like a movie!"

"No, ma'am," Shorty said. "By the other one. Ernie."

"Fat Ernie!" Caledonia agreed. "You wouldn't believe it. There I was jumping around . . ."

Caledonia had been on her two hundredth circuit of the cooler, skipping and singing and first beating her arms together above her head, then slapping them against her sides, when she heard a startled gasp behind her. She stopped in midstride and turned to see Ernie in the door, which now stood wide open: Ernie—gray-clad, grizzled, sweat-stained, and belching noisily as a result both of the beer he'd been sipping while he made his rounds and of the huge gulp of air he'd just taken in.

"Lady! Lady! I-I-Wha-wha . . . Whatcha doin'!"

"Oh, Mr. Morrison! Am I glad to see you!" Her gasp of relief was a frozen gust that hung in the air between them.

"Whatcha doin'!" he repeated plaintively. "You shouldn't be in here. They say it's bad for the food!"

"Bad for the food?" Caledonia choked out as she headed for the door, pushing Ernie's quivering paunch aside to get herself out into the warm night air. "Oh, that feels better! Close that freezer door, man. Close it."

"Yeah, bad for the food," Ernie said, his mind not working fast enough to do more than answer the previous question. "Germs. That's what Miz McGraw said. Germs. I suppose you got germs on you, too. As many as I do," he said accusingly. "She wouldn't want you in there, either, you know."

"Trust me, Mr. Morrison, I wasn't in there by choice!"

"Well, anyhow . . ." Ernie was still one conversational topic behind.   "I used to go in there on a hot day to cool off, see, an' I usually leave my lunch bucket in there. For a midnight snack when I'm on duty, see. But they told me it puts germs onto things in there, and I ain't supposed to leave it in there no more."

"You were coming in just now to get your lunch, weren't you?" Caledonia said. "That's your lunch box in there!"

"Yeah, sure. But please don't tell Miz McGraw, lady. She'd have my scalp, after she told me not to go in. Because of my germs. But I brung my lunch when I was on two nights ago, and I dint get around to havin' nothin' to eat that night, what with one thing and another. But I figured things was quiet tonight, and maybe it would still be good. So I come in and found you jumping around like crazy . . . What in blue blazes was you doin' in the freezer anyhow, lady?"

"Accident," Caledonia said shortly. "And it nearly killed me. Now I just want to lie down awhile. And I want to get w-w-w-warm!'' She was beginning to shiver in spite of the warm night air. As she told Angela, it seemed to catch up with her suddenly, and she was aware all at once of the cold and of her fatigue.

''But you had plenty of time to come upstairs to bed again,'' Angela said. ''Why didn't you?''

''I decided not to wake you,'' Caledonia said with dignity. ''It didn't seem like a good idea. I just came in here and lay down on the couch instead.''

''Don't be so modest, Mrs. Wingate,'' Martinez said. ''She's not telling you the rest of the story, Mrs. Benbow. Her Lochinvar wasn't about to let her out of his sight, after that. He followed her into the house, he brought her this quilt from storage, and he stayed right with her until most of the staff arrived, when he turned his charge over to Mrs. McGraw, who in her turn called us to come out early.''

''Ernie? Ernie Morrison stayed with you all night?''

''Only a couple of hours,'' Caledonia said. ''I told him that I'd been shut into the cooler by accident because I didn't want to explain in detail. And for all I knew he might have been the one who locked me in there. But he seemed to be genuinely worried. Maybe he thought I was crazy and might lock myself into some other strange place or something. I don't know. Whatever, he stayed right here and kept an eye on me for two, maybe three hours and a bit. Till someone else arrived to take over the duty.''

''All night?'' Angela asked again, and sounded amused.

''That,'' Caledonia continued, ''is another reason I didn't come up to our room. He wouldn't leave me by myself, and I had a vision of you waking up to your alarm and seeing my protector there in the bedroom . . . Believe me, Ernie belching beer bubbles and scratching his belly—that's not the first sight that should present itself in the morning to anyone of sensitivity. There are better ways to greet the dawn.''

''Well, he's gone now, isn't he?'' Angela said.

''I surely hope so,'' Caledonia answered. ''He gave me into the custody of Dorothy when she arrived. And Dorothy held the fort till these fellows arrived. Then she told me not to bother going in to breakfast, and she's gone to get me some.''

"And before she left, Mrs. McGraw charged us with keeping Mrs. Wingate safe," Martinez said. "The general opinion seems to be that you'll get into trouble if you're left alone, ma'am. And I can't say I disagree. Of course, Ernie and Mrs. McGraw believe you were just inept and locked yourself into the big cooler by accident, whereas I'm sure someone tried to kill you. Or at least to incapacitate you. To get you out of the way for a while, if not permanently."

Before either Caledonia or Angela could respond, the door to the hall opened and Dorothy entered with a tray. "Here we are," she said. "Prop her pillows up behind her, someone, so she can eat . . ." Angela and both the men sprang forward, Swanson winning the race to help bring Caledonia slightly more upright on her couch.

"There now . . ." Dorothy set the tray down across Caledonia's knees. "I checked the menus, Caledonia, and I saw that you've had the same breakfast every morning so far. So I got you a double helping today. I think you've earned it." And she swept the metal cover off to reveal a steaming bowl full of lumpy, taupe-colored oatmeal, swimming in skimmed milk and punctuated by brown islands of sliced dates.

"Eat hearty," Dorothy said cheerfully, and left the room quickly, so that she missed hearing Caledonia's heartfelt groan of dismay.

12

⊙

It was finally agreed, though over Caledonia's rigorous protests, that she was to remain in seclusion through the rest of the day. "And tomorrow as well, so long as we need to have you under our protection," Lieutenant Martinez said firmly. "We will tell everybody you are weak from what seems to be a severe chill, and you just stay in your room."

"A chill? Isn't that too vague an ailment in this day and age?" Caledonia, having lost the war, was still feeling prickly enough to continue the skirmishes. "Everybody who watches the TV news gets a medical vocabulary of sorts from all those special reports. Every Tom, Dick, and Harry can pronounce 'rhino virus,' and half of 'em even know what it means!"

"But if we're vague, then your attacker may believe you're actually in bad shape. He will find out soon enough that the attempt last night didn't dispose of you entirely. However, if you're out of commission with what might well turn into pneumonia, your attacker may decide that's enough to render you harmless and may leave you alone. Mrs. Benbow, if you could be suitably worried about her condition, it would help."

"Oh, certainly, Lieutenant." Angela was clearly delighted to have a part in the pretense. "I can shake my head and say things like 'You never know with a chill that bad . . . ' and maybe shed a tear or two."

"Well, there's no need to go that far," Martinez cautioned. "Be very careful not to overdo. We don't want Mrs. Wingate's attacker to decide it's all a charade—even though it is."

"Be dour, not desolate. Worry, don't weep," Caledonia added

her two cents' worth. Her sense of humor was gradually seeping back, aided by the mental picture of Angela in mourning dress, acting the grieving friend for the benefit of the other guests. "You go overboard too easily, Angela. Restraint. That's the ticket."

"I can be restrained," Angela protested. "I studied Richard Boleslavsky's *Six Lessons in Acting* when I was in theater classes at college. You know I ended up majoring in English, but I'm not sure I ever told you that I almost majored in drama."

"You didn't have to tell me!" Caledonia snorted. "I can spot an ex-drama major a mile away. Angela, believe me when I say, just forget about Boleslavsky and concentrate on the importance of being Benbow."

"Well, then," Martinez said, anxious to get on with business. "I take it you'll agree to stay quiet and out of sight for perhaps forty-eight hours, Mrs. Wingate."

"I guess so. The only question is, what do I do with myself all that time? It'll get mighty boring."

"Work a crossword puzzle. Read a book. Mend your stockings. Or don't ladies do that any more? Sleep, if you can. I'm sure you need it. And, Mrs. Wingate, don't answer your door. People may come and knock, but don't answer. Pretend to be asleep. If anyone tries to come in anyway, we want to hear about it."

"What about food? I have to eat, don't I?" Caledonia said, less grumpily than grudgingly. She had already conceded that she would obey his orders, but she wasn't letting go entirely without one more token show of resistance.

"We'll have trays delivered at mealtimes."

"See what you can do about that breakfast, then, Lieutenant. Somehow I keep forgetting to tell them in the kitchen that I'd sooner eat baked snake than choke down one more bite of oatmeal!"

"Oooh, Cal! Ick!"

Swanson laughed and even Martinez smiled, then put his reserve firmly back in place. "In that case, Mrs. Wingate, I'll do what I can."

"No, don't 'do what you can,' " Caledonia grumped. "Just do it!" And she stumped toward the door.

"Hold it a minute, Mrs. Wingate! Swanson," Martinez commanded, "take the point."

"Sir?"

"Check out the hall. Make sure there's nobody around to see Mrs. Wingate is healthy enough to walk to her room unassisted. Go ahead of her and check out the room. Make sure nobody's lying in wait. Then come back here right away. And, Mrs. Wingate, remember you've got a dead bolt on the inside of your door . . ."

"I believe so, Lieutenant."

"Use it. And don't open the door unless you're certain you know who it is outside. Even then, try not to let anybody else see that you're well enough to answer the knock. Clear?"

"I appreciate your concern, Lieutenant," was all Caledonia said before she followed Swanson meekly out of the room.

"I admire the way you handled her, Lieutenant," Angela said. "You just tell her the way things are going to be, and that's the way they are! She never lets me win an argument that easily."

"But in her heart she agrees with me," Martinez said. "She was undoubtedly locked into that big refrigerator purposely. And we don't need to let her assailant know she's fully recovered, or he'd simply try again."

"But, Lieutenant, if the person tried again, you'd catch him. Or her. Wouldn't you? I mean, it's the perfect chance to set a trap!"

"Is it, Mrs. Benbow?" Martinez's tone was one of polite interest, his smile pleasant but controlled. "Well, I really must take the idea under advisement. In the meantime, we have some questions to ask and leads to follow."

"Leads?" Angela said brightly. "From any of the material we found for you?"

"Naturally, Mrs. Benbow. We consider every idea, no matter how remote. Now, may I suggest you join the other women at exercise class?"

"Oh dear . . ." Angela's glance at her watch showed her that there was—unfortunately, in her view—plenty of time left for her to ride a stationary bicycle or row an imaginary boat. But then she remembered. "Oh! This morning I wasn't going to exercise. I was supposed to go to—"

"Mrs. Benbow, please join the others for today. It will make you seem less conspicuous. I'm worried about you, too, of course. And the more a part of the guests' regular activities you are, the safer you'll be. No need to turn the danger away from Mrs. Wingate and toward you. At the same time, you can do the job I need done."

"Job?"

"Yes. Remember that I'm relying on you to spread the word that the hundredth lamb has returned to join the ninety-nine in the fold. The lost is found. Mrs. Wingate is back, but is suffering from a severe chill. In fact, you might tell them the doctor will be checking on her later."

"Will he?"

"Oh yes. Mrs. McGraw has phoned for him. We want to be sure Mrs. Wingate is as undamaged by her exposure as she seems. But don't you tell anyone that she's in fairly good shape. We hope that doubt about her condition may make her attacker think he won't have to try again. Be sure to tell them she's too tired to get out of bed today."

Just then Swanson returned to report all clear: no watchers in the hall, no villain lurking under the bed, and Caledonia safe behind a bolted door.

"Thank you, Swanson. Now, Mrs. Benbow . . . if you'll begin your part of the plan, the informing of the others . . ."

"Oh, very well, Lieutenant. I'll have to reschedule a bit. Put my beauty appointments off and join the exercise group this morning, but I'll do it. For you," she added with a coy flutter of her eyelashes, as she turned to go about her assignment.

"Take the first watch, Swanson," Martinez said, when Angela was finally on her way.

"Sir?"

"First watch. I want you to be as inconspicuous as possible, but never to get very far away from Mrs. Wingate's room. I want her guarded every minute of the day."

"Gee, sir . . . How am I going to guard her and still be inconspicuous? You and me, we stick out around here. Everybody notices where we are."

"Shorty, do you suppose you could hear Mrs. Wingate if she was in her room and called for help while you were in this room?"

"Maybe . . ." Swanson was clearly skeptical. "But that's pretty far, even for a woman with her voice."

"Well, how about if you sat in the lounge near the bottom of the stairs? Could you hear her from there?"

"Sure. Her room's just at the top of the stairs, and the reception area is right at the bottom. Sure."

"Well, then, go and get a newspaper, sit in the chair closest to the bottom of the stairs, read your paper, and try to look like you're on a coffee break."

"Okay. But if I sit there all day, reading the same paper and drinking coffee, people will start to notice."

"You won't be there all day. We'll send for a couple of uniforms from the main office. Get them to come out here in civilian clothes and spell us on guard. We'll just make the reception area our break room today. And before you ask, the guard will not always sit in the hallway, right at the bottom of the stairs. No. From time to time whoever is on guard should, for example, lounge around on the back porch, up on the second floor."

"Doing what?"

"Feeding squirrels. Practicing birdcalls. How should I know?" Martinez said crossly. "Just doing something—*any*thing—that looks natural. But for God's sake don't go to sleep on the job. I want to keep that lady safe, as well as know about anybody who tries to enter her room. Somebody will have to be watching at all times, even if he has to lie across her doorway. But I'd rather our crew made themselves a little less conspicuous than that."

"You setting that trap? Like Mrs. Benbow said?"

"Not really. Certainly not without Mrs. Wingate's knowledge and permission. What I'm thinking is that her attacker might wonder about Mrs. Benbow's vague reports and may want to check up on Mrs. Wingate in person. In fact, I sincerely hope he does."

"You say 'he.' You got some ideas?"

"Not a one. I said that from habit, that's all. If our watch on Mrs. Wingate doesn't turn up something, I'm not sure what we'll do next. Just what I'm going to do now, I suppose . . . keep talking to people, hoping someone will make a slip. And hoping I notice if they do! Now, go ahead and start having your coffee break in the hall reception area, will you?''

''It would help if I had sweet rolls and coffee with me, Lieutenant. It would look more authentic like. How about if . . .''

Martinez nodded indulgently. ''Go right ahead. By all means, make your masquerade as authentic as possible. Just don't get so much frosting on your fingers that you couldn't draw your revolver, if it comes to that. And when you're relieved, see that the next watcher has a snack as part of his disguise, too, will you?''

Swanson smiled broadly and headed out the door and down the hall toward the dining room, and then presumably to the kitchen. At least, he was out of sight when Martinez came out of the parlor and went to the phone booth, where he called his office to request backup.

He appeared relaxed and casual, slumped on the stool with one foot propped up against the doorjamb. But he left the door open and from time to time leaned slightly outside the booth, as though to listen. But he heard nothing unusual.

The phone conversation ended, but still he sat there, the phone in his hand, as though he'd forgotten to hang up. Anyone seeing him would assume he was still making his call. In a short while, when Swanson came back carrying a mug of coffee, a Danish, and two fresh-baked bear claws on a plate, Martinez finally put the phone's handset in its cradle and stood up to stretch.

''Ruiz and Pickett will be here in about an hour. Till then, do the best you can. And look casual. Be a man on a break. Unless, of course, something happens.''

''Like?''

''Like Mrs. Wingate screaming, for instance. Or if you hear a gunshot! Come on, Swanson. Use your good common sense. You can hear footsteps in that hall quite clearly from here. And you can see anybody who heads for the stairs. If they just get to the top and stop, they're probably stopping near Mrs. Wingate's door. Clear? Then you start up the stairs yourself and take a look.''

''What if they come in by the back stairs?''

"You can probably hear them come through that back door, if you listen close enough. Don't go far from the foot of the stairs here. We'll go ahead and put a man on the porch, too, as soon as our help arrives. In the meantime, if you have the slightest doubt, you go park yourself right in that hallway. I'd rather find out who was coming and going without being so obvious, but Mrs. Wingate's safety comes first. Clear?"

"Yessir."

Martinez left, while Swanson began his patrol most enthusiastically with his coffee and sweet rolls.

While Swanson spread butter on his cherry Danish, Angela spread the word among her fellow exercisers. When she arrived at the Health and Fitness House, she found only two rowing machines vacant and rather grumpily plunked herself down on one of them.

"Did you ever find your friend?" Cracker Graham panted from the next rowing machine. In-out, in-out, in-out—her plump little form kept up the beat, her knees flexing in time with her elbows, her back bending with every stroke. "She was just out for a walk like we thought, wasn't she?"

"No, I'm afraid not. It was . . . really, it was rather serious." Angela worked at keeping her tone somber, without pushing it all the way to sorrow.

"She hadn't had a fall, had she?" Tilly Warfield said from the nearest exercycle. Her legs slowed and the wheel under her began to drag a bit.

"Keep going, Mrs. Warfield," Ginger called from the end of the room, clapping her hands in time to the music. "Keep going, girls . . ."

"I can't hear with this thing whirring and whizzing under me," Tilly called back. "I want to know what happened to Mrs. Wingate. She got lost this morning, but now she's found."

Maggie Randall was the next to defect. She left her trampoline and grabbed a towel to mop her brow. "Yes, we want to know about this," she called the length of the room. "Give us a break, Ginger!"

Frankie Cziok stopped bouncing on the trampoline next to Maggie's, then, nearly falling as she got herself onto stable ground, came closer to join Angela and the group that was forming around her. "Come on, what did happen to your friend?"

"Nothing serious, I hope?" Belinda Terry asked. She took another towel from the rack behind Maggie and mopped as well, tugging energetically at her gray curls as she did.

"Just imagine," Judy Daggett said, sagging her way closer to them, "if that moose of a big ol' woman fell and you had to try to get her onto a stretcher."

"Imagine having to *carry* the stretcher!" Carmen Sturkie nearly giggled.

The entire group had stopped their exercises. The machines were abandoned, as the women clustered around Angela. "It wasn't," she told Caledonia later, "that they cared so much about you, I'm afraid. It was that you gave them the perfect excuse to stop their sweating! They'd been at it maybe twenty-five or thirty minutes. They were facing another twenty before Ginger would let them go to the floor exercises."

"Though I'm sure they *were* concerned about your welfare," she added hastily. "I mean, who wouldn't be?" She did not repeat the remarks about Caledonia's size that formed a jolly exchange for a few moments as the group gathered around her in a tight circle.

"Okay, give," Marceline Richardson had said, with her accustomed sharpness. "Let's hear the story."

"Well, she nearly died, that's the story," Angela said. Surely that wouldn't be too much of an exaggeration. "She got herself locked into the big refrigerator at the back of the kitchen last night, and—"

To her surprise, three or four of the women burst out laughing. "Stealing a little bedtime snack, was she?" one of them said. "We've all tried that at one time or another," another voice chimed in. "Desperation."

"How on earth did she get locked into the freezer, though?" Maggie asked. "What happened?"

"There wasn't a wind last night," Cracker said. "I read my book rather late, and I'd have heard it . . ."

"The wind wouldn't move that big freezer door, anyway," Marceline said sharply. "Come on, Cracker . . . get serious."

"I really don't know exactly how it happened," Angela said. "She wasn't at all clear on it herself!"

"You have spokened to her!" Frankie said. "But that is good news. She is able at least to talk."

"Oh yes, but just barely," Angela said hastily, making sure she spoke clearly so they could all understand her. "And she's awfully weak and tired. We don't have any idea what long-term damage there may have been. To her . . . you know, to her insides. I mean, at our ages—that is, at *her* age—that much exposure to cold could be . . ." She hesitated, then decided to risk it, "Why, it could be fatal! The doctor's coming, of course. And in the meantime, she's sleeping. She'll probably stay in bed a couple of days at least. She's pretty nearly exhausted, poor thing."

"Who found her?" That was Carmen again, leaning forward so far that with her bright pink face she seemed to be standing ahead of all the other women in the circle. Cracker apparently thought Carmen was about to fall, and reached a hand out to steady her.

"The night watchman," Angela said. "He went in after a lunch he'd left in the refrigerator, I understand."

"Oh, my! How very fortunous," Frankie said. Everyone stopped and looked at her questioningly. "That his hungers should bring about her savings!" she explained.

"That handsome young watchman can rescue me any time he wants to." Belinda Terry picked up the conversational ball that had been lying there, dead, after Frankie's utterance. "What a wow he is! Don't you agree, girls?"

"A real chunk!" That had to be Frankie.

"Hunk," Maggie corrected her automatically. "But it wouldn't have been him last night. It would have been fat old Ernie. He was on duty last night."

"Ah, you *would* notice, Maggie," Cracker said, nudging her with a sly elbow. "I never thought to get their schedules, much as I enjoy watching the good-looking one!"

"He's the after-dinner floor show, all right," Tilly Warfield agreed. "I never mind getting a peek at Handsome myself!"

"Me, too. What a disk!"

"*Dish*, Frankie," Maggie said sharply. "Good heavens, but I wish you'd be more careful when you pick up new expressions. You drive me crazy getting things just to the right or left of correct . . . I'll bet you even drive nails in crooked."

"Well, is your fat friend going to live or not?" Marceline Richardson said, changing the topic abruptly back to the news item. She'd obviously had enough of the lighthearted banter.

"Marceline!" Judy Daggett was shocked. "You'll upset Angela! Of course she's going to live. Isn't she, Angela?"

"We hope so," Angela said piously. "But the doctor hasn't seen her yet. And she was so tired, I couldn't get any real idea of whether she was . . . you know, whether she was herself or not."

"You mean," Carmen said, leaning forward again, "that she might have suffered brain damage?"

"It's possible, of course," Angela said. That was a new thought, and she wasn't sure whether to agree or not. Perhaps she could keep Caledonia safer and help along the lieutenant's plan if she said Caledonia seemed mentally unsound after her experience. Perhaps . . . but she discarded the idea. She hadn't done enough research to describe convincing symptoms of oxygen starvation or hypothermia. Best leave details alone. Instead she concentrated on looking sad.

It was a pose she didn't need to keep up for very long. Ginger, waiting with ill-concealed impatience at the end of the room for her flock to get back to work, had finally decided to take a hand and came bouncing up to the group. "Ladies, ladies, enough of the rest and the gossip. Let's get those calories melting away again . . . get the fat burning itself off . . . let's go, let's go, let's go . . ."

Slowly and reluctantly, the group broke apart into its components, and each woman took one of the instruments of torture. Angela moved fast enough this time to snag a trampoline for herself, leaving an annoyed Maggie to take the rowing machine. "Hope you don't mind," Angela said smoothly. "You're so much younger

than I am, you can stand that kind of exercise. Not that you need
it . . .''

Mollified, Maggie bent over her oars. "Row, row, row your
boat," Angela sang smugly. Maggie looked up once to glare at her,
and Angela said "Sorry" aloud. But under her breath she muttered,
"Better you row, row, rowing your boat than me row, row, rowing
mine . . .'' but she didn't think it politic to say that out loud. Instead
she got quiet and concentrated on her jumping, letting the disco
beat of Ginger's tape player move her along what the Inn's brochures said was her "sure way to fitness and weight loss."

13

⊙

The day passed slowly, a day of routine, a day of boredom. Angela suffered through the morning's exercise classes, enjoyed her rescheduled beauty appointments in the afternoon, and generally kept up the pose of the worried friend, which, since it was not too far from the truth, was convincing. She even attended the cooking class in the afternoon, learning how to sweeten desserts with concentrated apple juice instead of with sugar and how to make an elegant banana flambé with very few calories. Each segment of the day's program seemed to her to take a year.

For her part, Caledonia found herself dropping off to sleep more than she meant to. Her night in the freezer had really tired her. She read, she washed out underthings and mended a pair of queen-size pantyhose (the waist seams always managed to let go and need reinforcing, she couldn't imagine why!), and then she slept again.

From time to time she heard a gentle knock on the door, sometimes a voice whispered her name from outside. "Mrs. Wingate . . . Mrs. Wingate, are you awake?" But true to her promise, she only sighed hugely and rolled over on the bed to produce sound effects—her heavy breath, the squeak of the springs—that might be audible to the listener. On each occasion, after a little wait her caller went away. As Caledonia told Angela later, that routine got old by ten in the morning. "I thought today would never end!"

Swanson, too, was bored. He was surprised to find he even became sated with sweet rolls and coffee, and he agreed to take the watch on the back porch, from time to time, for variety's sake. When he was downstairs in the reception area, he hid himself in the phone booth rather than continue the pretense of a coffee break. "I never thought I'd get tired of cinnamon and frosting," he told Martinez sheepishly. "But I sure did!"

The two auxiliary officers, Ruiz and Pickett, were similarly bored. Ruiz, slim and dark and smartly turned out in sharply creased slacks, paced while he was on watch, circling the reception area with restless energy that reminded Martinez, when he saw the man in action, of one of the jungle cats in the circus, confined in too small a cage.

If Ruiz was a jungle cat, Pickett was a walrus sunning itself by its pool and waiting for a keeper to bring a fresh snack of herring. Pickett was fat, balding, had a huge mustache, and whenever he was on duty, sat motionless in the largest available chair, staring unwinkingly ahead of him. "I thought he was probably asleep with his eyes open. That's a neat trick and some of our men have perfected its use," Martinez told Swanson. "Though not when they're told to guard our taxpayers, one hopes."

"Well, was he?"

"What?"

"Asleep."

"Oh. No. Just staring and apparently thinking of nothing in particular."

Martinez himself had the only interesting passage of the entire group, a moment in one of his interviews. As he reported it to Swanson later that day, he had been talking to Belinda Terry about her son Dennis.

"I understand he died of a drug overdose, Mrs. Terry."

She bit her lip and nodded. "I still can't believe it. That boy had such a sunny disposition . . . he was so popular and so successful at everything he tried. Why on earth would he want to use drugs? He had everything going for him. I thought," she went on in a tone that was almost accusing, "I thought it was losers who took drugs. People who needed drugs as a substitute for success and happiness."

"Unfortunately, that isn't the case," Martinez said gently. "Popular, successful people can get addicted rather quickly, too. They may start by playing around with drugs at parties—"

"Yes, he told us that's where he got the drugs first. Parties with his crowd from the office. Using drugs just for fun," Belinda said. She seemed wholly unconscious that one of her hands had crept up and now worked diligently at tucking the wisps and curls of gray hair back under her headband.

"But he got so he couldn't leave them alone. He started buying drugs in nightclubs, on street corners, in cheap hotels—wherever he could make a contact. He wept like a little child when he told us about it. He was spending every cent he made, and he couldn't keep his family going. He wanted us to help him and his wife financially. Just to pay his bills for him—the mortgage, the car loan, some clothing stores, the dentist. We believed him. We gave him the money."

"And did he pay the bills? Straighten himself out?"

She shook her head. "He spent that money on drugs, too. He told us when he came back for more. He confessed again and promised to do better."

She gasped at the pain of the reopened wound in her mind. "I think now that he knew all along, even when he asked us for the money the first time, that he was going to spend it on drugs. I think he was confessing just to get our sympathy so we'd be sure to give him money. I think by that time he didn't care for any of us—his wife, his brothers, his dad and me—he didn't care for anything by that time but the drugs."

"And then he killed himself?"

She nodded. "Not right away. Not that day. You know, we'd been advised to cut off his funds. To refuse him the money. One of those seminars for the parents of addicts told us that was the best way. So we did it. And we got the other children . . . I have two other sons . . . to do the same. And those of his friends we knew . . . we called and told them the same thing. To refuse to loan him anything. Not a dime."

"What did he do?"

"He sold everything he and his wife owned. Over a period of two months he sold the car and their television and their stereo. He sold his own jewelry, sold his wife's jewelry . . . He didn't have his job anymore by that time. They'd caught him taking money from the purse of a woman coworker. They didn't prosecute, but they fired him that same day. Finally, his wife told him to leave before he sold the house as well. By the end of that last two months on his own, he must have been desperate.''

''And then . . .''

''He didn't know how to be a good beggar, he wasn't very successful as a thief, he couldn't borrow from relatives and friends, and he knew . . . even as sick as he was, he knew that he was killing himself an inch at a time. So he just speeded the job up. He took a room at a hotel in San Diego and injected himself with a massive amount of heroin . . . he left a note to say he was sorry, but he couldn't see any other way out.''

She paused a moment, remembering, and then went on in a voice thickened with pain, ''When they called us and we came down to San Diego, we found we even owed for his hotel bill! Isn't that . . .'' She choked up again. ''You know, I'll always feel that *we* killed him. Our so-called cure killed him, and a lot faster than the drugs would have.''

''Don't even think that.'' Martinez resisted the impulse to put an arm around her and let her cry on his shoulder. ''Don't even think it. But, Mrs. Terry, I do have to ask you a question or two about that time in your life. Is it too painful to talk about it a little longer?''

She shook her head, though she didn't speak.

''Well, then . . . you said the hotel charged you for the room in which your son died?'' That seemed as good a way as any to bring up the hotel and its connections to the matter at hand.

''They tried. The desk clerk forced a bill into my husband's hand when we arrived. The police brought us in, let us see the room . . . and that desk clerk came bustling up as soon as he'd learned who we were, and he pushed that bill at us. Fortunately, the manager was there as well, and he simply reached over and took the bill away and refused to even consider our paying it. He was most gracious about it.''

''The Kimbrough was that kind of place in the old days, of course. I'm glad to hear all its grace and generosity have not passed into history. Although it's had its troubles, of course. You are no doubt aware there was another death there. A drug dealer named Gonzalez . . . or Guns . . .''

"Guns?''

"A nickname. Peter Guns. He was shot at the hotel right in the middle of one of his drug deals. Surely you read about that in the papers.''

"I think . . .'' She paused in tugging her curls about and passed a hand over her eyes. "Perhaps I have heard . . . or rather, no . . . I don't know.'' There was a pause, then, and she looked at Martinez from the corners of her eyes. "I think . . .'' She stopped again. "I think . . .'' she said again, and stopped once more.

"Yes?'' He tried to make the single word as gentle and encouraging a sound as he could make. "Yes?''

They sat motionless a long moment, but finally she broke the tension by getting to her feet. "Nothing. Nothing at all. If you're done with me for the moment, I really did want to get to the kitchen for today's cooking class. Is it all right?''

"Of course.'' Martinez could be gracious himself, even though he had reason to be annoyed. He almost had her there, for a moment, as he told Swanson. The mood had been right, she had wanted to tell him something. Well, perhaps if he let her cool a short time . . . Then if he called her back . . .

"Sounds like it would work,'' Swanson said. They were alone at the close of the working day, shut into the small front parlor behind its soundproof oaken door.

"Well, that's enough about my activities. Now, let's have it.''

"It?''

"The lowdown on Mrs. Wingate's callers. I've had a frustrating afternoon and I want some good news. So tell me you have found a suspect. Tell me someone lurked in the hall all day. Tell me somebody unauthorized actually went into that bedroom.''

Swanson shook his head dolefully. "Nobody much went in. Except the doctor, of course, and Mrs. Benbow. That doctor made a fuss about being called out for an emergency that he said wasn't.''

"I know. He told me. Mrs. Wingate is in reasonably sound condition, considering her age and all she's gone through. But surely he wasn't the only one.''

"Naaa. There's a whole bunch of people who fooled around outside her door or knocked . . . you know."

"Better tell me about it."

"Ruiz and I were on duty this morning when Bart came by. Ruiz was on the porch, and he saw Bart stop by Mrs. Wingate's door. But he didn't do anything—just sort of hesitated, knocked softly, waited, and when nobody answered, he went away."

"Interesting. The handyman came calling. Unusual, I'd say."

"No, not really. Ruiz also reports that about an hour later, Ernie came to Mrs. Wingate's door."

"Ernie!"

"That's right. He didn't knock, just stood there awhile and kind of leaned forward. Ruiz thought he was listening to see if there were sounds inside. I guess he didn't hear anything, though, because Ruiz says that after a while he just shrugged and went away."

"Sounds harmless enough. Maybe more curiosity than anything else, do you suppose?"

"Nossir. Because they both came back in the afternoon. Ernie came first and this time he knocked. But he got no answer, so after a while he went away. Bart came just a few minutes ago, according to Pickett. Same routine. Knocked, waited, left."

"Interesting," Martinez said. "And perhaps a little surprising. I didn't really think either of them was involved in this business. But I could be wrong. I have been, often enough. Better let me hear about the others, while you're at it."

"Well, all of the other guests except the Cziok woman, the one who talks so funny, and the beautiful one, Mrs. Randall, came by early, either after exercise or just before or after lunch. Each one either knocked and waited or else just stood and listened at the door. But nobody tried to go in. This afternoon, Mrs . . . let's see . . . Mrs. Daggett, Mrs. Sturkie, Mrs. Terry, that Mrs. Randall, and Mrs. Richardson all came back again. Or rather, Mrs. Randall came for the first time."

"But Mrs. Cziok hasn't come by even once?"

"Nossir."

"I wonder why? Everybody else came. That seems to have been the 'done' thing today. But not Mrs. Cziok. Well, I'll have to give that some thought. Now, what about the staff? Other than Bart and Ernie, I mean.''

"Mrs. McGraw told the maids not to disturb Mrs. Wingate's rest, and Betsy, the noisy one, didn't go near the room. But the quiet one, that Helena, she went in anyhow. Knocked at the door and after a minute she went on in. I guess Mrs. Wingate let her in, but I didn't see Mrs. Wingate.''

"Good." Martinez nodded his approval. "I told her to stay out of sight, and for once she must have listened to me. Any idea what the maid wanted?''

"She had fresh towels over her arm, so I figured it was just a routine call. Mrs. Wingate would have yelled, I figured, if there was a problem.''

"You said before only Mrs. Benbow and the doctor went in.''

"So sue me . . . I forgot to mention the maid! And Mrs. McGraw, of course. She brought the lunch tray up herself. Nobody else on the staff came by.''

"Well, most of them had their duties to attend to. They didn't have time for a social call. Now, this is the total of the notes? I mean, did you add Ruiz's and Pickett's notes to yours to make this report?''

"Yessir.''

Martinez looked faintly disappointed. "Well, we didn't find out much, did we? But, after all, our primary mission was to protect Mrs. Wingate, and we seem to have accomplished that.'' He rubbed his neck and one shoulder in a gesture that signified both fatigue and frustration.

"We'll keep up patrols around the place tonight, too. Get someone to spell Ruiz and Pickett for tonight's duty, and instruct them to show themselves as they stand guard.''

"Sir?''

"That's what I said. Be seen. At least enough so that nobody will get up to do any mischief at all during the night. We need a full night's rest. Tomorrow . . . well, we may have to do something a bit different tomorrow.''

Perhaps it was because of the highly visible guards that the night passed peacefully. Angela and Caledonia certainly began their next day calmly enough. Despite her getting a clean bill of health from the doctor, Caledonia assumed she was to continue playing invalid and kept to her room for the second morning in a row. But Angela dressed for morning exercise and, although she disdained the pre-breakfast walk, joined the others in the dining room and would, as she had told Caledonia, spend another dreadful day in stretching and bending. But her projected routine was delayed for a short time when, immediately after breakfast, Lieutenant Martinez beckoned her away from the others and into the small front parlor, his temporary office.

"The reason I called you in this morning is that I need an escort when I go to see Mrs. Wingate."

"Really, Lieutenant. How coy of you. Just knock, and when she answers, go right in. She won't mind."

"Ah, but she won't answer if I knock. Surely you remember that we instructed her not to answer when people came calling. She'll just pretend she's asleep, unless I identify myself. But someone else might hear me, and I'd rather be discreet about my call."

"Charming reticence, Lieutenant. And very unpolicelike. Or at least, what one always thinks of when one thinks of the police. By all means, Lieutenant, come ahead and let me act as your advance guard."

So Angela led the way up the stairs and into the room she and Caledonia shared. Caledonia still lay in bed, a book in one hand, a coffee cup in the other. When she saw the lieutenant, she made a face. "Oatmeal for breakfast again, Lieutenant. Oatmeal. I thought you promised . . ."

"I am really sorry, Mrs. Wingate. I was very busy yesterday. But today, I will certainly take care of that for you. Though I'm surprised you didn't mention it yourself to Mrs. McGraw."

"I hated to hurt her feelings," Caledonia confessed, a bit abashed. "You remember how pleased she was with herself yesterday to have brought me what she imagined was my favorite. I hate bursting the bubble, as it were. But I figure you can say it for me."

"Coward," Angela said. "I've never known you to back away before, Caledonia."

"Mrs. Benbow, if you would be so good . . ." The lieutenant's voice was satin-smooth. "You've done your duty in convoying me this far. Now I need you to run an errand for me at the Health and Fitness House."

"Oh. Oh, I'd be delighted!"

"Would you please tell Mrs. Terry to come over here to the small parlor? Just tell her I am anxious to continue our conversation. By the time she gets back to the house here, I'll be downstairs waiting for her."

"But I can do that after we talk to Caledonia."

"Certainly you could. But you'll save me so much time if you'll do it now." As he talked, Martinez inserted a gentle hand under Angela's elbow and pressed, ever so slightly, in the direction of the door, edging in that direction himself. "I also want you to tell the other guests that Mrs. Wingate is getting much, much better. Reassure anyone who asks that she'll be out and about tomorrow, as fit as ever."

"But that may be dangerous for Cal!" Angela said sharply.

"Quite the contrary," he said in a soothing tone. "I think she's relatively safe now."

"You didn't set the trap!"

"Of course not. I told you . . ."

"But it was such a splendid chance. I really thought . . ."

"All we did was to make notes on who tried to enter this room, who stopped and knocked on the door—that sort of thing. We had hoped perhaps someone might show unusual interest in Mrs. Wingate's condition. Someone unauthorized might try to enter the room, might try to find out if Mrs. Wingate had caught sight of him as he locked her into the refrigerator, perhaps. But that wasn't the case."

"Lieutenant." Caledonia had been listening with some care and now joined the conversation. "Am I to understand that you intended to set me up yesterday in the hope that the killer would attack me?"

"Certainly not," Martinez said. "Mrs. Benbow suggested we might try it, that's all."

"Without consulting me? Angela . . ." Caledonia's voice grew deep and resonant. In a moment, she would be rumbling *forte fortissimo*, and everyone in the building would know their business.

"Mrs. Wingate, we can talk about this in a moment. Just for now . . ." He turned to Angela.

"Please do go over to join the other ladies, as I asked you. You haven't forgotten, I trust, that I want you to continue looking very much a part of the group. I do not want you to be absent from activities any more than you must." He had her at the door now, and swung it open with a flourish. "And thank you so much for carrying my message."

And without her knowing exactly how it happened, Angela was on the outside of the door, Martinez remained on the inside, and he had closed the door between them. For a moment she just stood there with her mouth open. It wasn't often she was manipulated that easily. Then she turned and started down the stairs. There was nothing for it but to do her duty. Chin up, she headed bravely toward the Health and Fitness House for another vigorous morning.

In the bedroom, meanwhile, Caledonia was determined to make clear her annoyance. "Imagine Angela suggesting you use me as bait for a trap. What nerve that woman has!"

"Well, Mrs. Wingate, it wasn't altogether a bad idea, to tell you the truth. And that's why I'm here: to discuss with you the possibility of setting just such a trap."

Caledonia thought about that remark for a moment. "Okay, Lieutenant," she said, "please step aside. I'm going to get out of this bed and sit up in a chair. I need to be vertical to talk about something like this."

She heaved herself out from under the sheet and blanket. A startled Martinez was relieved to see that she was fully clad in a nightgown and a neck-to-ankle robe.

"Fully clothed, Mrs. Wingate? And a blanket? In midsummer?" The lieutenant, having got over his shock when he thought for a moment she was perhaps going to get out of the bed uncovered, was curious and just slightly amused.

"Out by the ocean where I live, we have to put a blanket over us at night, even in the summer. Sometimes I even wear a flannel nightie! I'm used to that. I like it. I couldn't get used to just a sheet, the way folks do inland here. So I turn the air conditioning in the room on full at night. Can't you feel the chill?''

''Now that you mention it . . .''

''Well, this is all beside the point. And the point is this trap idea of yours.''

He nodded. ''As I told you, that's why I'm here now—to ask permission to try a scheme of that sort.''

Caledonia had seated herself in a large chair near the desk she and Angela shared. Her customary good spirits seemed to have been somewhat restored by the prospect of action—or potentially exciting action at that. ''I see. I'm the cheese in the trap. Right?''

''That's about it,'' he agreed. ''Mrs. Wingate, if I could ensure your safety, would you act as our Judas goat? Knowing that there might be some small element of danger? Though I assure you we'd take every precaution—''

''I don't see why it wouldn't be all right. Provided you don't use that term, 'Judas goat.' It sounds so . . . so treacherous. I'd rather think I was doing a good deed for the community at large. What do I have to do?''

''Absolutely nothing. Or rather, exactly what you did yesterday.''

''I don't have to do anything but stay in here again, is that right?''

''Right. With one exception. Unbolt your door.''

''I already did. Didn't you notice when you came in? But that was because I assumed it was safe, now. Apparently you don't think it is. And come to think of it, I'm not sure why I thought so, either.''

''It may not be safe, but I still want you to make it possible for someone to come inside if they want to check up on you. Don't answer anyone's knock, though. Most visitors—innocent visitors—will assume that you're asleep and they'll tiptoe away. But what I'm hoping is that one person won't be satisfied with that. He'll need to find out for himself.''

''Because I'm supposed to be getting better all the time. Right?''

''Right. I hope that somebody will feel crowded by your continued recovery. I'm hoping that the reason somebody locked you in that refrigerator is strong enough that they'll consider trying another attack.''

"All right, now we come to the tough part. What if that really happens? What then?''

"If anybody should attack you . . . no, I'll make that stronger. If anyone even approaches you—actually enters the room without being told by you that he could come in—what I want is that you'll yell bloody murder.''

"I've got a pretty loud voice. If I yell, the killer will probably drop dead of a heart attack and save you a lot of trouble.''

"That would be fine with me if he did keel over,'' Martinez said. "But that's not the reason I want you to make plenty of noise. The reason is so that your guard will be sure to hear you and come running. I don't want you to be in any real danger. Not for more than a split second, at any rate.''

"Listen, Lieutenant. A split second is long enough to shoot somebody!''

"But our killer has always used silent weapons—the weapons readily at hand. It seems obvious to me that our murderer doesn't even have a gun.''

"Well, I'm glad *you* feel so confident. I'm not so sure . . .'' She sighed. "Well, where's this guard going to be? How close to me? Not right outside the door, I suppose. Not out on the porch in plain sight. So where?''

"There's a kind of loft off the back porch that extends over Mrs. McGraw's quarters, under the roof of that addition that runs down the west side of the house. It's a sort of attic over Mrs. McGraw's apartment that one can enter from a door that opens onto the back porch.''

"I don't remember . . .''

"Chances are you never even noticed it. It's just a small door. There's an unfinished space, and you have to stoop over in there, because the roof slants so steeply. It's really very cramped. I suppose the only time somebody goes in is to service the pipes or the wiring. But our man is going to be in there, nevertheless. He'll stay right by that door. If you shout loudly, he'll hear you and he'll get here in seconds. He's literally just around the corner.''

"I'll take your word for it, Lieutenant," Caledonia said. She sighed again and stood up, towering imposingly over Martinez, who got hastily to his feet. "You know, I racked my brain all day yesterday—when I wasn't asleep—trying to think of what it is that made me a danger to this person, whoever it is. I couldn't work it out at all. If I know something, I don't know that I know, if you see what I mean."

"But you might remember at any time. That's what our killer will be afraid of. At least, I hope so. And if that's true, I suspect he'll check on your health today, as soon as the guards appear to be removed and you seem to be improving enough to get out of bed soon."

"All right, Lieutenant. All right . . . I'm willing to be your bait. I'm as anxious to get this over with as you are. And now I suggest you'd better be on your way, completing arrangements for my safety. Because I need my privacy to make my own arrangements."

"Your arrangements?"

"Sure. I want to get dressed. If I'm going to meet this menace face to face, I don't want to do it in a robe and fuzzy slippers! I'll feel much more capable if I have on clothes and shoes!"

"Mrs. Wingate, promise you won't even think of trying to manage this by yourself. I mean, don't even contemplate ignoring us and striking out on your own."

"No, that isn't what I meant at all. I promise I'll call you as soon as the unauthorized guest arrives. Assuming he—or she—ever does." And with a gracious wave, she dismissed Martinez and set about choosing a suitable caftan to wear to an attempted murder.

14

◉

As luck would have it, Georgie Pickett was the man on duty when, in the late afternoon, Caledonia called for help. He might look like a walrus, he might not be the brightest man on the force, he might stare straight ahead unblinking (thereby convincing watchers that he was asleep on the job), but Georgie Pickett was essentially a good cop. He did not actually doze on duty, he was nowhere near as dull-witted as he sometimes looked, and he was doggedly determined to do what he was assigned to do: to keep Mrs. Wingate from harm.

For most of the day, Pickett sat doubled up under the low attic roof and suffered from the heat. Ruiz relieved him for three hours over the lunch period, but by two Georgie was back there in the enclosed darkness where no air conditioning could reach. He had scrooched along about four feet down the length of the space, away from the door to a spot where some plywood had been nailed down, so he could at least sit without the bare edges of the rafters cutting into his huge hams. And there he fought against sleep, occasionally stretching his cramped legs and shaking his head to clear the mental mists.

When Caledonia's call—"*Help! Police! Help! HELP!*"—vibrated through the superheated air, muffled though the sound was, Pickett tried to leap to the rescue. But he found himself scrambling along on his hands and knees, dragging a leg that had, in spite of his efforts, fallen asleep and was relatively useless. He was also trying, as he hitched awkwardly along, not to step down between the rafters, where he knew his foot (or a hand or knee) might go

159

right through the ceiling of Mrs. McGraw's place below, and he cursed mightily as he crawled.

It seemed to him like five minutes, though it may have been just less than thirty or forty seconds, when he got to the little exit door, but there he was delayed again. The door was barred. There was a wooden block about the size of a large bar of soap fixed by means of a huge nail to the exterior doorjamb, the kind of block that could be rotated to lie across the edge of the door and keep it from flopping open. Georgie had noted the block idly as he entered the attic. And now it had been swung at right angles to the edge of the door, and as effectively as a dead bolt might, it kept the door from opening.

At least, it did so for a moment. But Pickett, angrily ramming his body against the door so that it rattled in its frame, shook the wooden bar loose enough so that it was no longer pressed tight against the door and flopped freely downward, parallel to the jamb, freeing the door to swing open and allowing Pickett to fall through and out onto the open porch.

He picked his huge frame up, and still dragging his prickly, temporarily paralyzed right leg, limped thunderously down the porch and into the upstairs hall. He paid no attention to two women standing irresolutely about halfway down the hall, but charged straight into Caledonia's room.

Martinez and Swanson had also heard Mrs. Wingate's muffled but unmistakable bellow, although they were in the first floor parlor going over notes. The men had to take a moment to disentangle themselves from the mountains of manila folders, notebooks, loose papers, and index cards they had been studying, but they still entered Mrs. Wingate's room so close behind Pickett that they ran into him where he had stopped dead just inside the door. Martinez, as conscious of the curious onlookers as Pickett had been unconscious, shut that door firmly behind them.

"My Gawd!" Pickett croaked, pointing at the bed just beyond him. "He got her! He got her and he got away!"

In the bed was a huddled figure, covered with a layer of blankets and sheets against the icy blast of the air conditioning, which was turned on to full Arctic level. Martinez's eyes followed the line of

Pickett's pointing finger and saw the handle of a knife that protruded from the tangled folds of blanket and sheet.

"Honest, I came as fast as I could," Pickett was babbling. "My leg was asleep, and somebody locked the door . . ."

"Locked?"

"That little wooden bar thing was down."

"Maybe the wind," Swanson said doubtfully.

"No! It had to be on purpose. I think somebody was watching and knew I was in there. I think somebody needed time to knife Mrs. Wingate. And I think—"

"And *I* think you buzzards are talking through your hats!" a huge voice sounded from the direction of the bathroom.

"Mrs. Wingate! Mrs. Wingate, thank God!" Martinez gasped as they turned from the figure in Caledonia's bed toward the bathroom door, out of which came the real Caledonia, pressing a washcloth to her mouth, only her angry eyes visible above the red and white of her blood-spotted compress.

Pickett gaped, apparently speechless.

"Gosh, Mrs. Wingate, am I glad to see you!" Swanson blurted.

"I'll second that," Martinez said. "Are you hurt?"

"Only a little, no thanks to you," Caledonia said angrily. "I slipped getting out of the tub, trying to catch sight of my intruder, and I cut my lip. I figured I better yell at that point. Whoever she was, she wasn't going to stay fooled for long, and . . ."

"She? You caught a glimpse of her?"

"Just a bit of her dress as she went out the door. My yelling scared the blue beans out of her and she took off. You better start hunting for her . . ."

"We intend to, though it's almost certainly too late. Swanson, Pickett, see who those people in the hall are—make a note of names—and find out if they saw anybody come out of here and if there's anybody else around. Oh, and get them out of the hall. Tell them to go downstairs . . . get on with their business. You just take a quick look, and anything or anybody you find I want to know about. Report back here."

They moved out of the room quickly. "Out on the porch, Pickett," Martinez ordered, and as Georgie limped back outside again to search up and down and around the corner, Martinez turned back into Caledonia's room and again closed the door.

For his part, Swanson moved quickly along the hall to the little group, now increased to a total of three women standing at Maggie Randall's door where Maggie, her hair tucked under a shower cap and her bare shoulder gleaming wet, had put her head barely outside. "What's the racket, Officer?" she said, as she spotted Swanson approaching. "What's going on out here?"

"Trouble in Mrs. Wingate's room, ma'am," Swanson said vaguely. "You the only ones up here?"

"I don't know, Officer," Tilly Warfield spoke first. "I just got here."

"I think so," Judy Daggett said. "If anybody else was here, they'd be out in the hall with us, wouldn't they? What with all the noise . . . I mean, they're just as curious as we are."

Frankie Cziok just shrugged and shook her head.

"Well, did any of you ladies see or hear anything unusual? Someone running down the front stairs, for instance?"

"No. Well, at least—I ran down. But I ran right back up," Judy said.

"You ran down and then back upstairs?" Swanson was surprised.

"That's what I just said," Judy snapped. "I came up here to . . ." She hesitated. "You know . . . to do what I had to do before the cooking class started."

"Please, Mrs. Daggett, I don't quite understand . . ."

"Oh, for heaven's sake! She was in the john!" Tilly said grumpily. "We all go and . . . you know . . . wash up after jumping around, before we go on to the next activity."

"Yes, that's right," Judy took over. "I had an argument with Cracker Graham over who got the john downstairs and who had to climb the stairs to use the john in her own room. We flipped a coin and I lost. We don't climb those stairs if we can help it, you understand."

"Ah! So that is it! I try the door, and it is busy. Not the door— I mean the joan is busy. So I came up here," Frankie said cheerfully.

"Then Mrs. Graham stayed downstairs? She didn't come up here with you?"

"You don't listen, do you? I just said that. She won the toss!" Judy snapped.

"So you heard a noise and came out of your room . . ."

"No, that isn't what happened. I'd finished and gone back down the stairs when I heard some sort of pounding and bumping around. I thought maybe somebody'd fallen or something. So I turned right around and ran back up. I hadn't any more than got up here than you and your boss arrived. If you'd been one second faster you'd have seen me on the stairs!"

"You didn't by any chance see Mrs. Graham while you were downstairs? I mean, had she come out of the—"

"No. Of course, she may have gone on to the kitchen for class already."

"I didn't see her when I came through downstairs," Tilly volunteered. "And I didn't hear any bumping or any other noise up here, either. I came up because I was coming to . . . you know . . ."

"I heard some kind of noise, too, while I was in the shower," Maggie offered. "But what with the water running, I couldn't really tell what was going on."

"I hear bumpsing, too, but no yells. I was also in my bathroom—to making ready for class." Frankie pointed down and across the hall. "As I carried out, I see these others already in the hall."

"Not me," Maggie said. "You were already here with Judy when I stuck my head out to see what was going on."

"And not me," Tilly said firmly. "I told you, I just now got back to the house from our exercise class."

"Okay," Frankie said cheerfully. "If you say so."

"It's odd that you ladies who were up here already didn't hear more," Swanson said. "We could hear the yelling from the first floor, as well as the footsteps and the banging door."

Maggie shrugged a bare shoulder. "Maybe the floors aren't as thick as the walls, or something. I didn't hear any shouting, by the way, just the banging and heavy feet running. At least, I think that's what the noise was."

"I'll make a note to speak to Mrs. Graham about exactly where she was and what she heard,'' Swanson muttered. ''Now, we'd be obliged if you ladies would go ahead down to your cooking class. Unless you have anything else you feel we should know.''

The women shook their heads, clearly at a loss for anything worth reporting. Maggie, however, reached out a slim hand to grasp at Swanson, as though she feared he would be on his way. ''Slow down, good-looking. You haven't answered our questions. What's going on, anyhow? What's up?''

''Yes, what is going up?'' Frankie chimed in. ''If there is trouble . . . ?''

''You're absolutely sure, ladies'' —Swanson ignored the question, since he had no intention of explaining, ''that you saw or heard nobody else on this floor?''

They mumbled their negatives and shook their heads. Almost simultaneously Pickett came stumping back from the porch and also shook his head to Swanson's inquiring look. ''Ladies, we'll need to check out the whole floor, and we'd be obliged if you'd go ahead to that class, or whatever. Now, please.''

''My shower . . . '' Maggie protested.

''Please get dressed and vacate this floor as soon as you can, Mrs. Randall. Believe me, there's nothing to see, and we certainly will tell you all about it later. Pickett, check each room and each bathroom. Be sure there's nobody hiding in there.''

''Will you take my word there's nobody in my room? Or do you want to search my shower? I'd be glad to give you a guided tour.'' Maggie was clearly amused, and Swanson flushed dark red, as he tried to ignore her. She merely laughed and ducked back inside the room, closing the door with a thump behind her.

''I bet there's been a robbery,'' he could hear Judy Daggett's voice behind him. ''What do you bet?''

The three women lingered where they stood, watching with undisguised fascination as Pickett and Swanson, starting at the far end of the hall, moved quickly back toward Caledonia's room, opening doors and looking rapidly through the obvious hiding places (under beds, into closets and wardrobes, into bathrooms) before they went on to the next room.

At last Pickett and Swanson completed their tour. As they opened

Caledonia's door to enter, Swanson glared back over his shoulder at the watching women, who started guiltily and scuttled quickly for the stairway, following orders at last. Swanson then ducked quickly into Caledonia's bedroom behind Pickett and once more closed the door.

Martinez was coming from the bathroom with a clean, wet cloth, which he brought to Caledonia. She swapped her blood-stippled cloth for the fresh one rather ungraciously, though she said, "Thank you for the first aid, Lieutenant. I guess I ought to be grateful for the attention. Though in my view, it's a little late."

"I don't suppose you found anybody suspicious, Swanson," Martinez said.

"Nothing. Absolutely nothing, sir," Swanson said. "Mrs. Daggett, Mrs. Warfield, Mrs. Cziok—the one who talks funny—and that Mrs. Randall. They were all upstairs here. Say they didn't see anybody else, and we didn't find anybody."

"Me neither," Georgie Pickett said. "Checked the porch. Nobody there and all the windows closed. That Ernie's the only one I saw . . . putting gas into the mower." As he spoke, the sound of the engine started up. "There," Georgie said defensively, as though he feared contradiction. "There it goes now."

"Well, Mrs. Wingate, your attacker appears to have made a clean getaway. We can do some checking later. Someone downstairs may have seen something. Now, let's start with you. I'm not sure you'll need a stitch on that lip"— Caledonia lowered the cloth and showed the others a cut on her upper lip, already puffing up and turning an angry purple—"but the doctor can say better than I. Swanson, go get that doctor's number from Mrs. McGraw and call him to come out right away."

Swanson swung out of the room without another word.

"Never mind my lip. I want to know what happened to your great scheme to protect me. 'Don't worry, Mrs. Wingate. He'll be right around the corner, Mrs. Wingate. He'll hear you call and be here in a second, Mrs. Wingate . . .' What about all that malarky?"

"I was there. I was *there*! I tried. My leg was asleep and I was locked in . . ." Pickett was on the defensive again.

"Pickett, shut up!" Martinez was seldom so abrupt with a subordinate, but he wanted information, not an apology. That could come later. "Mrs. Wingate, it didn't go exactly as we'd planned."

Caledonia snorted but said nothing.

"I'm sorry, but the reasons we failed can wait. Let's get to what exactly went on here. You can scold me later if you like. To start with, who's that in your bed?"

"That," Caledonia said, striding forward to yank at the blankets, "is Amelia Earhart. Lieutenant, I'd like you to meet my luggage." The covers came sliding downward, at least as far as the knife, which held them pinned halfway along their length, to reveal two suitcases and several pillows mounded together to make a fairly convincing replica of a sleeping human being.

Martinez strode forward, and carefully rolled the bedding aside from the suitcase into which the knife had been driven, nearly up to its hilt.

"Pull it out, Lieutenant. Let's have a look," Caledonia urged.

"No." Martinez was sharp once more. "And don't you touch it, either."

"Fingerprints," Pickett muttered from the foot of the bed, and looked guiltily at his chief as though afraid of a reprimand for having spoken after being told to remain quiet.

"Certainly fingerprints," Martinez said. "Although there were no fingerprints at the other killings. People seem to have learned about wearing gloves. But fingerprints aside, the angle of the blow can tell us whether it was delivered with the left or right hand, and it may even tell us something about how tall the person was. I don't want to disturb things too much."

The door of the room opened again abruptly and an agitated Dorothy McGraw bustled through, followed by Swanson, who carefully shut the door yet again, although this time the hallway was empty of potential eavesdroppers.

"The doctor's on the way, though you should have heard him complain. It's a good thing he's a friend, and . . . oh, my dear, your lip! You look awful!"

"I'd look a lot more awful if I'd left my protection entirely to the police," Caledonia said. "Look at what happened to my substitute there." She pointed at the suitcase, trailing its draperies of sheeting and blanket from the knife, still embedded in its side.

"Good heavens! Our butcher knife!" Dorothy said. "At least, it certainly looks like a match for the big one from our kitchen."

"Big knife for a big target," Pickett muttered. "Oh, sorry, ma'am."

"Well, I forgive you for the insult," Caledonia said, "but I'm still sore at you for coming to the rescue late. Good thing I took steps to protect myself."

"Speaking of that, Mrs. Wingate, how did you decide to substitute the—the dummy for yourself in the bed? I'm grateful you did, of course. It stood up to the blow better than you could have."

Caledonia shivered. "Lieutenant, I got to thinking how fast this killer could do just what she did."

"Pardon?"

"Look, it doesn't take very long to slip a knife into the ribs of a victim. It made me a little . . ." She hesitated. "A little apprehensive. So I decided to do something about it."

Caledonia had felt a chill of dread when she considered the possibilities. Her reflexes were still adequate, and she was strong enough that she could probably defend herself if an assailant tried to beat her over the head with something, or if there were a frontal assault. But she wasn't sure she could react in time to stop an attack from behind.

Having showered quickly and put on a fresh caftan—grass-green sateen with glossy black jacquard trim—and replaced her fuzzy slippers with crepe-soled sandals, Caledonia was feeling much more capable and independent. She lay on the bed and read through the morning, though, as she told them, she was in no mood to let herself fall asleep.

But after her lunch tray had been finished off, Caledonia began to fret a little. The longer time went on, the more itchy and nervous she began to feel. Thoughts nagged at her—thoughts of a surprise attack, perhaps when she had dropped off for a little nap. Finally, she got up from the bed.

"The lieutenant said not to take on this job by myself. But surely he won't object if I add a little extra protection, over and above what he provided,'' she muttered.

Moving as fast as she could, but trying to keep from making any noise, she gathered a couple of the room's extra blankets from the wardrobe shelf where they were stored and some of the fluffy towels from the bathroom and packed them into her biggest suitcases. Both cases were of soft leather that bulged and deformed into more cylindrical shape with all the overstuffing. Using her extra pillows and her makeup case to add to the contours of the dummy, she shaped a fairly credible human form, aided by the lumps and ridges of blankets and sheets that softened the contours of her substitute, wherever a square edge threatened its verisimilitude.

When she finished her sculpting, the bed seemed to contain a figure, curled up slightly with knees drawn toward its chest, its back turned toward the door, the sheet and blanket carelessly lapping over its head. If an attacker drew down those top sheets, the deception was obvious. But surely he or she wouldn't risk waking the sleeper, Caledonia thought. "I wouldn't, that's for sure," she muttered.

Then she took more of the extra bedding from the wardrobe shelf and made herself a lounge in the tub. With sufficient padding, it was comfortable enough that she could relax and read a little, and once she even found herself dropping off to sleep.

"The tub, Mrs. Wingate?" Martinez said. "You've been taking your ease in the bathtub?"

"Sure. Why not? It's big enough . . . one of those wonderful old cast-iron jobs that every Victorian house installed when they first got indoor plumbing. Big enough for two my size. And the water comes right up to your chin, when you fill it up."

"Say!" Pickett's pudgy face lighted with interest. "I could use one of those. Boy do I hate those tubs that you sit down in and your knees are out of the water, or you straighten your legs and you're sticking up . . . What's the matter with the plumbing people they don't think we got to get wet all over at the same time?"

"Pickett . . ." Martinez was amused, but stern. "No time for that now."

"But you weren't really safe in here," Dorothy interrupted. "Good heavens, Caledonia, the killer could have come on in there—"

"I figured I could defend myself face to face, at least long enough to yell for help, if she did come into the bathroom looking for me."

"You said 'she,' " Dorothy said. "You saw her?"

"Not exactly. But I was lying there reading in the tub, as I told you, and I heard the outer door open."

Altogether, the door had opened three times during the afternoon. Once it was Dorothy herself, fetching away the used lunch tray. "You tiptoed in and out, so as not to wake me. I knew then the dummy was a success."

"But if you were in the bathroom, how did you know it was me?"

"Well, when I heard the outer door creak open, I got up and peeked through the crack in the bathroom door." Caledonia gestured.

The old house had settled over the years and there was indeed a fair-sized separation between the door and the jamb on the hinge side of the bathroom door. Swanson stepped up to it and pressed his face close. "Yep, I can see a little bit through there, all right."

"A person passes right through the line of vision as he comes close to the bed, you see? It's a perfect spy hole," Caledonia said. She had looked through and recognized Dorothy, then had quietly gone back to her impromptu bed in the tub.

After a short while, the door creaked softly open again and Caledonia repeated her maneuver, peering through the crack toward her own bed. But she saw no one, which meant that no one had gone near her bed. After another moment, however, she heard the *skreek* of a dresser drawer. "One of Angela's makes a noise of wood-on-wood like you can't mistake," she explained.

In a moment, Caledonia indeed recognized Angela's bright red slacks and shirt as she whisked past the bathroom door on her way toward the dummy in Caledonia's bed. Then Caledonia heard Angela whisper, "Stay asleep, Cal. Sorry if I disturbed you. I just forgot my bandanna—to use around my forehead while I exercise, you know . . .'' Then the door squeaked lightly again, and Angela was gone.

Another hour or so passed and there was silence through the old house. And then at last the room door sighed on its hinges one more time. But the sound was protracted, drawn out. Someone was opening the door slowly, slowly, with infinite caution. There was not another breath of sound, and Caledonia began to ease herself out of the tub so she could head for her viewing station and apply her eye to the crack beside the door.

One moment she was moving quietly and efficiently, the next she was dragged to a stop, held by the ankle. One foot was firmly on the tiled floor, but the foot still inside the tub was tangled in the bedding. Caledonia tried kicking free and moving forward at the same time, but the grip of the twisted blanket grew tighter as she moved. "Like one of those maddening puzzles you stick your fingers in, and the harder you pull to get free the firmer it holds you.''

"Chinese handcuffs," Pickett said aloud. Everybody turned toward him. "Well, that's what they call 'em," he said defensively. "Don't they? It's what we called them when I was a kid, anyhow . . .'' Nobody responded and he fell glumly silent, looking back at Caledonia again.

"I was thinking more of what the rope does when you hog-tie somebody," Caledonia said. "But anyhow, I couldn't get loose.''

She kicked and lunged, trying to free her foot without making a sound, all the while pulling herself forward toward her spy hole. "I thought if I could just get over there, even if I was still tangled up, I could at least get one quick look. I almost made it.''

But as she reached a point where she was leaning forward against the grip of the blankets on the one leg, straining toward the door, the knotted material suddenly let go. The folds slipped free of each other and with a horrid *THUMP* Caledonia fell forward, catching her head against the edge of the shower stall, and banging the door loudly with the heel of one hand, as her knees struck the floor.

"That's when I yelled for help," she said. "There wasn't a bit of use my trying to catch a glimpse of her before I called you in.

Not with all the noise I ended up making. So I hollered right then . . .''

"And I got there as fast as I could," Pickett again protested in his own defense.

"A comedy of errors," Martinez mourned. "But didn't you say you caught sight of the assailant? I thought—"

"Look, Lieutenant. I'm old, but I'm not stupid. I have my priorities in order. The cut lip could wait. The most important thing was to catch the killer, and if not that, then at least to identify her. So I got myself back up onto my feet and whipped that bathroom door wide open, but she was already out the door, closing it behind her. All I caught a glimpse of was a swirl of pink chiffon. Like the skirt of a fancy tea dress, you know?"

"That's funny," Dorothy said. "The women should all be at their last exercise class. Or no, wait . . ." She checked her watch. "They're at cooking class by this time. Or well on their way to the kitchen. Of course, they have about ten minutes between sessions to . . ."

The room door opened and Angela entered on those very words. "Dorothy! Lieutenant! What's the . . . Oh, Cal! Your face!" Angela raced forward to touch her friend's swollen lip.

"Ouch! Angela! That hurts!"

"You're turning purple. And there's blood all over your lip . . . You look *terrible*!"

"Thanks a lot," Caledonia said gruffly. "You'll be happy to know it feels even worse than it looks. Now just belt up, Angela, and I'll explain this all to you later."

"Mrs. Benbow," Martinez said. "You were at the exercise class just a moment or so ago?"

"Yes, of course."

"How many of the other ladies were there, too?"

"Oh, they all showed up. Except Cal, of course. But attendance was kind of ragged there at the end, with some leaving early for beauty appointments. Massages and facials, you know. I think one or two were only ducking out on the exercise, of course . . ."

"Who left early? That's what we want to know."

"Well, first to leave was Tilly Warfield. I know because she'd been standing next to me. I thought she looked pretty grim. Frankie Cziok took off sometime before we finished, too. Oh, and Maggie Randall left early. She may have had a facial coming up, or something.''

''No, she came upstairs to take a shower before cooking class,'' Swanson said. ''I saw her myself.''

''Really, Officer Swanson? You saw her in her shower?'' Caledonia was amused.

''Of course not!'' Swanson turned as red as he had when Maggie had invited him to search her bathroom. ''I only meant—''

Martinez shook his head. ''Later, Swanson. Go on, Mrs. Benbow. Who else took off from the exercise class?''

''Well, Cracker Graham did. Then Marceline Richardson went out for a breath of air and didn't come back . . . Come to think of it, I guess the whole class just sort of wandered away, along at the end. One at a time. I don't honestly remember. I—I left early myself and went over to see if I could make an appointment for another massage . . .''

Martinez shrugged. ''So much for alibis. I'll have to ask each of them where they were and what they were doing when Mrs. Wingate was attacked. But unless our killer is unusually careless, it's not going to do any good at all. Still, we must try . . .''

''Oo-oo-oo,'' Caledonia said, dabbing at her lip. ''The thing's oozing blood again.''

''Doctor will be here any minute, Caledonia,'' Dorothy said. ''Just sit down here . . .''

No sooner said than done, as it were, for the room door opened again and the doctor came striding in, black bag in hand. ''Your maid told me you were up here, Dorothy. Now, where's the patient?'' he said briskly. ''Answering service got me on my car phone when I wasn't too far away. I hope this is more urgent than the last . . . uh-oh! What a bruise you're going to have. Sit down here, my pretty young lady . . .'' His bedside manner made Caledonia wince almost as much as his touch on her aching lip.

''Can I have a little privacy in here, please? And a little elbow room. Turn the overhead light on as you leave, somebody.''

''But surely I can stay,'' Angela protested. ''She's my friend.''

"Well, she's my patient. And I want everybody out of here! Out-out-out! Go have your conference somewhere else. I may have to put a stitch in here, and I'll certainly want to clean this cut. And this little lady may want to yell a little when I do. She won't want an audience, and neither do I. Out-out-out . . . all of you . . .''

"Swanson,'' Martinez was saying as they trailed out the door and headed into the hallway, "phone the lab. I'll want someone to check the knife for prints and the suitcase for the angle and force of the blow and so on—anything they can tell us by examining our 'victim' there in the bed. Pickett, you go back on guard.''

"In that little room again, sir? I didn't do too well trying to get out of there last time.''

"No, the time for surprise is over. You stay in full view right out here in the hall. Get a chair and sit right near Mrs. Wingate's door, and if anybody tries to go in, you stop 'em and you call for me. Understood?''

"Yessir.'' Pickett fetched a folding chair from the back porch, put it squarely in the middle of the hall, facing Caledonia's door-way, and plunked his lardy bottom firmly onto the woven nylon webbing in its seat. He looked determined, and Martinez was sat-isfied he would guard Mrs. Wingate effectively this time.

"Mrs. McGraw, we're going on a treasure hunt. And I want your help.''

"Certainly, Lieutenant. What are we looking for?''

"Pink chiffon, Mrs. McGraw.''

"We're looking for pink chiffon? Why?'' Angela, pattering be-hind them, had not heard the explanation of Caledonia's only glimpse of her intruder.

"Because when we find it, we've found our killer, Mrs. Benbow. No need to look at me with such appealing eyes,'' Martinez said. "You're coming along.''

"I am?''

"I need both of you ladies to act as spotters. Find me pink chif-fon, that's what I ask. Come on . . . let's get working.'' And the three set off down the hall to start their search.

15

⊙

As Angela knew from her own explorations, the room next to hers and Caledonia's belonged to Marceline Richardson and Judy Daggett. She told her companions so as Dorothy led the way out of Caledonia's room and around the head of the stairs. As Angela also reminded them, she and Caledonia had searched through these rooms before.

"And I certainly didn't see anything like pink chiffon. Of course, we were looking for papers, pictures, check stubs . . . that kind of thing. Neither of us paid too much attention to the clothes except to search them. Still, you'd think I'd have remembered if I saw something like that!"

Martinez, a step or two ahead of the women, knocked at the door and, getting no answer, swung it wide. "Call out," he said to Dorothy.

"What?"

"Call out. Ask if anyone's home. Swanson told them all to go away . . . to leave the area . . . but we can't be sure. Call out."

"Hello . . . hello . . . are you in here, Mrs. Daggett? Mrs. Richardson?"

There was no answer.

"Okay," Martinez said. "Now we go to work," and he moved across the room directly to the huge freestanding wardrobes.

Almost at once it became obvious that neither Judy Daggett nor Marceline Richardson had brought clothing at all likely to include pink chiffon. Besides their leotards and flannel-lined exercise clothing, which both had brought in great amounts, Judy Daggett's closet held a small collection of drab dresses, classic cardigans, and plain exercise suits that sagged, as Angela whispered to Dorothy, almost as much as their wearer.

"Like owner, like dog," Dorothy said, nodding. "And look at these," she went on, pointing to Marceline's cupboard, where beside the casual clothes there hung two of the most masculine-looking business suits that ever came with skirts instead of trousers: pinstriped serge, knife pleating, expensive tailoring—hard and uncompromising.

"Just like the lady herself," Martinez agreed, going through the garments, all the same. But in a moment, having satisfied himself that there was nothing remotely resembling chiffon on either woman's hangers, let alone anything pink, Martinez led the way to the bureaus. Angela at once pulled out the top drawer and made as though to plunge her hands in to begin the search on her own, but he stopped her with a quick, "No! Please. Let me."

And as Angela told Caledonia later, she realized why as soon as he began to work. "I envy him his touch. And his eye!" she said. "He replaced even the wrinkles and folds so nearly the way they had been when he picked things up, I bet nobody knows they've been searched."

Careful or not, Martinez and his helpers found nothing in the bureaus or the nightstands or the luggage, which he took from and then returned to its storage shelf atop the wardrobes. The women headed for the door at that point, but Martinez was not finished.

"Remember," he whispered, "that the intruder, whoever she was, was anxious to avoid being identified. My guess is she would change her clothing as soon as she could and probably try to conceal the offending garment somehow, just in case she had been spotted."

"Just in case?"

"Well, she couldn't be sure what happened in that room, I suppose. She stabbed someone—some*thing*, as it actually turned out—but she can't even be sure of that! Then someone else—she didn't wait to find out who—made a racket in the bathroom and started yelling, and she ran. She's a cautious one . . . she'll take no chances.

That much I can tell about her without knowing who she is. She'd change her clothes, believe me. So don't just look in the closets. Look . . . well, follow me.''

With the women in rapt attendance on his every move, Martinez searched under, into, behind, and on top of every piece of furniture. He searched in the bathroom—inside the shower, under the big tub propped up on its eagle-claw feet, and inside the bathroom cabinets and the laundry hampers. He lifted the heavy bathroom towels and checked their folds.

Last, he returned to the bedroom and opened both beds, searching not only between the layers of bedding, but above and below the mattress as well. Finding nothing, he carefully remade the beds, again astonishing Angela by replacing the coverlets in an approximation of even the folds and wrinkles they had held before. Only then did he seem satisfied that they could leave the room and go to the next, which was Frankie Cziok's.

In Frankie's room, the whole process was repeated. They called, they entered, and finally they searched. But here they had results of a sort. They found a rose slip, a pink shorty nightgown, and a pink blouse of silk brocade. ''But they don't seem to fit Cal's description,'' Angela said doubtfully.

''Nevertheless, we'll remember and make a point of mentioning these things to Mrs. Wingate, if we find nothing else,'' Martinez said, and led them on next door to the maids' closet, where linens and cleaning supplies were kept. Searching newly pressed sheets was relatively easy work. Anything interleaved would have made bumps in the silky-smooth surfaces, so though Martinez lifted each sheet and pillowcase individually, he did not open the linens out. But the three searchers felt confident when they left that there was no pink chiffon there, either.

Across the hall in Tilly Warfield's room, they had their first piece of real luck. Pink chiffon, indeed—a blouse with a large collar edged in lace and with long, full sleeves that Angela identified as ''Russian sleeves. I love them. So smart . . .''

At the lieutenant's suggestion they took the blouse, still on its hanger, down the hall past a silent and watchful Georgie Pickett, to Caledonia's room. The doctor had gone, but others had come to take his place; Swanson stood at one side as though supervising, while three large men moved silently and purposefully around the bed that held the murdered suitcase.

"We had some good luck," Swanson said to Martinez. "They were on a job down the valley. Got right over here."

The men were photographing everything before they moved it, then lifting it as gingerly as though it were Ming Dynasty porcelain, making it ready to transport to the lab to be examined further.

Caledonia sat at one side, a book dangling idly in her hand (she had been reading when Swanson brought the crew in, but abandoned her story to watch the proceedings). When Martinez led his little parade in with the pink blouse, she hailed them with obvious amusement.

"Come in, come in. It's like the Marx Brothers in *A Night at the Opera* already. I expect room service, a steamer trunk, and a manicurist to arrive at any minute—three more people can't hurt."

"We've found it, Cal," Angela bubbled. "Here-here . . . here it is . . ." She grabbed the hanger from Martinez's hand and thrust it under Cal's nose.

"Well, I see 'it,' all right. But what's the point you're trying to make? Why am I supposed to be thrilled by a see-through blouse?"

"Pink chiffon, Cal. See? See?" Angela was waving the garment close enough to brush Caledonia's cheek.

"We're hoping our search is over, Mrs. Wingate," Martinez explained. "Is this anything like what you saw disappearing through your door as your intruder fled?"

"Gosh no! I told you. It was a *swirl* of chiffon. And it was low . . . I mean, I saw the material around the bottom half of the door, below the knob. Obviously a skirt or something like that. Unless some crazy woman was wearing her blouse hanging loose and was crawling on her knees, this thing wouldn't swirl low to the ground! Besides, I don't think it's dark enough pink. What I saw was more . . . rosy. Less like cotton candy."

Angela was plainly disappointed, but Martinez was philosophical and led his troops back to the hunt, returning Tilly Warfield's blouse with great care to its place in the closet. The rest of the Warfield room was disappointing, and so was Maggie Randall's, although Angela was fascinated by and commented sourly on the state of the bathroom (splashed with water and littered with damp towels) and the unsuitability of Maggie's clothing (which ranged from color-coordinated velour exercise outfits to a sequin-covered dress cut low in back and which included several dramatic negligees).

For one exciting moment, Angela thought she had found something and plunged recklessly into Maggie's overflowing closet, reaching with a loud "Ah-ha!" for a flash of rosy pink she'd spotted on the floor. But she came out with a silver lamé and rose satin jumpsuit with huge palazzo legs.

"Oh! I thought for a moment . . . but this is what she wore today to exercise class."

"To exercise class?" Martinez moved to her side and gazed in awe at the elaborate garment. "Isn't that a little dressy for the kind of activity . . ."

"Oh, absolutely. But quite typical of the woman, Lieutenant. She had matching outfits for everything. Even the tie she used to hold her hair back matched her slacks. She'd wear a black satin set all day long, then dress it up for dinner by adding a gold lamé sash and bolero jacket . . . and voilà, a smart dinner outfit! I realize this is not what we're looking for, of course, but," she said wistfully, "it's certainly stunning. I'm too short for something like that, of course. Besides, I can't stand jumpsuits because you have to get all undressed when you want to go to the bathroom, and that's awkward, especially if you're out at a restaurant . . ."

She saw out of the corner of her eyes Martinez's quick reaction and assumed he was about to laugh. "Sorry, Lieutenant, if that amuses you, but that is one of the biggest drawbacks to a jumpsuit. Designers don't think about mundane things like using the bathroom, I suppose. And they couldn't exactly put a drop seat like a Dr. Denton into something like this . . ."

She waved the elegant satin garment before his eyes. "I always wonder, when I see some gorgeous fashion plate wearing a jumpsuit—does she avoid drinking iced tea at lunch or something? How on earth some women manage to not have to . . ."

"Angela, please! You're embarrassing the lieutenant," Dorothy said.

"Not at all, ma'am," Martinez said, his smile—if he'd ever had one—fully controlled. "I appreciate the fashion commentary. But I would ask you, are you sure this material doesn't qualify as Mrs. Wingate's 'swirl of pink chiffon'?"

"I suppose not," Angela conceded. "Besides, this is in need of some repair. She must have torn it taking it off." She held the garment aloft and pointed to a ripped underarm seam and a missing button. "It wasn't like this when she had it on earlier. We'd have noticed. That's why it had been dumped on the floor, of course. All right, all right . . . She seems to dump everything. I agree."

Carefully she put the garment back on the floor of the closet where she'd found it and went on with the search in silence and in disappointment. Because although Maggie owned "enough clothes to stock the May Company," as Angela put it rather sourly, and although Maggie was incredibly careless (there were garments jammed in a jumble on the rods, fallen to the floor, piled on the foot of the bed, and draped over chairs), the searchers were able to conclude eventually that Maggie had nothing more in pink than that satin jumpsuit.

It was in Belinda Terry's room next door that they finally struck gold. Martinez had warned them to hurry. "That cooking class won't last forever," he cautioned. "And although we're searching legitimately on the premises of a murder, and I am here with the owner of the premises—and though we may be covered by something like the 'Doctrine of Hot Pursuit'—the courts might be a bit unkind about our invading these ladies' privacy. So I'd rather finish without them being aware we'd even been in here."

Martinez went straight to Belinda Terry's bureau, while Angela took her wardrobe and Dorothy began looking through the bathroom. In a few moments, they converged in the center of the room and began searching under, in, behind, and above the furniture. When they got to the bed, it was Dorothy who spotted the fluff of pink foaming out from beneath the carelessly draped bedspread. She pounced and pulled . . . and from under the lumped-up spread there emerged the flounces and folds of a full-length, rose-pink chiffon dress.

"Or is that a coat?" Angela said. "It's got sleeves and it's full length, but it's open down the front." She held it to herself, but it dragged the floor. Its owner was taller than she, but then everybody at The Time-Out Inn was taller than Angela's four-foot-eleven. "Is this a negligee, do you think? It looks like it."

"Possibly so," Martinez said judiciously. "Do women still wear things like that?"

"Lieutenant, what do the women in your life wear, if not negligees?"

"The women of my acquaintance," he said seriously, "wear robes that conceal what is underneath. They do not wear man-made cobwebs."

Angela grinned. "Lieutenant, I do believe that's the first personal remark I've ever heard you make. I really have been meaning to ask you . . ."

"Not now, Mrs. Benbow. Someday you'll have my complete autobiography. I promise. Right now, we need to have Mrs. Wingate look at this . . . this *thing*."

"You bet that's it," Caledonia trumpeted, when they delivered the garment to her. "It has to be. There can't be another piece of clothing like that at the Inn!"

"We're about to test out whether or not this is the only one of its kind," Martinez said, "by checking out that last room." He laid the negligee gently down across the foot of Caledonia's bed, now emptied of bedding and of the remnants of the makeshift dummy, thanks to the lab crew, who had finished up and gone.

"Oh dear, I must get you fresh sheets and a new bedspread," Dorothy fussed.

"A blanket, too, please," Caledonia said.

"Blanket? In the summer?"

"Yes, I'm used to its weight. Angela is, too." Caledonia gestured at Angela's bed, and she launched into her explanation of her bedding preferences.

"You stay here and do your work, Mrs. McGraw. Mrs. Benbow will help me." Martinez beckoned a delighted Angela to accompany him and went across the hall to examine the contents of the last guests' room. Just in case, as he put it. He searched quickly and efficiently in the room occupied by Cracker Graham and Carmen Sturkie, but found only one pink oxford cloth shirt and a pair of pink-and-white striped shorts. No chiffon at all.

"Ladies," he said as he and Angela returned, "I must ask you to say absolutely nothing about this. We have enough reason, I think, to justify our asking Mrs. Terry to come with us to headquarters where we can talk quietly, at length, and without interruption. Mrs. McGraw, you probably should tell the other guests only that she's with us to help out and you don't know when she'll get back. Provided they ask. Don't tell them if they don't get curious."

"Will she be back?" Angela asked.

"I don't know. To be candid, it looks very bad. She admitted when I interviewed her again this morning that she recognized the name of Peter Guns. Yesterday she wouldn't admit it. She said today that she thought he was one of the men from whom her son bought a supply of drugs once."

"I thought Guns was a big-time dealer, not a pusher. Would he sell in such small amounts? Like to some poor fellow who just wanted to get high?" Caledonia asked.

"Probably not. But there's nothing like goodwill advertising. Creating a market, as it were. He just might have sold to the Terry boy, if they ever ran into each other. Or he might not. But the connection has to be explored. And now this garment . . ." He picked up the chiffon coat and started out the door.

"You'll let us know what happens?" Angela said.

He bowed without agreeing or denying. "The ladies are in cooking class now?" He addressed Dorothy.

She checked her watch. "For another five minutes, I think."

"And Officer Swanson. Did he . . ."

"He left here with the others, Lieutenant," Caledonia said. "I believe they went down the front way."

"Mrs. Wingate, I think you're safe enough now. But to be sure, please stay with the others. Don't be alone for a moment. And under no circumstances go for a midnight stroll alone."

"Then you believe we have our killer, don't you? Then why the warning?"

"Well, it really looks as though we've solved the murders. And even if Mrs. Terry weren't guilty, the killer has never operated except when her victim was alone and unguarded. So all I'm asking is that you should take reasonable care."

"The body system!" Angela crowed suddenly. "Of course."

"What?"

"Nothing, Lieutenant. I just mean that I'll watch over her personally."

"I'm sure you will, Mrs. Benbow." The lieutenant bowed again and opened the door to the hall. "Pickett, come along with me. Your guard duty is over for now." And as they went down the stairs, Martinez's voice was audible calling lightly, "Swanson . . . I need you. Swanson . . . ah, there you are . . ." Then Angela closed the door.

"It's almost over, Dorothy," she said. "Almost over. You'll be relieved . . ."

"That's putting it mildly," Dorothy answered. "I suppose I'd better go to my own quarters and gather myself together. I'll have to tell the women something tactful about Belinda Terry's absence. And I'll need to think it through in advance, because I want to be very, very careful what I say."

"Will they all know about it by dinnertime?"

"No," Dorothy said. "I thought I'd make a short announcement at the meal, tell them they don't have to wait for her before they begin and say just a word or two more to explain. If I do it at dinner, I'll only have to do it once. I don't tell fibs too well."

"Okay, then," Caledonia said. "We'll see you down there. I want to freshen up. I suppose it's safe for me to leave the room and join the others, now . . ."

"I wish you wouldn't, Cal," Angela said.

"It's safe now. You heard the lieutenant."

"But . . . well, it's just that . . . well, things aren't really over yet. Not till we hear from the lieutenant that Belinda's confessed or that he has the final evidence."

"I'd call that pink chiffon thing pretty convincing evidence, myself!"

"So would I," Dorothy agreed, bewildered. "What's bothering you, Angela?"

"I don't know," she said. "But there's something . . . I'm trying to think . . . It'll come to me, eventually."

"Fast, I hope. I mean, 'eventually' could be years and years. What good will that do?" Caledonia said.

"Oh, I'll work at it," Angela promised. "I usually get my good ideas when I'm in bed at night, just before I drop off to sleep. So maybe then."

But in fact, Angela's mental lightbulb turned on a whole lot sooner than that.

16

⊙

It was a shame, really, that Dorothy worked so hard creating an announcement that warned the guests not to expect Belinda any time soon—one that told them she had been called away unexpectedly—and one that told them nothing of Belinda's problem and the suspicion that surrounded her. She really needn't have bothered with her careful wording, because Dorothy followed her careful speech with the news about their evening program, and pandemonium broke loose, with everyone totally forgetting poor Belinda.

They also forgot completely about Caledonia's split lip and facial bruises, which had occasioned a great deal of comment at first. Of course, as Caledonia said later, she wasn't really lying when she told them all that she'd merely fallen in the bathroom, it wasn't anything serious.

"Oh, and one more thing before you begin your dinner," Dorothy concluded. "Please go promptly to the lounge at seven, because tonight we have our hairstyling program, and Mr. Desmond hates it when you come in after he's started to speak."

"Desmond? You don't mean Morgan Desmond!" Maggie Randall's voice was thrilled and breathless.

"Yes. Morgan Desmond."

"Not really! Marvelous Morgan?"—"You mean Desmond of 'Desmond's Designs'!"—"Coming here? For real? Coming here?"

The babble of voices rose in a wave that completely swamped Dorothy's attempt to explain that the program would last longer than usual, as well, and if they wanted their sleep . . .

"Who is this guy?" Caledonia growled to one of her tablemates.

The nine remaining guests had been sorted out three to a table, and Caledonia was sitting with Marceline Richardson and Tilly Warfield.

"You don't know?" Tilly's face had flushed and her voice, like Maggie's, had climbed very high up the scale. "He's just the handsomest, most devastating . . ."

"He's supposed to be a hairdresser," Marceline Richardson said, a bit more soberly. But Caledonia thought her voice was not as firm as usual, and her eyes looked bright. "He has his own TV show. Don't tell me you never saw him with 'Desmond's Designs'?"

Caledonia grunted. "Uh-uh. I'm more the type to watch reruns of the old 'Dick Van Dyke Show.' Or of the first 'Bob Newhart Show.' "

"I guarantee you'd be a fan if you ever watched him," Marceline said. "He absolutely makes love to the camera. And he's the handsomest man on the air! Without a doubt."

"He shows the latest cuts and styles each week," Tilly Warfield said, and to Caledonia's annoyance, she giggled. "But nobody watches to see the hairstyles. They watch him. What an incredible . . ."

"I think I've seen him once or twice," Angela was saying doubtfully at her table. "But I don't know . . . the program didn't seem very interesting to me, though."

Carmen Sturkie, her face pinker than usual, said, "I think that must be a local program. I never heard of him."

"What you have missed," Frankie Cziok sighed. "He is so gorgeous, it burgles the mind!"

In the general anticipation of Desmond's performance, Belinda's absence simply disappeared from consideration. But even Desmond couldn't keep the ladies from their food very long. A little plate of tomato aspic was served as an appetizer, and the room fell silent, except for Frankie, babbling happily away as she ate.

"I love this aspect. This is the first time I ever tasted it before. Is that not wonderful? The food here is really state of the ark!"

But even Frankie fell silent when the main course arrived, a veal marsala accompanied by snow peas and followed by a dainty pineapple mousse. As she made the rounds picking up empty dishes half an hour later, Betsy raised her voice with a warning. "Don't forget, ladies. The program starts promptly at seven. If you want to change your clothes to something comfortable, get a move on. Desmond won't wait . . ."

The suggestion sent half the women thundering up the stairs to their rooms to throw on soft trousers and pullovers. "I may get chosen to demonstrate one of the hairstyles," Judy Daggett explained to Caledonia, by way of apology for pushing past her at the exit. "I don't want water on this nice blouse. Because he's bound to wet down your hair before he cuts and sets it, you know."

Angela, Caledonia, Frankie Cziok, and Carmen Sturkie were left alone to head for the parlor while the others changed. "Well, we'll be able to find the best seats for ourselves," Angela said, moving across the length of the room to sit where she faced the entrance—on the far side of the fireplace centered on the interior wall, the most likely area for their guest to use as a stage, since it was clear of furniture and the chairs and couches seemed to form a natural half circle around it.

"I'm not changing any clothes," Carmen said a bit defiantly, as she plunked down on a couch. "I couldn't be more comfortable than I am right now." She indicated her sweat suit with its outsize shirt. "And if it gets wet it doesn't matter a scrap. Does Judy really think he'll choose her as a model?"

"I'd say they all thought they might be chosen, to judge by their speed going off to change," Angela said.

"That's just wistful thinking," Frankie put in.

"Wistful . . ."

"Let me refrain that. They *hope* it is so. You see? But we know better. He will choose Maggie for his model. The rest of us have no chance."

"What makes you think that?" Carmen said. "It could as easily be me. Or you."

"No-no-no. They always choose Maggie. It is her beautiness, of course. And she dresses in such a way to make herself stand out. You have not notice? She has a different outfoot for everything."

The other women began to come back to the parlor wearing clothing suitable, as Tilly Warfield said, for getting wet around the neck. "Just in case Desmond decides on one of us as his model."

"See? Didn't I say?" Frankie called gaily across to Angela.

Even the fresh clothing was casual, however, except for Maggie Randall's. Maggie made an entrance after all the others, forcing her way into the center of the couch directly in front of the open area, and it reminded Angela of nothing so much as Rita Hayworth playing Salome, entering the court of Herod.

"You remember," she whispered to Caledonia on her left. "Herod was played by Charles Laughton. He was so delightfully lascivious when he looked at her! Of course, Maggie didn't dance in here, or anything. It's her clothes. What Frankie called her 'outfoot.' "

And it was an "outfoot" to catch the most reluctant eye. Maggie was dressed in lavender and gold silk lounging pajamas, low cut on top and supported by a pair of rhinestone straps, her shoulders swathed in a cloud of matching tulle that floated up around her neck and ears to frame her exquisite face.

"She must have chosen her clothing with a lot of care," Angela whispered to Caledonia. "Though I wonder how she could find what she wanted so fast in that tangle of stuff in her closet!"

Maggie had contrived to flatter both her coloring and her figure. She stood out from the women on either side of her, huddled as they were into drab, baggy, flannel-lined knits. Furthermore, she would be able to serve as a model without getting her costume wet simply by removing the tulle scarf surrounding her shoulders and neck.

"Damn," Judy Daggett muttered. "I wanted that new hairdo. But he's bound to choose her. She had that cosmetic makeover, too. I was hoping— Oh! Oh my!"

What stopped Judy's complaint was the entrance into the room of the handsomest man Angela had ever seen in the flesh. A bronzed, smoothly muscled, black-haired vision in a mint-green salon coat two sizes too tight, so that it clung to his broad shoulders and hugged his incredibly small waist and hips. The Devastating Desmond had arrived.

"Good evening, ladies," he caroled, turning as though to address them all.

"He looks like Stewart Granger in *Caesar and Cleopatra*. Nothing less than marvelous, and he knows it," Caledonia whispered.

"He isn't moving around to let his voice reach us! He just wants to give us all a good view of his face!" Angela whispered back.

"Are you ready for 'A Do with Desmond'?" the vision sang out and flashed his white, even teeth.

"Huh! Capped, I bet," was Angela's sotto voce summary. "I bet he had aspirations as an actor and didn't make it!" Caledonia grinned and turned her attention to the show.

"Who is going to be our model tonight?" Desmond said, continuing his pirouette before his audience. "We need to get started. Any volunteers?"

"Me"—"Me"—"Me"—"Me" . . . the chorus babbled around him.

"How about you, my dear?" Just as Frankie had anticipated, Desmond's melting eyes had focused on the incredible beauty of Maggie Randall, seated in her lavender silk cloud.

"Shall we have this lady model a brand-new hairstyle, created just for her? Let's give her a little applause and encourage her . . ."

Maggie had actually begun to rise in her place, beaming, when she very obviously changed her mind. Her face closed down almost sullenly, her inviting smile died, and she shook her head firmly, settling back in her place with a finality in her movements that allowed of no argument.

Angela, like all the others, was mildly surprised at the about-face, but she was given no time to think it over. Desmond was not going to let a minor disappointment mar his performance, and he reached over to grasp hold of Judy Daggett's hand.

"Well, then, how about this lady here?" he said, pulling the beaming Judy to her feet and moving a straight chair around for her, so that when she sat as he directed, she faced the audience. "After all," he chuckled, "Desmond adores a real challenge!"

"She should pop him one for that," Angela whispered to Caledonia. "And I hate people who refer to themselves in the third person! It's so . . . so incredibly conceited!'' But Judy was obviously delighted and quite beyond taking any offense.

Desmond reached into the leather case he'd brought along, bringing out a gaily colored throw, which he fastened around Judy's shoulders. ''These preliminaries are not very thrilling,'' he advised them. ''Please forgive . . .'' The women seemed inclined to watch every move he made, thrilling or not, and he did everything with such a flourish that Angela was certain he expected the admiring reaction.

She, on the contrary, was experiencing a strong distaste. ''I never liked peacocks in the zoo either,'' she whispered to Caledonia, who gave her a silent thumbs-up sign.

Then, as Angela settled herself for the show, she glanced at the entryway. What had Maggie seen, she was thinking, that made her decide against being tonight's model? Helena and Betsy were there, as was the chef, gazing with rapt attention as Desmond made his preparations. Then Angela caught sight of Bart just behind the standing women, his blond head towering above theirs. But his expression was not like the women's, who looked adoring in varying degrees. Bart's face was thunderous, his lips compressed and his brow furrowed. He glared with narrowed eyes into the parlor, concentrating on one spot.

Angela followed his glance as best she could and decided he was glaring straight at Maggie Randall. At that moment he turned and started away down the hall. Then he hesitated, came back, and very obviously jerked his head twice in a ''this way—follow me'' movement.

Angela was fascinated. Here was a show far more worth watching than Desmond, who having brushed Judy's hair forward, backward, and forward again, now combed it, pulling it hard and straight. He reached into his bag and pulled out a handful of hair clips with which he sectioned off various quadrants of Judy's limp hair. ''Now the first step . . .''

From her place at the center of the audience, Maggie Randall rose and moved quickly toward the door. ''Pardon . . . beg pardon,'' she murmured, as she pushed the maids aside and slipped between them to leave the room.

"Ah," Angela breathed. "I thought so."

"Did you say something?" Carmen asked.

"Nothing, dear. Keep watching," Angela whispered to her. "Just got to go to the bathroom." Then she too rose, and bending over double the way people do when they hope nobody will notice them sneaking in or out of a crowded room, she made for the door about twenty feet behind Maggie.

Desmond didn't miss a beat in his lecture. "The first step is to determine the basic shape of the face. Oval? Square? Round? The diamond shape with the broad cheekbones? Now this lady seems on first glance to have a round face. Note, however, the narrow brow . . ." But Desmond's eyes were angry as he pulled Judy's hair this way and that. Angela carefully avoided meeting his annoyed glance for even a moment.

Once outside, having squeezed past the maids and the chef packed so tightly into the doorway, their eyes fixed on the dazzling Desmond, Angela walked quietly down the hall. She saw Maggie's lavender silk just disappearing around the corner of the staircase. Presumably Angela's quarry was headed upstairs.

Angela moved slowly so that she would not catch up, though not slowly enough to lose Maggie. The stairway being enclosed, she was even more cautious on the steps and as she turned the landing corner. For all she knew, Maggie might have stopped for some reason right at the head of the steps. But there was nobody at all in view along the length of the hall when Angela emerged from the stairwell. From two doors to her right and across the hall, however, she could hear angry voices.

"Don't you order me around, little boy," Maggie was saying bitterly. "I'll do what I please."

"You were flirting with that . . . that barber!" It was surely Bart's voice Angela heard. With infinite caution, she edged across the hall and down toward Maggie's door, which she noticed stood just ajar. Angela silently thanked her stars. She would never admit it, but her hearing was faulty enough that a closed door would have muffled the sounds beyond intelligibility for her. But as it was, the words were perfectly clear. Closer she edged and closer . . .

"What if I was?" Maggie sounded arrogantly cold and every bit as angry as he. "You don't own me. If anything, it's the other way around."

"I don't want you looking like that at other men!" His voice was thick with emotion, and Angela thought he might have reached out to grab hold of Maggie, for she responded sharply.

"Don't be such a fool. You have no right to be jealous. I've had a marvelous time with you, of course. You've made the dull hours here pass more quickly. But we'll be leaving here eventually. Soon, I'd guess."

"But, sweetheart . . ."

"Knock it off. Start right now calling me 'Mrs. Randall.' Better get in the habit of being formal."

"Aw, honey, not when we're alone . . ."

"Well, we won't be alone in the future. And if we are, it doesn't matter. I'm still 'Mrs. Randall' to you."

"But what about us? What about after you leave here?"

"Bart. Grow up. If you can. There is no 'us' after I leave here."

"But you said . . ."

". . . whatever came into my head, my handsome lover. I thought you understood. It's exactly the same for me with a good-looking man as it is with you and some woman you want to drag into your bed. You say anything you have to. So do I. That's all. I didn't believe you and I thought you had enough sense not to believe me!"

"But I wrote you letters . . ."

"Ah yes, those wonderfully vulgar letters. You can really be very amusing, and I'll enjoy reading them again, years from now, and remembering . . . You have several good points. For instance, you have the most beautiful body of any man I've ever known. In a way, I'm sorry this is all over."

"But—but—honey, I just don't understand."

"Okay, I'll explain it. You're not the brightest man around, even though you are certainly the best looking—except for that TV hairdresser, of course. Though I'll bet he's not one bit smarter than you are. Anyhow, I'll use simple words so you'll get it. Here's the thing . . . I always have a man around."

"Sure you do. Beautiful women like you always do."

"It's more than that, Bart. I need . . . I really *need* to see men look at me like you do. Sometimes I think I don't really exist, if I can't see my reflection in some man's eyes."

"That's nuts. A great-looking old gal like you? You've got a terrific body, even for somebody your age."

"Why, thank you, my dear." Her voice was colder than ever, heavy with irony. "What a touching compliment. Have you been so delicate with all the other guests you've made love to here?"

"I told you that was business with me. They were . . . you know . . . grateful. And they gave me presents. I told you—it's been different with you." His voice was agonized. "And I thought . . . at least, I told Jenny that we . . . you and me . . . we have something special going."

"Not so special. You aren't even very good at the only thing you're good for, if you see what I mean."

"That isn't what the others used to tell me," he said sullenly.

"Well, you've had a customer for your services in almost every group of fat ladies who came through here. So maybe the customer knows best. I won't argue the point."

"My girl Jenny thought I was a good lover." He was still sulky and defensive.

"She was a professional hooker, you simpleton. She'd said that to every john she ever hired out to."

"No! She meant it. And she was in love with me. We were going to get married."

"Okay, maybe you're right. Maybe she did love you. Or she wouldn't have come up here to tell me to leave you alone, would she? She didn't seem to worry about your other women, but she roared up here shouting she'd tell Mrs. McGraw, she'd tell my husband, she'd make a scene in front of the others . . ."

"I tried to stop her, didn't I? She didn't tell anybody! You told me to take care of that and I did, didn't I?"

"True. I'll give you that. You know, I don't know which threat annoyed me more—losing my marriage and my meal ticket or being embarrassed in public."

"How do you mean, embarrassed?"

"You don't think I want to show off my dirt-common taste in

public, do you? I like being taken as an equal by these rich old girls. I like being one of them. It's just . . . I want to have my fun, too, that's all.''

"Fun! Oh God . . .'' His groan was racked and painful. "I wish I'd never met you.''

"Well, I don't feel that way about you, you good-looking thing. Provided you behave yourself. Don't get in my way and don't act like you own me. Oh yes, and be reasonable.'' Her voice grew soft and coaxing. "When the time comes, just shut up and wave good-bye like a good boy. Okay?''

"I can't . . .''

"Sure you can. Sure . . .'' Her voice dropped almost to a whisper. "In the meantime, of course, here we are . . . for a little while longer. So I don't see why we shouldn't enjoy each other while we can. Everybody's busy downstairs, so . . .''

Bart's voice got even huskier. "Honey, we really shouldn't. Late at night is one thing. But with everybody still wide-awake and roaming around . . .''

"They're busy with Desmond. Besides, don't you enjoy a little bit of danger? Tell you what, lover. . . .'' Her voice dropped to a cozy mutter that Angela could not make out, even though she strained to hear.

Angela had been frozen in her fascination. But now she backed away from her position near the half-open door, heading for the stairs, where she turned and tiptoed down to the reception area and the phone booth. Her hands trembled as she checked the phone book for the number of the county police, and her eyes were not focusing quite right. She adjusted her glasses and found the listing.

"Lieutenant Martinez, please,'' she quavered to the voice that answered. "Please!'' She closed the phone booth door more tightly to be sure she couldn't be overheard.

"Oh, Lieutenant,'' she quavered when his soft baritone came on the line. "Get back here to the Inn as fast as you can. You've got the wrong person. Belinda didn't kill those women . . . it hasn't anything to do with the Kimbrough Hotel. At least, Belinda didn't kill Jenny. I suppose she didn't kill Bunny either, but I'm not as sure. And if you don't get here soon, the killer might get away.''

"You're very excited, Mrs. Benbow, and you're talking entirely too fast. I can't understand you."

"Oh, please . . . there's somebody coming and I can't talk!" Angela had picked up a flicker of movement in the hallway, down toward the parlor. "They're busy for the moment. But you have to come fast, they can't stay occupied forever. And I think it's dangerous here. If anyone knew what I'd found out . . ."

"I can be there within the hour. Probably less. But if you're in real danger . . ."

"I don't think so. I don't think either of them knows that I know."

"Good. Then listen to me. Stay where there are plenty of people around you—don't be anywhere alone. And when everyone retires for the evening, go to your room with Mrs. Wingate and the two of you bolt your door and stay there until I arrive. Promise me."

"Oh, I promise. But please hurry." Angela cradled the phone, slid the phone booth door open, and looked around outside to be sure the area was still unoccupied except for herself. Then she moved quickly back down the hall to the parlor, from which a burst of laughter was sounding as she approached.

"And that's approximately the way it will look," Desmond beamed, pulling Judy's hair up and back away from her face. "Now comes the acid test of my theories: we cut!" He began to spray water from a plastic bottle, thoroughly wetting Judy's already lank hair until it hung in sodden streamers.

"Now, my dear lady, are you really sure you want to do this thing? Once I cut, the hair can't be glued back, you know!" Desmond reached into his bag once more to get a wicked-looking pair of shears, which he flourished with his free hand as he posed and simpered, and the audience laughed with delight.

Then he caught sight of Angela, hovering in the door between the two maids (the chef had moved politely aside to let Angela have a better view). "You're back, I see. Well, come in, come in . . . you've missed much of the fun, but you're here for the main event, at any rate."

Angela tried to look like a lady who'd been to the bathroom and was deeply embarrassed by having attention called to her, and slipped across the room to her seat between Caledonia, who looked amused, and Carmen Sturkie, whose pink face was shining with enthusiasm.

"Oh, Angela, you almost missed the most wonderful show," she whispered.

"Never mind. I made it in time. So there's no harm done." Desmond cast a reproachful glance in their direction. He obviously wanted everyone's undivided attention—and adoration—and complete silence. "Now . . . the first cut," he sang out, flourishing his scissors.

"I have something to tell you later," Angela whispered to Caledonia. "I went to a show of my own!"

Desmond glared, and Angela dropped her volume to a mere breath of sound, putting her mouth next to Caledonia's ear. "This was a very special show. And I wouldn't have missed it for the world!"

17

⊙

"**Y**ou understand," Desmond said, his teeth twinkling and his dimple appearing and disappearing with his smile as he worked, "this style will look ever so much better after a real shampoo and some conditioner to give the hair life and body." He toweled the excess moisture out of Judy's hair, snapped the comb through, took one more snip, ran his fingers along the sides, then stood back to let the audience admire his creation.

Judy Daggett looked, if not young and smartly turned out, at least not old and frazzled anymore. Somehow the hair that had been so stringy and lank before now looked sleek and purposeful, hair that knew what it intended to do for its wearer. Her face had taken on a sophisticated look. It was a cunning piece of work that deserved the hearty applause Desmond's audience awarded him.

"He *is* good!" Caledonia whispered in awe. "Who'd have thought that woman could look like . . . like . . ."

"Like an After!" Angela said softly, equally awed.

"After?"

"You know, from the Before and After in the women's magazine makeover sections. Maybe I'll make an appointment with Desmond myself."

"Now," Desmond went on, after gesturing back into the audience a delighted Judy, who could hardly be induced to stop looking at the mirror over the mantel long enough to return to her place. "Now," Desmond said cheerily, "we have another half hour, so suppose we do one more. And how about this delightful lady!" His choice for a model this time was Tilly Warfield, who giggled with excitement.

"He spotted her as the senator's wife while you were out of the room," Caledonia whispered. "She said something about how things were up in Sacramento, and he pounced. Now I think he'll expect to get some customers from among state officials' wives. Don't you bet?"

Angela nodded and said nothing. As time passed, she had become more and more tense, waiting for Martinez to arrive.

" 'Smatter?" Caledonia asked her. "Don't feel well?"

"Oh, no . . . I'm fine. Tired, maybe . . ."

Caledonia shrugged and they watched the second demonstration in silence. But Angela's active little brain was whirring away with other matters, and she wriggled impatiently as Desmond snipped and combed and snipped again, punctuating his work with anecdotes about famous clients and turning his torso this way and that, as though to be sure his audience admired him from all possible angles as he worked.

Eventually, near nine-thirty, the second demonstration ended. "It isn't the cutting that takes so long," Caledonia muttered in Angela's ear. "It's all the preening and posing in between cuts! I bet that at his salon back in town, Desmond gets 'em in and out of his barber chair in no time flat!"

Referring to Desmond as a "barber" brought Bart and Maggie to Angela's mind again, and she shivered. The women around her rose and clustered around Desmond to offer congratulations and to get his autograph on one of the tasteful little advertising brochures he had brought out and laid on a nearby table.

"I'll be happy to give you an appointment for my personal attention . . . you just tell them I said so when you call," he was telling Cracker Graham, who dimpled and simpered as he signed her brochure.

"Cal, do you mind if we just go on up to bed now?" Angela asked.

"You go, if you want to," Caledonia answered. "I intend to wait up for the snacks. We've missed out, going to our room night after night without sticking around for the program . . . or at least without waiting a few minutes, when we did sit through the entertainment hour. While you were gone just now, Carmen was telling me that they have popcorn every night!"

"You won't like the popcorn, Cal. I've heard it's unsalted and unbuttered."

"No butter?"

"No oil at all. That's why it's a good diet snack."

"But without salt . . ."

"That's what Frankie Cziok told me."

"Are you sure that's what she meant? Sometimes she muddles what she says."

"Not this time. Marceline was there, too, and she made an awful face and said just about the same thing."

"Not in the same words, I bet." Caledonia grinned. "Okay, I can live without dry, unsalted popcorn. To bed it is. Hey-hey . . . what's the rush?" For Angela had grasped Caledonia's hand and was towing her along as fast as she could manage.

"Tell you in the room," Angela said. "Oh, there he is! Thank heaven . . ."

The front door had swung open just as Angela and Caledonia reached the hall, and Swanson was there, holding the door open for Lieutenant Martinez to enter. "Ah, Mrs. Benbow. Let's go into the . . . into my office, shall we?" Martinez said briskly, turning left into the small parlor and ushering the ladies in ahead of him. "Close the door firmly, Swanson. I don't feel Mrs. Benbow wants to be overheard! Now, dear lady, what is so urgent that you bring us back here at . . ." He checked his watch. "Oh! I didn't realize it was so late! Nearly ten o'clock! No wonder you were anxious to get away and go on your date, Swanson. I'm sorry. I hope you phoned an apology to your fiancée, Miss Cassidy."

"Sure did." Swanson seated himself and took out his notebook.

"Go ahead, Mrs. Benbow," Martinez urged.

"Well, I was suspicious from the minute she refused to have her hair done. Then I saw him looking through the door at her, and he kind of gestured, and she got up and followed him . . ."

"Lieutenant," Caledonia interrupted, "I haven't the least notion what Angela wants to tell you. I didn't even know she'd summoned you out here. But I can at least interpret part of that for you. It's

Maggie Randall who refused Desmond's offer to have a new hairdo and ended up leaving the show, though who 'He Who Peered Through the Door' is I can't explain.''

"He's Bart, of course," Angela said impatiently.

"The handyman?" Caledonia asked. "I didn't see him . . ."

"He just looked in at the door a minute and left. I almost missed him myself," Angela went on. "But Maggie went to meet him. And they went to her room. I know, because I followed them. And then I listened in the hallway."

"Eavesdropping, Mrs. Benbow?" Martinez was amused at the picture of Angela with her ear applied to a keyhole.

"Don't mock me, Lieutenant. You're going to be grateful I did!" And with unerring accuracy, Angela repeated the dialogue she had overheard, her mimicry of Maggie's cold and scornful voice so exact that she held her audience spellbound.

"I see. And you're sure they mentioned Jenny?"

"Positive. He said he and Jenny were going to be married . . ."

"I knew she had a serious boyfriend. Mrs. McGraw told me. But I didn't know it was Bart."

"Maybe nobody knew," Caledonia suggested. "I'd guess that Maggie wouldn't be exactly proud of her association with him . . ."

"That's putting it mildly!" Angela said.

". . . so maybe Jenny wasn't advertising it either," Caledonia finished.

"And maybe," Martinez said, "she kept it quiet because he asked her to. The implication I get from the conversation you report is that he made it a practice to cultivate at least one woman in each group of guests here. Sometimes, apparently, to make love to her and to receive handsome gifts in exchange. Apparently Jenny didn't object. Perhaps she even encouraged him. She'd done pretty much the same thing herself, after all. And letting folks know Bart was engaged to a pretty young woman who worked right here might have cut into his business arrangements."

"The Inn offers a lot of services," Caledonia said. "But I bet you anything you like *his* services weren't on the list Dorothy Mc-Graw planned for the guests."

"Oh, Cal, of course not," Angela said. "Dorothy wouldn't have stood for what he was doing! Not for a minute."

"Well, if what I gather from your story is correct, Mrs. Benbow, she won't have to put up with him around here after tonight. Let me be sure you heard correctly. You heard Mrs. Randall mention that Jenny had threatened her . . ."

"Right."

"And then Bart said that he'd taken care of that for her?"

"Right."

"In just those words?"

"Truly, in exactly those words."

"Well, Swanson, I think we had better go to find our handsome handyman, don't you? Would he still be on the second floor in the main house here, do you suppose? We should try there first, at any rate." And Martinez, with Swanson in his wake, made for the door.

"But, Lieutenant," Angela said. "What about the killer?"

"Mrs. Benbow, that's what we're doing right now. Going to arrest him."

"Oh, no, not *him*."

"Mrs. Benbow, he's the one who said he'd 'taken care of' Jenny. You repeated that to me yourself."

"Well, I don't know what he meant by that, of course, but I bet he only meant he'd had a talk with Jenny. Maybe he meant he cautioned Jenny to lay off Maggie. Anyway, he isn't the one who killed her."

"How do you figure, Angela?" Caledonia was as puzzled as Martinez was.

"Well, I think we're agreed that whoever killed Jenny was probably the one who locked Caledonia in the cooler as well, aren't we?"

"That could have been Bart," Martinez said. "He might have been on his way to visit his ladylove, and he might have been afraid Mrs. Wingate had seen him. Anyway, when he tried to knife her this afternoon, it was surely for the same reason. And also to be certain she hadn't seen him locking her up in the freezer."

"Well, that's the way it was—except it wasn't Bart. In the first place, he wasn't even here that night. Remember? Ernie was on duty, because he's the one who let Cal out of the cooler.''

"Bart could have come back," Martinez said, but he didn't sound very sure of himself.

"Somebody'd surely have seen him. Ernie, for instance. And besides, Caledonia was attacked because of something else . . . Cal, do you remember how you found out that wasn't Judy Daggett's pocketknife and flashlight in her handbag?''

"Sure. Lieutenant, we reasoned that whoever fiddled with the lock on the steam room door had to have used a flashlight and a screwdriver. We found only one of each when we were searching the other guests' bags. The screwdriver was inside the pocketknife I mentioned. One of the blades, you see.''

"I don't remember your saying anything about a flashlight or a screwdriver," Martinez said, his tone slightly accusing. "You didn't tell me about them.''

"Well, I suppose I should apologize," Caledonia said. "But there was so much else going on that they didn't seem the most important clues we found.''

"Perhaps they weren't clues at all," Martinez said.

"Oh, but they were! They were!" Angela was bubbling with excitement. "Because Cal found out they weren't Judy's at all. Somebody must have dumped them into her purse to get rid of them . . . just in case!''

"Did Mrs. Daggett tell you that?''

"No-no-no. She keeps so many things in her purse, she probably hasn't noticed that pocketknife or the flashlight in there yet!''

"A regular pack rat, is our Judy Daggett," Caledonia agreed. "Whoever dumped them there, they had figured out that was a safe hiding place, all right.''

"Which meant," Angela went on, "that it was probably one of the other guests or one of the maids. Someone who'd seen the inside of the Daggett purse and knew what a mess it was in!''

"That all makes sense," Swanson said. "But what I don't understand . . . excuse me, Lieutenant . . . what I don't understand is how you figure they weren't Mrs. Daggett's.''

"Because Cal did such a clever thing. She pretended she'd lost a contact lens . . ."

"I don't wear 'em," Caledonia said proudly. "That was just a spur-of-the-moment invention. Pretty smart, huh?"

". . . and she asked Judy to borrow the flashlight to help her hunt on the dark carpet," Angela went on. "Judy said she didn't own one, never had. Then Cal asked her about a screwdriver and it was the same thing—Judy said she didn't have one. But, Cal, don't you remember that there were other people there at the same time who heard the whole thing?"

"Yes, but I'm darned if I remember who."

"You said two people. The maid Helena and Maggie Randall. She told me all about it later, Lieutenant, but so many things happened in between then and now, I haven't thought of that again till tonight. But you do see that Maggie has to be the one you want, not Bart."

"A flashlight you don't even know for sure is Mrs. Randall's . . . a screwdriver blade on a pocketknife . . . and that's enough to make you suspect murder?"

"That and the pink chiffon garment someone wore while they were attacking Caledonia. You forgot about that."

"I certainly have not forgotten it. But we found it hidden in Mrs. Terry's room. There's no reason to connect it to Mrs. Randall."

"They're right next door to each other!" Angela said. "But Belinda's room is closer to ours. Suppose I'm right and it was Maggie who stabbed Cal—or anyway what she thought was Cal. Suppose she hears all that noise in the bathroom and wants to get out of sight quickly. What would she do? Maybe she'd duck out quick, across the hall, and into Belinda's room, where she'd quick strip off that telltale coat. That bright pink chiffon was certainly the most likely thing to identify her quickly if she'd been spotted."

"And I *had* spotted it, all right," Caledonia said.

"Well, then, I think she probably got into her own room by merely going out Belinda's window, down the porch, and in at her own window. All those rooms have windows onto the porch, just like ours does. She certainly wouldn't want to go out into the hallway again."

"Sure, I see," Swanson said. "Then she ripped out of that suit and pulled on a shower cap and got herself all wet..."

"...and she went to the door and she fooled you into thinking she'd really been in the shower all along!" Angela said accusingly.

"I guess I did what you said not to, again, sir. I took it for granted..." Swanson sounded seriously annoyed with himself. "But I don't quite see how I could have checked on her story."

"If that's true," Martinez said thoughtfully, "don't blame yourself. I'd probably have done the same. Well, Mrs. Benbow, it all sounds logical enough. But Belinda Terry's room is the second door along, isn't it, and not directly across the hall from Mrs. Wingate? So why wouldn't Maggie have ducked into that first room, if she was in such a hurry?"

"Because that first room belongs to *two* women," Angela said triumphantly.

"Graham and Starkie," Swanson confirmed quickly from his notebook. "But I don't see..."

"I bet," Angela said smugly, "that Maggie figured it would be just fine if the coat was found, and if—as a result—you suspected someone else. But it would have to be hidden in a single room, where there was no roommate to get suspicious of all the night prowling the murderer must have done. Otherwise you'd never believe the coat belonged to the murderer. Do you see?" Angela was almost crowing with her excitement. "So Maggie went past the first room and ducked into the next door along, which belonged to someone who had no roommate... Belinda Terry."

"That would be awfully fast thinking," Martinez said, his tone still reluctant.

"Well, she's a very sharp woman," Caledonia said.

"Think about it," Angela said. "The coat really wasn't very skillfully hidden, was it? That could mean she wanted it found, couldn't it?"

"All right. I'll agree that all your guesses are possibilities. But only if that coat really is Mrs. Randall's and not Mrs. Terry's."

"Oh, it is, all right. I'm sure."

"Mrs. Benbow, I don't see how you can be positive. Did you ever see her wearing it?"

"No, but it's a matter of style. To begin with, never in a million years would dumpy, motherly little Belinda Terry have worn such a glamorous outfit!''

"She's right about that, at least, Lieutenant," Caledonia said.

"Everybody else brought exercise clothes. Maybe one or two dressy outfits to travel in or in case there was some sort of gala dinner or something. But only Maggie wore lace and chiffon and things like that every day. Then when I saw Maggie in her outfit tonight—in silk lounging pajamas with a swath of matching tulle—it made me think of that pink chiffon. That would have made a glamorous duster-style coat draped over a rose satin jumpsuit . . . very much in the style of tonight's creation."

Caledonia took up the argument. "Belinda simply never changes for dinner, Lieutenant. Most of us don't. The most the rest of us do is put on a fresh sweatshirt. But Maggie changes into something elegant and stylish nearly every night, and a lot of times she does it by just dressing up the outfit she wore during the day. I should have thought of that myself. Who else would be wearing pink chiffon right after exercise class was over?"

"That's what I was trying to think of earlier," Angela said. "I've had some picture nagging at me, just out of reach, all through dinnertime. That was it. Maggie in pink satin topped off with flowing chiffon . . . Lieutenant, the idea of Bart being the murderer, of Bart running around disguised in that pink chiffon . . . well, that's too ludicrous to consider!" Angela finished with triumph.

"All right. Maybe it figures. But I don't see why Mrs. Randall wouldn't have got rid of that jumpsuit, too," Martinez said. "Why dump the coat in someone else's place, but take the jumpsuit back to her own room?"

"She'd worn the jumpsuit earlier in the day," Caledonia said. "We all saw her in it. I expect she put that coat on to dress up for dinner. And then, of course, when she decided to stop off in my room—"

"To kill you!" Angela breathed excitedly. "Oh yes. She was wearing the coat then . . .''

"And if anything was seen, it would be that froth of chiffon," Caledonia nodded.

"Besides," Angela said, "it only takes a second to get rid of a coat, but it's much more difficult to strip out of a tight jumpsuit. Remember, she would have been in a terrific hurry."

"And she went right to her room and pretended she'd just got out of the shower!" Swanson said again. "I can't believe I fell for that."

"Besides . . . think," Caledonia said. "If she took off the jump-suit as well as the coat in Belinda's place, she'd have had to run to her own room in just her underwear. That would be hard to explain, if anybody saw her going along the porch."

"Once in her own room, she must have ripped that suit off so fast she tore the buttons loose," Angela went on. "Remember it was ripped when I found it where she'd thrown it in the closet?"

"Maybe," Caledonia said, "she meant to take the thing out somewhere later tonight and bury it. Or maybe she just thought nobody would realize it went with that bright chiffon coat."

Martinez was thoughtful. "I still am not really sure . . ."

"Well, then, what about this?" Angela said. "It's been nagging at me since the first . . . When Jenny was found, she was wearing nothing but a towel done as a turban. Now, Lieutenant, how many men could wrap a towel into a turban and make a twist that would hold it securely? I think I've known all along that the killer had to be a woman. I told you it was statistics—because there were more women than men around the place. But I knew all along it was more than that. I just couldn't think why I felt that way."

"Swanson," Martinez said, "I think maybe we'd better have a serious talk with Mrs. Randall. We'll just go upstairs and ask her about all this. It's worth looking into, at the very least. And you two ladies will oblige me by going up to your room and staying there. Please keep yourselves out of the way and safe." And the two men left the room, striding down the hall toward the stairway.

After a short while, Caledonia and Angela made their way out of the parlor and up the stairs. But though they hesitated a long time when they got into the upper hall, and though they waited with their room door ajar for some time, nothing else happened. At last, with some sense of disappointment, they closed their room door, bolted it securely, and made themselves ready for bed.

18

⊙

"It's all your fault," Caledonia was saying grumpily. "I've told you and told you to remind me to say something about that breakfast. And you know what my memory's like. But no! I get oatmeal again this morning, while you go your merry way . . . Are you listening to me?"

Caledonia was sitting in the large chair in their bedroom watching Angela stuff clothing into her suitcase. It was, in fact, the only chair left available as a seat, since Angela was using the others to sort clothes for neat packing.

It was the next morning, the day after Lieutenant Martinez had gone off to talk to Maggie Randall, and after Caledonia and Angela had, much to their own disgust, gone off to sleep without finding the outcome of Angela's detective work.

All they knew for sure was that Maggie had been missing at breakfast, and they had been told to begin their meal without her.

"I don't know how you can be so sure we'll be out of here today, anyhow," Caledonia said. "We haven't heard a word from Martinez. You don't even know you were right about Maggie. But be that as it may, let's talk about my breakfast. Now I think . . ."

"Listen, Cal." Angela dumped a load of clothing into the case in a jumble and crossed the room to confront her friend. "I don't mind you harping on the horrors of oatmeal. You're making yourself a bore about that, by the way. But just don't make it all my fault if you get nothing to eat for breakfast. You could eat oatmeal if you wanted to!"

"No, I couldn't. Not without being sick."

"Plenty of people do it." Angela turned back to the drawer to get another pile of underwear and nightclothes.

"Sure. And plenty of people jump out of airplanes without parachutes. A few of them even live through it. But I don't want to do it myself, even if it's possible! *Possible* and *pleasant* are two different things!"

There was a firm knock at their door. "It's the lieutenant," Angela cried with excitement, hastily dumping her burden on her bed and turning to answer the door.

"Sure! Now she can see through doors before they're opened! Sure it's Martinez!" Caledonia said. "And I'm Marie Antoinette!"

But the door did indeed open to show their handsome policeman, standing metaphorically hat in hand on their doorstep. Angela made a triumphant face at her friend, then turned back to Martinez. "Come in, Lieutenant. Come in. We were just getting ready to leave. At least, I was making a start. Cal hasn't even begun. Now, are you here to tell us how everything came out last night?"

Caledonia rose and emptied a chair for Martinez by simply dumping onto the floor the clothing it held, but Angela was too excited to complain. With a quick smile, Martinez moved into the vacated place, while Caledonia plopped back down in her own chair and Angela perched her tiny frame on the foot of her bed.

"Well? Was my little Sherlock Holmes on the right track?" Caledonia asked. "I confess I'm curious. Have you made an arrest?"

"And it was Maggie, like I said, wasn't it?" Angela added.

"Yes, yes, and to the last question, yes," Martinez said. "I won't tell my captain about the reasoning that brought me to the answer to our puzzle. And I don't want him to know that you, dear lady, came to a correct conclusion faster than I did. But you were absolutely right!"

"She's confessed!" Angela cried, delighted.

"Oh no. Not her," Martinez said ruefully. "She's still claiming she didn't do it. She says it was Belinda all along, it was

Mrs. Cziok, it was you, Mrs. Benbow—it was an unknown trans-
vestite with a passion for pink chiffon who just happened to wander in, it was the chef, Bart, one of the maids, Ernie, Mrs.
McGraw, and/or all of them together, she isn't sure. She's only
sure that she was otherwise occupied on all the relevant occa-
sions—with Bart.''

"Then how did you finally . . .''

"Bart told us everything he knew,'' Martinez said. "And it was
enough. More than enough, really. She bruised his ego worse than
she even imagined, in that conversation you told us about. When
we got to her room, she was lounging on the bed, still yammering
at him, and Bart was sitting on the floor with tears leaking down
his face.''

"If he really knew about all she'd done, why wasn't she nicer
to him?'' Caledonia said.

"I suppose she thought she didn't have to be. I suppose she
thought she could handle any situation, especially if men were involved. And it had all worked out satisfactorily for her up to that
point. She believed she'd been clever, hiding everything that might
have pointed her way—the flashlight and screwdriver, the chiffon
coat—she had killed or tried to dispose of the people she regarded
as threats. Of course, she'd missed getting rid of you, Mrs. Wingate,
but little Bunny . . .''

"She killed that girl from the kitchen, too?''

"Oh yes. So Bart tells us. It seems that Jenny and Bunny were
friends, in a quiet sort of way. Their shared background, I suppose.''

"There was a connection with the Kimbrough Hotel business
after all, then?'' Caledonia asked.

"Not really. Only peripherally. That business got the two girls
acquainted, and when they got here, Jenny made a confidante out
of the other girl. Jenny had special worries, after all, that nobody
but another graduate of the sisterhood would understand.''

"Like?''

"Like her tolerance of Bart's extracurricular activities with the
guests.''

"If it had been me, I'd have punched him right in the nose!" Caledonia rumbled.

"Well, Jenny felt differently, and she needed a friend who could be sympathetic with her . . . uh . . . less orthodox viewpoint. The girls had become friends, and Bart knew that his Jenny told Bunny just about everything that concerned her love affair with Bart."

"Bart must have mentioned that to Maggie!" Angela said.

"Yes, but let me back up a bit. Bart threatened Jenny several times, and once he knocked her down in a rage, arguing over his association with Maggie. Jenny hadn't minded the others, but this affair was different. He was going to leave her and form some sort of permanent arrangement with Maggie."

"Well, that isn't exactly what Maggie had in mind, Lieutenant."

"Bart didn't know that, did he? Anyway, he told Jenny he'd be leaving the Inn when Maggie left. He thought that ended the matter, even though Jenny kept making threats . . . threats he told Maggie about."

"And I suppose Maggie wasn't convinced that Bart could really handle his ex-fiancée and she took matters into her own hands, right?" Angela was smug.

"Apparently. According to Bart, Maggie invited Jenny up to talk it over, gave her a glass of drugged wine . . ."

"She had wine in her room? At a diet spa?" Angela was shocked. "That's cheating!"

Martinez grinned. "So it is. An indicator of true character, I suppose."

"We didn't find any wine when we were looking through her things," Angela said. "Are you sure?"

"Maybe she'd drunk it all up by the time we searched," Caledonia said. "Do you suppose?"

"We haven't been able to find it yet, and I suppose it went out with the trash. She certainly got rid of every other bit of evidence as soon as possible. I've got Pickett searching the county landfill for the bottle, right now. It would make good circumstantial evidence, though not absolute proof."

"Poor Pickett!" Caledonia said, and Martinez smiled quickly, then went on.

"Anyway, once Mrs. Randall drugged Jenny, she walked the half-conscious girl to the cabana, got her clothes off her, and put her neatly into a locker there—yes, and tied her hair up into that turban."

"I knew it," Angela crowed. "I told you, didn't I? No man could make a towel-turban stay on her head . . . that's a thing only a woman would know how to do!"

Martinez nodded. "Well, then Mrs. Randall put Jenny in the steam bath, undid the panic bar so it wouldn't operate if Jenny came to, turned the controls up, and just walked away."

"But she told Bart, apparently?" Angela asked.

"Obviously."

"It didn't bother him that his new girlfriend had done away with his former girlfriend?"

"I'm afraid he's not the sort of young man whose loyalties run deep. What happened next was that he began to worry about what Jenny might have told Bunny in one of their sessions of girl talk. And therefore what Bunny might guess about Jenny's murder."

"He told Maggie about his worries, didn't he?" Angela asked.

Martinez nodded. "He says Maggie said not to worry—she'd take care of it—and the next day Bunny was found stabbed to death on the path by the lake."

"Maggie apparently has a passion for neatness," Caledonia said grimly. "Leaving no loose ends. It wasn't too long till she locked me into that refrigerator—"

"Because of your curiosity about the tools she'd put into Daggett's purse," Martinez said. "Bart tells us Maggie knew getting rid of them that way had been a mistake. Then when you got curious . . ."

"And she overheard me asking questions! But how did she find me to lock me in? I thought I was pretty quiet, sneaking downstairs."

"Apparently you let the door slam as you went out. She got up to investigate, recognized you tiptoeing down the stairs, and followed you."

"I might have known. This is a back that would be hard to disguise, even in the dark! I guess I'm lucky she didn't give me a push down those steps."

"Bart says she had taken along a pair of shears as a weapon, but she was glad to use the freezer instead. She thought it was another easy solution to a vexing problem. That's one lady who doesn't like to just sit around getting worry lines. She takes action."

"But it was dumb! I wasn't anywhere near guessing the truth."

"Oh, I agree. The attacks on you were not very well thought out, compared to the caution with which she had acted up to then. She seems to have lost her head completely over what she thought were your suspicions."

"And Bart told you all this, Lieutenant?" Angela said.

"That's right. He's very angry and very bitter. His dreams of a comfortable life as a rich woman's kept lover have vanished. He may even have felt a measure of real love for the beautiful Maggie, who is now busy cursing the day she met him. Very loudly and in inventive terms."

"I won't remember her as being half so beautiful as I thought she was when I first saw her," Angela said.

"And rightly so," Martinez agreed. He stood gracefully and moved toward the door.

"Ladies, I have much work to do. To begin with, I must explain all this to Mrs. McGraw. You have your packing to complete, and in addition you will want time to say farewell to your friends here . . ."

Their good-byes to the lieutenant were affectionate, their packing rapid, and just before lunchtime the limousine service brought around a stunning car with a stunningly uniformed driver to take them back to Camden-sur-Mer.

Dorothy McGraw said good-bye to them privately and with heartfelt thanks. "I've told them all about you. The other women, I mean. They know you two were helping. They don't seem to mind a bit. And by the way, all of them but Tilly Warfield are going to stay and finish out their four weeks! Furthermore, instead of scaring people away, the publicity about the murders has brought us more inquiries and reservation requests in the last week than we've had in any four weeks before put together!''

"What's wrong with Tilly Warfield?'' Angela said. "Why is she leaving?''

"It's her husband. He's going to run for governor, and he wants her at the press conference when he announces his candidacy. Oddly enough, it wasn't the possibility of publicity from the murder that bothered him. It seems strange to me. Here we were, so worried about publicity . . . I still can't get over the fact there weren't hordes of reporters hanging around here.''

"Dear Dorothy, don't be silly.'' Angela was at her most tart-tongued. "Murder is an everyday occurrence in Southern California. It barely rates two column inches on a back page, unless the victim is a movie star. I suspect that instead of scaring folks away, what publicity you do get—now that the murderer is caught and not a menace—is going to mean more reservation requests than you've ever had before!''

"Well, whether it does or not,'' Dorothy smiled at her friend, "I can't thank you two enough. You know that . . . if you ever need anything . . .''

Saying good-bye to the other guests involved a lot of hugs and many promises to meet again. "Call me if you're ever in Houston,'' a revitalized Judy Daggett said.

"Or if you get to Phoenix,'' Carmen Sturkie put in.

"San Diego isn't far away from you,'' Marceline Richardson said. "We'll have lunch. I know some of the best restaurants . . .''

Cracker Graham wept quietly, her dimples obscured, and it was left to Frankie Cziok to sum it all up.

"I will invite you *all* to visit me . . . all at the same time . . . soon. We will have a runyon!''

"Reunion,'' Cracker sobbed. "Oh, it would be nice!''

"But expensive,'' Judy Daggett said doubtfully.

"Yes. A get-a-gather. Don't worry. I will just charge it on my American Express card, you see, and no matter what it costs, they will not dismember me!''

Even Cracker could not think of a word that would substitute and listened with the others, struck speechless.

"It only goes to follow suit that we developed a comradeness for each other here. I feel for all of you a big love," Frankie paused for emphasis, "love absolutely out the gazebo!"

After that there could be, of course, nothing to add. The farewells were over. The other guests went inside to their lunch, luggage was loaded into the limousine, and Angela climbed in. Caledonia was bent over, following her friend into the backseat, when she heard a hesitant clearing of the throat behind her.

She backed out again and turned, full height, to face a round, red, shining face that for a long minute she could not even recognize.

"Ernie," she said, suddenly realizing who this spotlessly attired man really was. "Ernie! I didn't even know you!"

Ernie had shaved. His face was pink from razor scrape. He had bathed, and he smelled not of beer, but of the mingled aromas of flowery soaps, talcum powder, scented deodorants, and some violently insistent aftershave. Ernie had even changed clothes, and his ample belly strained against the buttons of a new gray work shirt. (One of the packing clips still held the corner of its collar tightly.)

In Ernie's hand was a frazzled nosegay of daisies, begonia, and leaves from a dusty miller, obviously picked from the Inn's own gardens and held together by a red rubber band.

"Ernie, what are you doing here?"

"I brung you something." He pushed the bouquet into her hand. "I come to say good-bye."

He hesitated, cleared his throat again, and finally—shifting nervously from one foot to another—burst out, "Lady, you're one helluva handsome old broad. I'd be proud if you'd come out with me some evening. We could have dinner . . . no two-bit joint, you know. There's a great spaghetti place in town. I wouldn't take you bowling or to no beer joints. Not a lady like you. We could do something classy . . . see a movie maybe. If you ain't spoken for . . ."

"Ernie," Caledonia said kindly, "I don't know when I've been so flattered. I am not, as you put it, spoken for. But neither do I want to get involved with a gentleman friend, at my time of life. All the same, you've made me very happy by asking, and I thank you. I'll treasure these flowers to remember you by. I'm sorry . . .''

"Aw . . .'' He scraped a foot in the grass. "That's okay. I didn't think you would. But it ain't gonna hurt to ask. You're really something, lady.'' And he turned, heading toward the back of his house and his mower. But he was whistling as he went.

"I didn't exactly break his heart, did I?'' Caledonia said, as the car whirled off, headed back toward the coast, bringing them home to Camden-sur-Mer. She held out the flowers. "Isn't that just the sweetest . . . who could have imagined Ernie was a sentimentalist?''

"Or that he had an eye for a 'handsome old broad' like you?'' Angela was laughing, but her laughter was delighted, not mocking. "I'm a little sad about leaving,'' she went on. "I feel sad for poor, stupid Bart.''

"And for those girls . . . Jenny and Bunny. Don't forget them.''

"I haven't. It's always sad, thinking about the end of such violence. And I hate leaving those nice women at the Inn. They were such a good group.'' For a moment there was silence in the car. The engine purred, as limousine engines do, barely audible over the road hum of the tires.

After a moment Angela went on. "If Frankie Cziok only knew about your invitation from Ernie!''

"Good heavens, why?''

"Because she'd have a way to sum it up. She'd probably say,'' Angela decided, "that you should have been flatterized by his invitation.''

"Yeah,'' Caledonia grinned. "You know, she's a lot of fun. We really should think about going to visit her. San Diego isn't very far.'' She set onto the car seat the little bouquet she'd been holding and sighed.

"Cal,'' Angela said after a moment. "Cal, there's something I've got to tell you. And I'm not sure how. Something . . . well, I don't think you're going to like it.''

"Something else? Something I don't know about? Come on, Angela. Tell me. Don't keep me in suspense.''

"Cal,'' Angela said, her voice almost a whisper. "I . . . I

weighed myself before we left, and I've lost four and a half pounds this week.'' She waited.

"Well, that's terrific! Why did you think I wouldn't like that? Congratulations.''

"Oh, I haven't got yet to the part you're not going to like! It's . . . well, here's the thing. I know how you feel about diet and exercise, but I've been thinking . . . it might not be such a bad idea if we both tried it. Now, you're not mad at me, are you?''

Caledonia chuckled softly. "No, I'm not angry. Angela, I weighed myself, too.''

"You did!'' Angela was delighted. "Oh, Cal. And what did you find out?'' Her voice was breathy with anticipation.

"You know I didn't exercise, so you have to take that into account. But I also didn't eat breakfast all week . . . because of that oatmeal misunderstanding. And you know I ate only about half the amount I usually eat. You know I also had no snacks, no liquor, no chocolates, no mashed potatoes in butter—none of the things I like. I was really on a diet, and I kept it faithfully. And, Angela, I didn't lose at all.''

"What? Cal! Nothing?''

"Nothing. Well, a quarter pound. That's all I have to show for my self-deprivation.''

"Cal!''

"Oh, I'm used to this . . . I gain easy and lose hard. So, Angela, you can diet and exercise if you like, when we get home. Speaking for myself, it would be agony, and to no avail. And I never did go in for masochism. Besides, at my age, I figure I've earned the right to just let it spread!''

Caledonia raised her massive wrist and checked her watch. "As I figure speed and distance, we should be back at my place just in time for a lovely glass of sherry before dinner. What about it? Are you going to be virtuous and start your weight loss program, or are you going to live it up and join me?''

"Oh, Cal. I . . . I . . .'' Angela bit her lip, and then a little smile escaped from one side of her mouth. "Just give me time to unpack and I'll drop by your place for that sherry.''

"Atta girl. As Frankie would say, 'I'll break open the Welcome

Wagon for you.' '' Caledonia chuckled again, and her chuckle rolled up and out into an open, happy laugh.

Wordlessly the two friends looked out at the countryside as the car whispered along. The road rolled out before them, yellow with sunshine and bright with the delight of going home once more.